Catch An Honest Thief

Maria E. Schneider

Bear Mountain Books

A Bear Mountain Books Production
www.BearMountainBooks.com

Catch An Honest Thief
Maria E. Schneider

Printing History:
POD printing June 2011
E-format August 2009, 10.26.2011

Cover Art from Dreamstime
(Danomyte)

ISBN-13: 978-0615485003 (Bear Mountain Books)
ISBN-10: 0615485006

Catch An Honest Thief

Chapter 1

Dr. Alexia Zimmerman wondered, not for the first time, why people believed that burglars always wore black. Efficiently, she donned white gloves to match her outfit and slid through the doorway into the first chamber. That particular stereotype was about to cost the City of Haven its livelihood. Again.

Of course, she didn't really intend to steal the crystals that powered the experimental city; this was her way of proving that they weren't being guarded carefully enough. Locked away in the mountains of the Cibola National Forest in New Mexico, various experiments utilized abundant sunshine and wind to provide much of the electrical needs for the city. The crystals, a serendipitous discovery, provided the rest.

Carefully, she launched an electric current to confuse the listening devices that recorded noises as quiet as breathing. The steady hiss would cover any minute sounds she might make and fool the alarms that triggered on sudden noises.

A white reflective shadow, she crossed the room to the second door and organized her tools for final penetration into the chamber that actually housed the crystals. She drew a white hood over her head. It did not sport eye or breathing slits, but if all went well, she wouldn't need it long. Like a phantom, she dodged through the invisible light beams that crisscrossed the room, her stark white suit reflecting the beams back. The illusion was complete. No sirens sounded, and Alexia allowed herself a small smile of triumph.

As lead psychiatrist on the case of the thefts, she was supposed to help profile the mind behind the thefts. As part of the team of experts, she had access to the specifications for the security system--a fact that wasn't supposed to help said thief.

It helped her.

Above the room, she knew that a real person watched a camera feed. His pulse was monitored so that if he began to snooze, a jolt of electricity would awaken him. Five minutes ago, Alexia had blocked the camera feed with a computer-simulated picture of this very room.

Using lasers of her own, she bypassed the more complex light beams surrounding the package. The computer she carried could produce up to forty beams, and she had memorized the necessary pattern before she entered the chamber. She set the device, feeding light into the receptors just long enough for her to grab the small package. She swapped the crystals with an empty bundle, removed her computer and scooted through the doorway.

Hurrying now, she placed the crystals in the first room where they would still have minimal protection. She removed her gloves and hood, shook her blond hair free and tucked her tools away.

The outer door opened onto a hallway. Her watch indicated that she had just over a minute before one of the "random" electronic sweeps would detect her presence. Listening to the tiny microphone she had planted outside the door, she heard nothing.

Good.

With the clock running down, she quickly inserted a metal strip that would keep the door contact sensors happy.

Just as she was about to open the door, she heard noise.

Voices.

It took superhuman effort, but she held perfectly still and listened. The voices weren't coming closer, nor were they fading. Her hand, turned to keep the doorknob in position, cramped.

Her heart beat faster and she licked sudden beads of sweat off her upper lip. She didn't dare look down at her watch. Doing so would twist her hand, and she couldn't chance the knob moving. As long as no one glanced directly at the door...

She counted without moving her lips. Thirty seconds...forty. There was going to be a blue screen of death coming if she didn't get a break soon. She had perhaps fifteen seconds, maybe ten.

Voices fading slowly or not, she had to get out or she would be caught, and that would be the end of her legitimate career as well as her extra-curricular activities.

Edging through so that she could watch the hallway, she eased the contact strip out as the locks re-engaged.

She held her breath as the two people who had passed continued talking. They were not facing her and took no notice.

Alexia put her shaking legs to use by walking steadily away from the scene of the crime. People might see her now, but would think nothing of it. This hallway was quite populated in the daytime, and it was only just after lunch.

Another myth: burglars always work in the darkness of night.

Chapter 2

Alexia removed a sandwich from her pocket and chewed as she made her way through the hallway. Fingerprint readings for the doors would show her taking her lunch break in case anyone tracked her movements. As soon as the package was found, tracking would be required. The scientific community of Haven couldn't exist without the crystals. Without them, energy would have to be drawn from polluting materials just as in the rest of the world.

Contrary to her current activities, her life before Haven was not that of a thief. She had never actually stolen anything. It was just that when she was told she could not go to a place because it was closed, she had a tendency to…disobey. She went to the library after hours, museums and anywhere else that presented a challenge.

Of course, the Corporate Board of Haven had approached her because of her degree in psychiatry, not because of her undocumented penchant for sneakiness. Her ability as a thief could easily cost her everything she held dear. There were other psychiatrists at Haven that would have a field day with her career if they found out about her side activities, even though she had a very good reason for her actions.

Reaching her desk she typed "zap," onto her console. The picture of the room disappeared from her machine and from the camera feed. The blank hallway shot suffered the same fate. No one would find any crucial evidence tied to her person because it no longer existed.

She checked her appearance in a hand mirror, trying to erase the triumphant twinkle from her brown eyes. It might have been smart to change out of her reflective spider-silk outfit, but if someone had seen her as she made her way back through the corridors, it would seem odd that she had changed. As a psychiatrist, she knew how unlikely it would be that anyone would remember, but there were always exceptions. Her suit was as common as any other at Haven, except that most women preferred regular silk rather than threads woven by spiders.

Much to Alexia's surprise, it took the guard over twenty minutes to notice the package sitting in the outer room. He must have gone down to check personally because when the alarm finally did sound, it was the opening of the hall door that caused the system to respond.

Always ready to conform to other people's expectations, she remembered to breathe hard and look panicked as she ran back into the hallway and joined the flurry of people.

"What happened?" a voice demanded from within the crowd.

"Not again." A gasp or two and then someone accidentally fired a stun gun into the crowd.

Alexia pushed forward, her white suit now serving the purpose of identifying her as medical help. "Calm down. Please move back." She pushed until she reached the package.

A guard was holding it, his eyes roving in wide-eyed panic. He waved a stun gun aimlessly, unable to pick a target in the crowd. Spittle dripped from his mouth. "Can't...ca..n't..get it on my shift!"

"Mr. Miller--George." Alexia read his name from his tag and edged closer to the distraught man. "With this many witnesses, I don't think you have to worry about the package disappearing. Set it down and take my hand." She stretched out her own in a friendly manner.

Before George could respond to her overture, a harsher voice intervened. "The package has gotten this far. Who is to say it won't keep walking?"

George turned quickly, shouting, "Sir! Darren!"

As soon as George shouted the name, Alexia knew that the head of security, Darren Westmore, had taken charge. Darren's arrival caused her patient, and she was certain she had a new patient, to panic anew.

"George, who do you trust with the package?" she asked.

George, beyond an answer, shocked her with his next movement. "Sir. Darren. Mr...Westmore, sir." Reaching for a lifeline, he stumbled to Darren and dropped, not only the stun gun, but the precious package. He grabbed Darren's shirt and hung on desperately.

For a moment, Alexia forgot the psychiatric condition of George. She stared at the package, thanking God it was wrapped. In the future when she took it, she would double-check the outer covering.

Darren's harsh voice broke the silence. "Dr. Zimmerman, if you would be so good as to remove this--individual, I'll take charge." He ripped George's offending digits from his shirt.

Numbly, Alexia gathered her wits. "George, why don't we go sit down?" Fortunately, he needed no restraints. His own action of dropping the package, coupled with the disapproval in Darren's voice, had frozen the poor man in his tracks.

Alexia was happy to spot Dr. Brandon, her mentor and colleague standing by, ready to help. She got George to the door. Dr. Brandon offered to take over. "I'll get him settled. You finish up here. Come along, George."

Dr. Brandon led a mumbling and shattered George away. The man would have to be kept away from sharp objects for a while. He obviously viewed his defeat as worse than treason to his country. She sighed and rubbed her eyes. Haven, and the crystals that made the place possible, was like a country. It was truly its own territory with patriotic citizens that sometimes went too far in their beliefs and their actions.

Looking up, she found herself staring into the handsome, but malignant blue eyes of the man who now held the package. His black haircut was on the long side, allowing a slight wave to his perfectly combed hair. He was dressed in dark slacks and a white shirt, the collar of which was slightly crumpled from George's assault. For a fraction of a second, she wished that she had opted to follow George under the pretense of treating him.

"And you are waiting for?" Darren pointed his chin at the door in insolent command.

"The investigation. I'm part of the newly assigned team of psychiatrists that is helping to profile the thief." She pointed to her badge, which gave her name, rank and title.

His blue eyes flashed with irritation, but he turned his attention elsewhere. "Surround this package and take it directly to--"

On what Alexia suspected was a rare occasion, Darren was out of words. She filled in the blank for him. "How about the last secure area?" She kept her voice low so that only the closest guard could hear. "We've finished gathering anything useful from the theft that occurred there. Place extra guards outside that area, the battery storage area and Darren's office."

Darren slanted his eyes and then nodded his approval. "The thief may assume from the extra guards that I have the crystals or that they are charging the battery system that supplies Haven with electricity. Let's do it!"

His troops moved in quickly to obey his orders.

As soon as the crystals were out of sight he bellowed, "I want this floor scrubbed." Arms waving, he ushered people out before they could so much as breathe more contamination into the room.

Alexia barely held her temper. Scrubbing the outer room was

already useless because so many people had entered when the alarm went off. In fact, scrubbing at all was useless because she had worn no special clothing. Everyone in the complex wore natural fiber clothing. No chemically processed or dyed clothing was allowed at Haven. "I would think you could skip that step and move on to the mechanical records."

Before Darren could reply, a new voice broke the staring match between her and Darren.

"Ah, but that would imply that the mechanical devices detected something. In which case, the jewels wouldn't have been successfully taken," the new speaker chortled.

Alexia turned to find merry green eyes watching them.

The man pointed a finger at Darren and wagged it, scolding a naughty child. "This was the perfect trap, you said. Your own people watching and wired like robots so that they couldn't fall asleep on the job." He shook his head in a not-so-convincing show of sorrow and moved towards them. He narrowly missed a technician that was scrubbing the room with a monitoring device. When he reached Alexia, he stuck out a hand. "Chris Appleton, here."

Alexia stared. He was impossibly nondescript. She could have seen this person a thousand times and never noticed him. In fact, had he not spoken, she probably wouldn't have noticed him in the room. He was of medium height, medium coloring and medium appearance. His blue jeans were not fancy, nor did his dark blue polo make much of a statement. They were merely functional. Only his green eyes stood out in an otherwise unremarkable face. They were grinning at her.

Chris Appleton reached out his other hand, the one that wasn't held in a shaking position, grabbed her own and deposited it in his slightly larger hand. "Glad to meet you. You're the local shrink, right? Trying to study the inner working mind of the thief." He leered at her, tapped his forehead, and then glanced around her shoulder at the towering man whose face was frozen in a glare.

"You!" Darren finally managed to strangle out. "How...Get out!"

"I don't think so," Chris said. "You know as well as I that father said I could take over if you failed again. He didn't want to give preferential treatment, but he has no choice but to admit that even I, his son, could perform at least as well as you have."

"Uh," Alexia began, realizing that Darren was not going to take the insult well.

"Imbecile! I have not yet proved that I don't know the culprit!" His face was gaining color at a rapid pace, going blotchy red all the way to his dark wavy hairline.

Alexia began to worry that Darren might suffer a heart attack, complicating the investigation and certainly her own day. "Uh..."

"And do you?" Chris challenged, cutting her off. "Have you apprehended anyone?" He displayed his own two empty hands and turned in a circle, finding no one except Darren's men. The laughing eyes of the man who had identified himself as Chris Appleton turned cold. "I think not. And that means you're off the case."

He treated Darren to a final mocking eyebrow before he turned and walked through to the inner chamber. The lasers and infrared beams in the doorway had been turned off, but after standing in an area not protected by the beams, he used a remote control to re-activate the alarms.

Alexia halted midstep in her intention to follow him. She still had on her reflective suit. If she walked through the first set of lasers and they didn't go off...

As if reading her mind, his eyes caught hers. She held her breath until her chest ached. She was too good a doctor to allow any expression on her face, but only because she had sat through so many bizarre confessions of patients. The green eyes that had been so friendly before stared into hers with the intelligence of a hunting cat.

"Mirrors," he muttered and turned away. "Could have been mirrors or--" he wheeled around on one foot. "Come in here."

Like a deer caught in headlights, Alexia merely stared. He beckoned her forward impatiently.

With a hard swallow, Alexia moved her foot forward.

Chapter 3

Behind her, confusion reigned. Darren shouted orders from somewhere down the hall. The sweepers collected particles and people milled about. The world carried on despite her predicament.

She was still wearing her reflective spider-silk outfit. Only her hands and head were exposed. Her bare skin would be enough to break a beam, so long as her head or hands interrupted one. She considered waving her arms to force the beams to break, but that would be a touch too obvious. If she walked quickly, she would cross more of the beams. The more she crossed, the more likely one would hit her head or neck and trigger.

Instead, she forced a serene smile. With apparent nonchalance, she moved forward, stepping inside the room.

The hardest part was not breathing a sigh of relief when the alarms registered.

Chris held her gaze for another fraction of a second, and then began walking around the various traps, muttering. "Too easy. If I knew where these beams were placed, I could walk around them." He paced the room, stepping over one of the lasers. "And he calls me an imbecile."

The man who had done just that reappeared as if called, rushing back into the room and yelling at the top of his lungs. "Remove him! Now!"

Alexia turned again, this time to stare at Darren with surprise. Chris came from behind her and gently moved her from harm's way. He flashed a card at the approaching guards. "Sorry, gentlemen. No fun today. I have a pass, activated when the alarm went off." He addressed Darren. "I was willing to deactivate my own pass, assuming that you had actually arrested anyone, but you did not." His smile had all the warmth of an iceberg. "The security of the crystals, as of a few minutes ago, is mine."

Darren nearly suffered apoplexy before he managed to get the next phrase out. "I have made an arrest! I want you out! Out!" He came at

Chris with fisted intent.

Alexia put her head into her hands. She had led the wrong patient away. Obviously she should have subdued Darren.

"Oh?" Chris met the bigger man face to face. "Who? Who is the culprit?"

"George Miller. It's the only possible solution."

Alexia nearly fell down. "What?" She took a deep breath to stop her next words. Until the report was compiled she had to maintain her facade. After that, she could point out fallacies. For now, she couldn't afford to defend anyone, even if it meant that Darren arrested the wrong man.

Thankfully, she was saved from risking herself. Chris did it for her. "You're claiming that the man who discovered the package, that nearly incapacitated man, is guilty? How was he supposed to have carried that off? The alarm that sounded was this one." He pointed to the outer door. "You're saying he stole the package and then set off the alarm by coming back into this room? What was he going to do, return the crystals?"

Darren didn't back down. "Of course he was putting it back. He took it with the intention of leaving it here to be found and then came back in to guard it personally. That way the package wouldn't be damaged or stolen by someone else. He set off the alarm to let us know he had finished successfully."

Alexia couldn't just stand by. "This is the same George who was so organized that he triggered his stun gun when people came running? The same guy that then dropped the package at your feet?" She shook her head. "Not even close to the medical condition that I witnessed when I arrived. Sorry. I can't back up that data."

Darren glared at her. "Of course you can. The man became so worried that a hostile person would actually gain access to this room and steal it that he," Darren waved his hands in an attempt to come up with the medical terminology.

Alexia supplied a few of the terms that she knew he was holding back. "He blew his stack? He lost his marbles? He short-circuited the network?"

Sarcasm was lost on the man. "The photographs will prove it." Darren pointed to the camera. "Ollern, my second in command, will escort you out."

Ollern was a smartly dressed man, obviously emulating his master. He stepped forward to do Darren's bidding. He was shorter than Darren, but no less focused. His light hair was military short, and his fatigue dress perfect. He moved towards Chris like one of the laser beams.

Alexia wanted to scream. This was precisely the attitude that was putting the crystals in so much danger. Darren cared more about his career and saving face than setting up protection that might stop a real thief. What was he going to say when the film showed a blank? She rolled her eyes heavenward and stomped to the door.

"When you two figure out who is in charge, let me know. I'll be waiting for the report." She slammed the door shut behind her and fled to her office.

After pacing uselessly for fifteen minutes, she decided to head home. This new development was far worse than she had anticipated. Her actions were supposed to improve security, not negate it completely.

She shut and locked her office. Guilt assailed her as she contemplated the fact that she may have actually ruined George's life. Of course, any person that could not accept fallibility had problems. Men like Darren played upon the pride of people like George by telling them they were trustworthy, offering them chance upon chance to prove it. It was unfortunate that George had picked her territory to guard. Since her sixteenth birthday, she hadn't met a lock she couldn't pick.

"What else could I do?" She hadn't known George was near an edge.

Plagued by guilt, the first thing she did when she arrived home was call the hospital and check on him. "How is he?"

Sally, the ward clerk, checked the chart. "Sedated and resting comfortably. Will you be in?"

Alexia shook her head at the video screen. "There isn't much point until he sleeps some of it off."

"Okay doc, see you in the morning."

Guilt caused stress. She flexed her hands and tried to put off worrying about him until tomorrow. Normally, after a break-in, she was relaxed and, if she was forced to admit it, a little smug. This time, however, all she felt was dismay.

She sighed and got ready for bed. There was a lot of work to be done tomorrow, especially now that a new player had been introduced. Chris' appearance changed the picture entirely. Darren had been in charge of the security for some time now. He played consistently by the same rules. Until today he had never shown his face this early in an investigation. Apparently Chris' arrival had challenged his effectiveness, if not authority. Darren now had something to prove.

Too little, too late, in her opinion.

Unfortunately, Chris wasn't necessarily an improvement. He had taken on the other man with all the subtlety of a bulldozer in a nature preserve. That technique had proved so effective she now had not only a patient, but an accused patient at that.

"Thank you, Chris Appleton."

And what if the only way to save the patient was to confess her part in the theft?

That thought sent her heart plummeting and kept her awake most of the night. If she had to leave Haven, she would be the one who went insane.

Chapter 4

By morning, Alexia had decided on a plan. Her new patient took precedence over her other projects, including the crystals. Truth to tell, Haven wasn't the type of place that generated a lot of psychiatric patients. When Haven offered Alexia a job, it was to study the effects on a society that lived within the false scientific bounds that Haven had created, not to take care of patients. Alexia earned a comparable salary to what the outer world paid, but like all members, she gave up social security and public funds for such things as schools, roads and other amenities. No outside incentives, including government subsidies or political contributions that might influence decisions, were accepted. People reacted differently when the rules they understood were suddenly replaced. It was her job to document and study the patterns.

This morning, however, she had to find a way to convincingly argue that George was innocent. If she confessed that she had taken the package, it would certainly exonerate him. Of course, Darren would then arrest her and although he would save face, she would have even bigger problems.

She sighed as she pressed her hand into the security reader at the hospital. It was a small building; more of a clinic and laboratory wrapped into one. The physician community performed high level research here and developed new machines, medicines and techniques for various illnesses.

Alexia made her way to the patient floor. Sally, a petite brunette, was on duty again. She had a reputation as a prankster in the ward, but she took her job seriously as long as she didn't have a grudge to settle.

"Anything new on George Miller?" Alexia asked.

Sally shook her head. "Nurse said he slept through the night." She pulled up a copy of the record and added, "All his data has been updated. He's current."

"Thanks." After noting his progress, Alexia handed back the electronic chart display and made her way to his room. Even though she knew George's problems went deeper than a single failure, guilt nagged. She made a mental note to talk to Darren about his training methods. No one should be brainwashed into believing that personal worth was equated to guard duty performance.

After a fruitless hour of talking to George, Alexia called Dr. Brandon. The picture seemed off in its color match, but Alexia knew better. He really did have hair that red-orange, and his skin was almost transparent.

"How's George?" he asked immediately.

"Not so great. I wondered if you..." George was really her responsibility. She didn't have a good excuse to ask for help. She couldn't tell Dr. Brandon that she simply knew too much about the robbery to treat George effectively.

"Sure, not a problem. I'll check in on him."

"Can I list you as primary?" She didn't give reason. She couldn't.

He looked surprised, but didn't ask any questions. "Sure. That's fine." The screen blurred with red-orange as he nodded.

Glad he hadn't asked why, she signed off. She updated the chart before leaving.

Feeling nearly as much a failure as George, Alexia headed to her office in the main complex. The report on the theft awaited, as well as a surprising development. The first page of the report informed her that Darren had been "reassigned" on the case, and Chris had been given the lead. The most interesting part was that Chris, unlike Darren, did not have an entire agency of people working for him. He worked alone. The message conveyed by Corporate was that because he did not have a professional entourage they had hesitated to assign him the project. However, the report pointed out, "Thus far, the Agency has been unable to provide for the safety of the goods in a manner which is acceptable."

Great. Darren was going to need psychiatric help now. With a loud plop, she sat. Before she could figure out a plan of action, her office door flew open.

"Hi!"

She nearly jumped over her desk before her brain registered that it was Chris in her doorway. "What?!?"

"Didn't mean to startle you. Just stopped by to get your opinion." Chris grinned and pointed to the report showing on her console.

Alexia took a deep breath and settled back into her chair. "That's it? From your entrance, I thought maybe the building was on fire." She waved at the screen. "Congratulations. I'm sure you can be proud."

With open amusement, he clarified, "I mean about the robbery, not me being in charge. I want your opinion on what kind of mind could perpetrate such a crime."

"Oh." Alexia blinked, switching her train of thought. Concentration was critical now. "I haven't read the entire report. I did compile a set of documents from the previous thefts that detail, in my opinion, the mind behind the crimes."

"Yes, I've read them." His green eyes were watchful.

She stared blandly back. As a psychiatrist, she knew the signs of guilt. As a thief, she knew how to hide them. "And, what did you think? Do you agree with my analysis?"

He waited a moment longer, like a quiet statue. "It's as good a guess as any other," he finally allowed.

Alexia had to be very careful. The line between a psychiatrist who demanded respect for her ideas warred quietly with the thief who demanded total silence to keep from getting caught. "There are two or three other reports from my colleagues available. I assume you have read those also." At his nod, she continued. "In my opinion, we can dispense with Phillip Teldman's report; whoever is committing this crime is definitely not insane."

Chris came in and sat in the chair across from her desk. He leaned forward, his eyes bright. "I quite agree. Whatever mind is behind the crimes is brilliant, responsible and clever." His fingers worked the edge of her desk as though he couldn't wait to get his hands on the criminal. "Though an insane person can be diabolically clever, there has been no sign of an unbalanced mind. No odd sacrifices to the crystals, no attempts to draw them too far from the base. Dr. Teldman's conclusion that the thief is at war over wanting to possess the power and wanting to do what is right makes no sense. The thief has never taken the crystals and brought them back, he has only removed them from protection."

Alexia nodded, unable to keep herself from being drawn into his enthusiasm. "Dr. Teldman's argument that the challenge of outsmarting the best minds of Haven could be closer, but that doesn't necessarily show a tendency towards insanity."

"And what about Dr. Ann Reven?" Chris asked.

Alexia sighed. She liked Ann, but the woman was very idealistic. "Ann has some valid points. The thief could be trying to warn Haven against misuse of the crystals. However, I would have expected some type of note demanding proper behavior if that is what the thief had in mind. Additionally, leaving the package outside the confines of protection belies the underlying premise that the thief wants to see the contents protected. By taking the package, it is vulnerable for however short a period of time."

Chris nodded. "Her idea that the thief is homeless is totally incorrect. Whoever has been breaking in has access to Haven and is a member. I refuse to buy the theory that a stranger could walk in here."

Alexia grinned at his misunderstanding and had to hold back a real chuckle. "Uh, I don't think she meant homeless in quite that manner, Chris."

"Oh?" He sat forward, his face wrinkled in disapproval. "Hidden meanings within the text? I thought she was supposed to be clarifying the matter."

Alexia laughed. "I'm afraid I have prior knowledge. If you had ever met Ann, you would know exactly what she meant." Alexia got up and sorted through the information chips on her bookshelf. She grabbed one, inserted it into her computer and quickly found the page she wanted. She turned on the console that was located on his side of the desk. "You'll note that almost every time she refers to 'homeless' the word 'soul' follows within the next word or two. She is referring to a state of the man's soul, not his physical amenities. A homeless soul is a man in search of God, not a man who is homeless, as in without a physical structure."

Chris groaned. "How did I miss that?"

"Ann is subtle. She doesn't want to give the impression that she is a Christian zealot. Otherwise, people discount her from the start. Once you meet her, however, or hear her talk, it's no contest."

"So." Chris was obviously suspicious now. "She didn't exactly give her true opinion."

"What do you mean?"

"Her analysis is flawed. For one, she is taking into account her own consideration of the universe. She assumed things about the thief based upon her own views. For two, she hides her real point, which, now that you've mentioned her ideals, is obviously that we are all poor souls in search of--" he stopped and then waved a hand, "in search of whatever she feels souls search for. A kind God, salvation, whatever."

Alexia couldn't disagree with his assessment, because she knew that every psychiatrist had to fight against including personal views. "That's a fair statement. Although Ann does look at the facts, they tend to take on a religious coloring."

"Interesting that someone who is supposed to study other people's minds would lie about what is in their own."

Since Alexia's own analysis contained half-truths, she squirmed. "Sometimes a psychiatrist has conflicts of interest, just like everyone else." She forced her hands to relax even though she felt a need to grip the sides of her chair. In her imagination, Chris was able to see inside her head, and she shuddered at what he would find there. "I'll be sure and let you know if I have anything to add after I study the rest of this report more thoroughly." He would get the most convincing report she had ever written.

"Hmm." Chris didn't look entirely satisfied, but he stood and handed her a chip that he had brought with him. Her assumption that it was a copy of the security report was incorrect. "I'd like your opinion on this proposal, also. It's the next plan for the location of the crystals. I want to know whether this mind," he pointed to the psychological analysis, "will be able to break into this new location."

She stared in dismay at the proposal. He hadn't even asked her opinion about security measures before compiling his ideas. She was more than a little tired of lame proposals. "Certainly," she replied halfheartedly. "I'll get back to you tomorrow."

He nodded and turned to go. As an afterthought he looked back and asked, "How is George?"

Alexia grimaced. "Dr. Brandon is going to help out with that. It may take a while, and George probably won't be getting back into the same line of work."

Chris grunted. "I don't place much belief in people guarding objects anyway. Too vulnerable. They can be killed or corrupted."

With that uplifting, optimistic remark, he disappeared down the hall, leaving Alexia wondering. She wouldn't have expected such a cynical remark from the happy Chris Appleton.

Chapter 5

The rest of Alexia's day was filled with reports. Her hands had a tendency to shake when she thought of Chris' green eyes boring into hers, questioning. She tried to convince herself that Chris had no way of knowing she was guilty and no reason to even suspect her.

Unfortunately, she couldn't get her work done in her current state, let alone consider Chris' plan for protecting the crystals. Grabbing the reports, she headed home. It was imperative that she study her newest adversary. It was also important that she find out what security had learned about the most recent theft. She would have an easier time keeping her tracks covered if she had all the facts.

To her relief, the theft report contained exactly what she expected. Security had easily figured out that the outer door had been bypassed by use of metallic tape. There were several inconclusive theories about the camera malfunction and George's apparent lapse. Once they figured out that she had inserted a blank picture of the room, George's real treatment could begin. Dr. Brandon could tell him that it wasn't his fault he had been fooled.

Chris' proposal for security was an entirely different beast. After only the first few pages, she groaned.

Chris Appleton had decided to set a trap that few people in the world could break. His conclusion: the egotistical thief would try to break through no matter what. Chris Appleton would be there to catch said thief.

Alexia found herself plagued with doubts. Chris may have researched her background; then again, he may not have. She didn't know enough about him.

That was a problem she could solve. Most medical records were available to her because she was a psychiatrist, but she wasn't going to be that obvious. She bypassed the normal logon system, copied his records and exited. It took less than thirty seconds.

She chewed her lip, wondering if Chris had set any traps on his file.

Once assigned to protect the crystals, it would be normal for the thief to investigate the new security expert. She found herself wishing she had used a machine other than the one in her home, just in case Chris found a way to unscramble the mess.

She took a deep breath. It was too late to worry about it now. Tomorrow she could go into the complex and remove her false user name and create another one.

Meanwhile, she got down to reading.

His file absorbed her for the next two hours. His education was normal, his upbringing normal and his career normal. He had taken various technology courses as an undergraduate, and several years ago when his father had founded Haven, he began to seriously study biology.

By the time she had finished reading, she had at least part of her answer.

Chris was too normal. Therefore, his file was a lie. He had to be more than he appeared, and the answers weren't going to be found in the folder.

Frustrated, she turned off the computer. It was nine o'clock, too late to accomplish much else.

She ate a quick snack pack and headed to bed, but her misgivings and Chris' plan refused to leave her alone. His sketch for protecting the crystals was pure genius. He wanted to keep the crystals at Haven, but put the instructions for creating them elsewhere. The crystals had to be at Haven in order to obtain the energy, but the instructions for creating and refueling them did not. A thief needed both, because with just the crystals, the crystals couldn't be recharged or reproduced.

She sighed and flopped over, but there was no point in trying to sleep. She got up and put on her hiking shoes. She had skipped karate practice today. Better to do her required amount of exercising now than have to double-down tomorrow.

Darkness did not bother her. As a precaution against wandering coyotes, she carried her knife and rifle. She didn't care to become an easy dinner.

The breeze was mostly cool, although vestiges of the hot air that was trapped in the valley during the day buffeted her gently as she hiked upwards. Even climbing as straight as possible, her favorite perch was almost a mile away. If she were a bird, it would have been half that.

The view it afforded was worth the climb. Haven was nestled below. The protection of darkness kept her from feeling too much a part of it. The main complex shown with a few lights. Mark, Ed and Sam worked into the night, every night. Higher up, another light winked, and she knew that Grace had stayed late again. Grace was only an occasional night visitor, but frequent enough that Alexia had bothered to find out who left the lights burning.

She shifted the rifle and sat on her boulder. A like rock, covered with desert lichen, rested on another mountain on the opposite end of Haven. She grinned. Her thief instincts kept her watching from several angles.

Not that she knew what she was watching for. If Chris had his way, she would be spending her time watching her own tail rather than the peaceful valley of Haven. His plan couldn't have been tailored more perfectly to challenge her talents. In fact, maybe Chris' idea of protection was good enough.

She tried to stifle the next thought, but it was like trying to keep an ice cube from melting in the desert sun. Could she break-in? Was there a real need to do so, other than to prove that she could? Chris' plan was certainly safer than any of the others.

She shook her head to clear it. The motion caused her to notice a flickering light. This time the light wasn't in the main office building, it was near her house. In fact…she stood up on the rock for a better look. It wasn't unusual for people to be out and about at night. Haven was a safe community. Eccentric scientists weren't likely to steal, rob or mug anyone.

But…there was a flicker again, right near her bedroom window!

Now why would anyone be at her house? And shouldn't they be near the front door? She blinked and carefully measured the distances that appeared smaller from her vantage point. Fully alert now, she readjusted the rifle across her back and worked her way down the first slope. Knowing the terrain, she ran as quickly as possible, but it didn't really matter. Whoever was at her window would probably be gone long before she could get there.

Once on level ground, she cut through the lot where an experimental house made from gelatin had once stood, nicknamed little piggy house one. She took another shortcut through Anderson's garden, one end of which bordered her own yard. She hoped that her occasional trip-up in the dark didn't hurt the numerous desert grasses. If so, she would hear from her grumpy neighbor come morning.

At her gate, she paused and tried to breathe quieter.

Slinging her rifle into place, she crept cautiously through the entrance. The baked-brick garden wall was too high to allow her to see anything from outside the yard. Moving carefully, she edged near a twisted scrub oak and peered anxiously around the corner of the house.

Unbelievably, a male figure still stood in front of the window. The intruder did not move.

Alexia eased back, confused. If he was thinking of stealing, what was he just standing there for? Was he some kind of pervert who wanted to peek through her curtains? Shouldn't he at least wait until she was home to do the peeking?

As a psychiatrist, she was familiar with a rather long list of fantasies, but nothing in her experience allowed for a man who showed an inclination to stand around and watch an empty bed.

So, what--

While she stood uselessly speculating, the man let out a yell, jumped and spun around. Assuming he had sensed her presence, she raised the rifle. Fire first, ask questions later.

Before she could pull the trigger, another figure came from behind the first and tried to wrestle the guy to the ground. She tried to aim the rifle again, but there wasn't much light filtering through her bedroom window. Her hands were none to steady either. All she could see was a tangle of arms and flying fists. She had no idea whether the second intruder was her savior or another thief. Her window cracked ominously as the first man's head smacked against it. His hair, she saw from the light of the window, was dark, nearly black. The other man was smaller and possibly had lighter hair.

She readied her rifle again and then slowly, the smallest of suspicions leaked into her consciousness.

"No," she argued with herself, "it can't be." They weren't that stupid. Were they?

Never being one to wait for things to sort themselves out, she fired her rifle and watched in satisfaction as both parties froze.

The grunts were reduced to harsh breathing. The struggle diminished to whatever effect gravity had on a raised arm or leg.

"I suggest that neither of you move. I can't see very well in this light, so if I hear movement, I'm going to assume it's hostile." She kept the rifle pointed in their direction and knew full well that the reflection from the stars and half-moon was enough to glint off the barrel. "Identify yourselves."

There was silence for another moment, even quieter than before. Then, sounding somewhat defensive, a voice broke the silence. "He was lurking at your window and--"

"Lurking?" The second voice sounded strangled. "I," claimed a voice filled with self-righteous indignation, "do not, lurk. I have every right to be here!"

"What," panted the other voice, "came over to discuss business through her window? Then you change your mind and decide to be a peeping tom--"

"Peep--peeping--" The man was so affronted, he couldn't get the word out.

It didn't matter. She lowered her weapon. Chris and Darren screamed at one another, and she couldn't make heads or tails of the conversation. She shrugged. They were bound to tire themselves out, and it was long past her bedtime.

The door was set to automatically lock behind her when she entered, but, given the bizarre circumstances, she checked the light pattern. It indicated security was on, so she put the rifle back into her gun safe. Turning back to the security panel, she turned the window settings to "black" so that no one could see in. Since the black setting also dimmed her own view, she usually left the window setting at its lightest, but it hardly seemed the thing to do tonight. There was no telling how long those two might be outside her bedroom.

In the kitchen, she pulled a package of milk from the cabinet and broke the heating element. She wasn't cold, but she was thirsty, and she had the strangest feeling that she was going to have a bit of trouble sleeping. Granted, the yelling had finally stopped, but a round of cursing had followed before an uneasy silence settled.

Sipping her hot milk, she walked to her bedroom. She turned out the light, lightened the electrochromic window setting and peered out. The tangled bodies had removed themselves, but she pressed the button for the outer shutters anyway. She had installed them herself over protest of the builder. He had insisted that with the auto-darkening windows, she didn't need shutters.

What did he know? He didn't have strange men arguing outside his house.

She looked at her watch and counted the seconds.

The first knock sounded after about thirty seconds. A second, louder one, occurred less than half a second after the first. They were obviously still arguing. Too bad. Grown men too.

She turned down the covers, shut off the lights, and, contrary to her expectations, immediately fell asleep.

Chapter 6

Alexia hummed happily as she arrived at her office the next morning. She didn't need to borrow anyone else's machine. She fully intended to look up the files from her own computer. After last night, surely no one would question why she obtained Darren Westmore and Chris Appleton's files.

She would have gotten straight to her task, except that a bright, gift wrapped package waited by her office door. The wrapping was silk, reusable. The bow was a coarse material that she didn't recognize.

She shook the box suspiciously. It was silent. She smelled it. Who would leave her a present?

There was only one way to find out.

Carefully, she carried it down to Sam's lab. He wasn't in yet, but that wasn't a problem. The first time he had found her using his lab, unauthorized of course, he had laughed and showed her how to use the equipment. He had even offered to show her the cadavers he worked with, but Alexia had wrinkled her nose and declined. Dr. Sam Olstein, nice though he was, happened to be in charge of autopsies, suspicious deaths or otherwise.

After seeing Alexia's interest, at least in his x-ray equipment, Sam had added her name to the access list.

She exposed the mysterious package and processed the film.

What she saw left her more confused. There was no mistaking its distinguishing lines. She stared at the outline of the film incredulously. Why would someone send her a gun?

She studied the shape, but didn't recognize the model. At least it wasn't a bomb.

But a gun? She had several. Was this a new twist on a death threat?

That unpleasant thought made her frown. Perhaps there was a card.

She retrieved the package from the x-ray room and made her way back upstairs.

There was a card, but it had been slipped underneath her office door. The scrawled handwriting said, "Love, Chris."

Chris had left her a gun? Even more puzzled, she turned her full attention to unwrapping the package.

It wasn't until she had opened it that she understood. Her grin turned into loud laughter and then giggles. Ann, from across the hall, must have heard her mirth. Her matronly face peered around the corner of the door. "My dear, whatever is so funny?" She rolled her wheelchair into the room. "A present? Who is it from? It isn't your birthday."

Alexia wiped her eyes and sat up straighter. "No, it isn't my birthday. I don't know why I found it so funny. It's a stun gun." She lifted it out of the box and showed her colleague. "Just enough volts to startle a person." Apparently Chris wanted her to have something around her house that was a little less lethal than a gun with real bullets.

Ann's slash of bright red lipstick turned down in disapproval. "We shouldn't need weapons of any kind. I suppose someone knows that you actually have those things and thought to add to your collection." She shook her head and her hair, curled in giant round cylinders around her ears, bobbled like water-wings. "It's a thoughtful gesture; Lord knows that whoever sent it meant well. At least it isn't a killing weapon. That would be sinful."

Alexia sighed, her mirth dissipating quickly. "You're right, it isn't that funny. I didn't mean to disturb you."

"Not at all, my dear." Instead of leaving, however, she rolled her wheelchair further into the room. Her toenails matched her lipstick, as did the bright red circle of leather on her thong sandals. She always wore flowing robes, either because she was trying to hide her disability or because she thought it made her look mystical. Alexia rather thought it was the latter.

Ann said, "I assume that you've read the latest report? Can you even believe it?"

Alexia immediately focused. It was crucial for her to remember what security had discovered versus what she knew because she was the thief. "I did read it, but I need to spend some more time on it." Alexia also didn't know whether Chris had copied everyone on his new plan, so she didn't mention it.

Ann cleared up the question, however. "What do you think of Mr. Appleton's suggestion?" She pursed her lips worriedly. "I hate to see anything that belongs to Haven moved off elsewhere."

Alexia nodded, knowing how Ann felt. "Yes, I know. However, I think it might actually be for the best. He has some good points."

"He can hardly know the human mind like we do, Alexia. I'm sure that Corporate must see that the perpetrator will only commit these offenses again, further away from where we can reach him. We have to find a way to reach him, a way to save him. Given the time, I know we could make a difference!"

Before the older woman could get any more distraught, Alexia sinned and interrupted. "We do need to discuss the possibilities, but I think Chris may have a point. The instructions may be safest away from the complex." She hadn't even known for sure that she felt that way until the words were said. She had been thinking about Chris' plan all night and the more she considered it, the better it appeared.

"But what if it draws the thief away? How can we help him?"

Corporate, Alexia knew, could give a rat's ass if the perpetrator left the complex for good. Not a single one was overly worried about helping the thief find salvation either. Of course, Alexia could hardly tell Ann that. For one, she wouldn't hear it and for two, it was unthinkable that everyone else didn't want to help their fellow man. It was the sole reason Ann had become a psychiatrist. The woman probably should have been a priest instead. She would likely have been a happier person.

"Give me a chance to do some more research," Alexia said. "I'm sure we can come up with something."

Ann looked like she might argue further, but then she relented. "Okay." She drummed her fingers on her chair. "Think of how important it is to repair the mind behind the deeds. Can you imagine how rewarding it would be if we succeeded?" She smiled at the thought and rolled her wheelchair out into the hallway. Her hopeful voice floated back through the doorway. "I know we can save him."

When silence reigned again, Alexia couldn't help but spare another grin for the stun gun before turning her attention to the files. She wasn't as interested in Chris' file since she had already seen it, but she retrieved it for appearance sake.

Darren Westmore was, in her opinion, a far more interesting individual. She had glanced through his file once before, but it had been a while. His parents were military, and he had served in the army for twelve years right out of high school, making his way up the ranks faster than finishing a boot camp jungle course. He had left the army only when he came to Haven to help arrange the strategic layout of the "town" and keep tabs on the crystals for the United States government.

The man was used to success and heavy backing. He wasn't going to sit idly by and let someone else try to do his job--even if that someone happened to be the son of Haven's CEO. Additionally, to have failed, but still be alive indicated less than an actual defeat. It simply meant that the war wasn't over.

Darren's file contained assessments on the various thefts, and it was obvious that he regarded the thief as the enemy that had yet to be conquered.

Alexia had managed to put herself in front of a tank quite nicely. And it wasn't going to stop firing until she had been run over, shot or captured.

From his record, she could see that containment wasn't part of his plans. He went to great lengths to point out that capture was a "remote" possibility since Haven was dealing with a deranged criminal. He would have to "subdue" the creature in whatever way possible.

She was thus engrossed when a very tentative knock sounded. Looking up, she saw nothing but a hand waving.

Eventually, a head of brown hair poked slowly around the corner. "Can I come in?" Chris asked.

She scrunched her eyebrows in attempt to appear stern and folded her hands primly on the desk. "You'll find that I usually let people in when they are reasonable and knock."

He slid around the corner. The side of his face had a long red welt, one that would probably blossom into a full bruise. "So," he said rather too loudly. "Finished reading my report?" When she nodded, he handed her another information chip. "The last section outlines a test of my security methods by having someone actually try to break through. I was going to be that person since I knew the setup and everything about it. I assumed that if even I couldn't break through, no one could."

Alexia raised an eyebrow. "Except for the fact that you already know your design from every angle. You would have to hope for inspiration along the way. It would be better to let someone else try."

Chris grimaced. "That was pointed out rather forcefully."

"Darren?"

He nodded. "He'll be attempting the break-in. I will be doing the evaluation."

"Oh." How could she invite herself along? Worse, if she did, Darren or Chris was bound to notice her skills. Then again, if they had actually decided to put their security through a test, why should she bother at all?

The answer was simple: ego. She couldn't help but believe that she might be better than Darren or Chris. Until she couldn't do it, she wouldn't know that she had done everything in her power to protect the crystals.

Her consideration made her miss his next two or three statements. The last one must have been a question since he was staring at her with a less than patient expression on his face.

"What did you say?" she focused on Chris again.

"I said, I'd like you to go with us."

"What? Me?" Did he know?

"I just explained," he said irritably. "Weren't you listening?"

"No." She smiled sweetly. "But, you owe me a favor or two since I didn't shoot you last night. Why don't you try your question again?"

He stared at her warily. He opened his mouth, shut it and then opened it again twice. Finally he mumbled, "Last night was an accident."

"You still haven't told me what you were doing there." She was stalling for time. She had no idea how to respond to his request. Why in the world was he inviting her in the first place? Did he suspect her?

"I told you, I saw someone, and it turned out to be Darren. The real question is, what was he doing there?"

Alexia shook her head. "You couldn't have seen him from outside the wall. You already had to be inside the gate or standing on the windmill." Alexia happened to have one of the water-pump windmills right outside her yard.

"I was coming to see you about the plan, just like I'm doing now. I wanted to ask you to come along. I want outside evaluation about how the original thief might try to break in."

And do you think I am that thief? "Why me?"

"Because I've read all the psychiatric evaluations of the thief, and yours is by far the closest possible match. You know this guy's mind as well as anyone. You've had a security course; I want you along to use your imagination and help Darren break in. One of you is going to have to be creative, and it sure as hell isn't going to be Darren."

Her eyebrows arched. "I can't deny that I might be a tad more creative than Darren, but the security course that I took hardly qualifies me to break through your defenses." She waved at the plan. "I don't even understand most of that stuff." Truthfully, she was going to have to do some research on many of his methods before she could break through them. On top of that, Chris had obviously watched Indiana Jones a few too many times. One of his security methods included burying the instructions in a cave that was booby-trapped with large holes covered with false ground.

Not that booby-traps worried her. Outdoor traps could always be set off falsely, and they were not usually automatically reset. Already her mind was planning how to get around the electronics.

Chris interrupted her thoughts with more persuasion. "The security course is enough for you to understand the basic principles, which is all you need. I want you there for your creativity and understanding of the human mind, not as one of Darren's soldiers."

"Soldiers wouldn't work. For one, getting across that expanse of desert would be too noticeable. One or two people could make it without being spotted by the radar fly-by, but Darren isn't going to be able to take a tank in there with him."

Chris shrugged. "He gets three tries. If he wants to waste them by trying to get a tank through, that's his problem."

"A small army from different directions might work," she mused. "Then, if you could trip up the electrical system, you could sacrifice bodies setting off your other traps. Darren might try that."

"That would be try number two," Chris sneered. "He's going to have a hard time finding volunteers to jump into the traps."

She shook her head and thought of George. Darren had the ability to make people follow him, either by working on their expectations or by generating fear. "You'd be surprised. Of course, he would have to find not only nut cases, but ones that could actually make the trek across the desert. All in all, not an easy task."

"Nut cases?" Chris repeated, feigning shock. "That would be the medical term, I suppose."

Instead of being embarrassed by her own comment, she laughed. "No, it would be a general statement, not a psychiatric analysis."

He shared her smile. "So you'll go?"

"I'll think about it." She made sure to keep her sweating palms quiescent.

"That's all I can ask." He stood. "Remember, I will be there to help break through the security, so for any plans you come up with, I'm going to offer my assistance. I won't tell you anymore about the security than you already know, but other than that, I'll be along to help."

"Tanks are out then." She pretended to be gravely disappointed.

He gave a wicked laugh and turned to leave. "Oh yeah. You might consider bringing the stun-gun rather than one of your more lethal weapons, in case you have to break up any fights." His green eyes were wide, but guilty.

"You mean in case I should find myself wanting to use an almost harmless weapon?"

"You never know when the occasion might arise."

"Don't worry. I don't hit anything by accident. If you want me along, I suggest that you and Darren put your differences behind you. It's going to be a long, hot trek across some rough miles. If we are going to make it, it will take cooperation." She tilted her head. "And if I take a weapon, it will be there for me to use."

He nodded solemnly, the last trace of humor gone. "Glad you'll be on board."

His assumption probably should have made her angry. Instead, it left her staring at his retreating back with a worried nagging. He knew her well enough to know she wouldn't back down from the challenge.

What else did he know about her? Worse, when would he decide to use it?

Chapter 7

Much to Alexia's amusement, Darren took her addition to the project as an extreme nuisance. She heard from Ann that he had been bellowing about having to coddle a young woman and what real thief would bring along such a detriment?

Alexia ignored the situation and began her own preparations. It would mean a trip to the outer world to the nearest town, Socorro. The name of the town was the Spanish word for "help." She wasn't certain if the town had been named that because someone had once received help there or because the town needed help. It was a dusty, mangy settlement with little to recommend it other than one battered college campus and a few storefronts that looked like they belonged on an old western movie set.

Nevertheless, there were some things that Haven didn't supply and a store of ammunition was one. Socorro was her closest option, so after she finished up work for the day, she headed there.

She should have known that Darren would also make the trip for the same reasons. If she had thought of it, she would have contrived to avoid him entirely. Unfortunately, there wasn't more than one store at which to buy ammo. When she stepped inside the store, Darren spotted her before she could change her mind and come back later.

"Hello." His voice was a good deal colder than the warm air outside.

"Hi, Darren."

"Surely you don't mean to go through with this." It was not a question, so Alexia chose to ignore him and went to pick out her purchases.

"This isn't a picnic complete with servants." With her peripheral vision, Alexia could see that his face was deepening in color. He finally put his hand out to stop her from walking away. Alexia looked up. Piercing eyes stared down at her. His expression was as hard as his body, and Alexia had no doubt that he could make the trip. He could probably carry her the entire way if it became necessary.

"No, I didn't think it was going to be a picnic." She gave him a half-smile. "We'll have to meet and make plans. Bring the topographical maps. I've broken down Chris' defense plan. I'll bring that."

She turned to go. His sigh of exasperation lifted the hair off the back of her neck. "Dr. Zimmerman." She would have stopped and faced him, but movement outside on the street caught her attention. The sun was setting, and it was almost dusk. The storefront faced east, so the street outside was already in shadow. She very nearly missed seeing the girl's body being jerked back into the alley.

But she didn't. Neither, apparently, did Darren miss the girl's scream. He beat Alexia to the door, only because he pushed her out of the way. Since one didn't win against something of his mass, she was forced to allow him to go first.

He reached the alley a scant second before she did, and busied himself with the three large men that were not holding the girl. The young woman was no longer trying to scream. She was too busy trying to breathe. Her eyes bulged against the pressure of a man's hands that were wrapped around her neck.

Alexia kicked the man hard. His leg didn't break, but she did get his attention.

He let the girl go very quickly. Alexia barely caught a glimpse of dark blue eyes and long black hair before the girl disappeared around the side of the building. She probably wouldn't be able to scream any time in the near future, but she was able to breathe again, a process the man had been about to stop.

Even with his knee hurt, the man attacked. He pulled a weapon of some sort, but in the dim alley light, Alexia couldn't tell exactly what it was. She kicked at it, sending it spinning against an adobe building. He lunged towards her in a crouch designed to smother.

She grabbed his head and helped it into her knee.

He crashed down, out cold.

Instinct provided another warning, and she spun low. Darren should have been the only one behind her, but that was not the case.

There was only one man tall enough to hold a knife to Darren's throat. He had only gotten in that position because another man had entered the alley with a gun. The gunman was comfortable with his weapon. It showed in his relaxed stance and in his eyes. She couldn't reach any of the thugs without considerable movement--during which time, she would no doubt be shot.

The man with the gun studied the body behind Alexia. "He dead?" The guy leaned sideways, trying to see the body.

"Friend of yours?" Alexia asked. She had misjudged his age. The gun made him appear older, more menacing. Behind it, the "man" was a teenager. So were the four or so others that crowded into the alley behind him.

The youth shook his head, both sides of which were shaved. The top of his head sported long, orange hair. "Nah. Belongs to the Barracks." He spit to emphasize his feelings.

Unlike those that had attacked the girl, he was young, as was the guy holding a knife at Darren's throat. This gang was also better armed. "You mind if we take our business elsewhere?" Alexia asked.

Darren stared at her as if she had lost her mind. The kid smirked. "Why should we let you?"

"Why shouldn't you? We were passing through, saw a young lady that needed help. I'm sure that you would have jumped in had you come along first," she added, her voice the very spirit of good will.

The one with the knife shrugged, causing Darren to grunt with pain. "Why should we help anyone? What's in it for us?"

She glanced at him while keeping the gunman in sight. "Women should be protected. What's the point in being a man and being stronger, if you don't do anything useful with your strength?"

No one seemed to have an immediate answer to her question. Finally, the one holding the gun announced, "I think if we let you go, you'll owe us a favor."

When the knife holder heard this, he relaxed. This was familiar ground.

"What favor exactly are you doing for us?" Alexia asked.

The gunman was surprised again, either at her question or at her lack of fear. "Letting you go without hurting you." To emphasize the point, he pointed the gun towards her middle.

She shrugged. "We had that much accomplished before you came along."

He blinked several times without saying anything. He was a good leader; he didn't glance at any of his followers to see if they had answers, nor did he allow his uncertainty to rule.

Finally, not knowing how to counter the argument, he started one of his own. "You think because you work on the hill, you're better than us? You think all that pretty schooling, made you special?" He drew out the word special in a high mocking voice.

"Sure. My education and my job make me useful to society and worth my share of the air I breathe. You're worth as much as you choose to be." As her glance passed over the youth with the knife, she noticed Darren's eyes. They bulged. He did not look particularly pleased with her. The knife wasn't close enough to his windpipe to be causing the choking noises he was making.

The leader said nothing. These guys weren't hungry, they weren't strung out on drugs and they weren't desperate. They were just bored, and that made all the difference in the world when compared to the original thugs that had attacked the girl. Those guys were hunters. The girl's death may have meant another meal for them, more drugs or plain survival if the girl somehow represented a threat.

By contrast, the boys who stood here now were from middle class families, and they were restless. They were making their own excitement.

"Next thing you know," the kid drawled, "you'll be telling us to go to school, get us a preeetty ed-u-ca-tion and be like yooou." He took one hand away from his gun and did some kind of complicated hand signal and then proclaimed, "Life ain't living unless it's dangerous."

"So you pick up a gun and suddenly it's worth living?" Alexia stared at him and muttered under her breath. How was she supposed to argue with such lack of logic? How to convince him there was better excitement elsewhere? "What are you going to do with this exciting gun? Hunting for a living is out these days, unless you want to hunt the vermin of the street. Hard to do when you're one of them."

He watched her. He might be considering her words, then again, he might be trying to figure out how best to kill her.

She nodded in Darren's direction and noticed that Darren's eyes were now glazed. "Let him go. Find something else to entertain you."

"Why?"

Darren gargled.

"Because there isn't any point at all in killing us. I assure you, it won't be fun." She tried to look threatening, but she was running out of ideas. She couldn't fight them all.

"You think it's us that makes decisions about what we'll do?" the leader asked. "Would you hire us?"

"That depends. What can you do that I can't do myself? When you find that skill, come find me. I live at Haven."

Those standing the closest moved back. She had openly admitted what the group had already guessed. She and Darren were from Haven. It was as good as confessing that she was a freak. Haven had a reputation for housing insane old men who could blow up the world.

Apparently further coercion wasn't needed. The leader gave another hand signal. The guy holding Darren pushed Darren towards her. She stepped aside, letting him hit the wall, keeping free should she need to move. Her sideways jump brought her close to the edge of the circle, next to a knife and the kid holding it.

He stared at her for a moment and then backed away, slowly. If he attacked, his age wouldn't matter, and he knew it.

Darren, now that he was free, suddenly loomed a lot larger in the shadows.

The alley was alive with movement for a moment and then only the gunman stood there. Alexia knew that he would be gone in another second.

"Keith. Keith Sandoval."

The light swallowed him. Alexia remembered to breathe, and she flexed her knees. She searched the alley, but it was empty. Slowly, followed by Darren, she edged back out into the open street.

Now that the danger was over, she felt much more like a helpless female. Her hands shook, and she was tempted to clutch Darren's arm for support. Knowing that they were probably still being watched saved her as she marched back across the street to her car. Darren followed her to it.

"I want you to drive me home," Alexia said.

He didn't answer, but after she got into the passenger side he slid behind the wheel. She couldn't tell if he was angry or not, but it didn't matter. She had to tell him about her problem. "I tend to faint after a crisis or get violently ill." The black haze was already forming a tunnel, calling to her. It was better than usual since she was sitting down. "Could we stop and get a milkshake? Protein and sugar are best at settling my stomach and getting my blood sugar stable."

"Milkshake? You can't eat that junk." He glanced at her out of the corner of his eye. "Are you really going to faint?" He sounded distinctly uncomfortable as well as bewildered. She didn't blame him. How often did he watch a woman stand up to several armed men and then do an about-face and sit white-faced, looking like death?

"Are you okay?" Real concern touched his words, and he reached out a hand. Her own was like ice. "My God." He started the car. "You definitely can't have a milkshake!"

"Please. It would help." She hated the weakness in her voice, but by God she had been in danger, and her body wasn't going to accept it and blithely move on.

He probably shook his head, but she couldn't tell. Her cold hand trembled with reaction. Inside her mind, she felt fine, but her body refused to believe it. The problem had plagued her for her entire life. No matter how much she controlled her mind, her body insisted upon reacting.

By the time Darren arrived at the complex, she was feeling distinctly ill. Her stomach did not approve of his driving. Eating would have helped, but she hadn't had the strength to convince him. She stumbled out of the car. "Should have taken me home."

His arms came around her to support her before she fell. "No one is going to hurt you. I would never have let them hurt you."

She didn't mention that he would have had a hard time protecting her if he had been shot full of bullet holes. Even her body muscles, which had no brain of their own, had made that connection. Strangely, his holding her helped. He smoothed a hand down her back, rubbing warmth into her body.

He continued to murmur reassuring phrases and hold her.

She sighed and relaxed. When Darren decided to give a woman attention, he didn't go by halves. "Thanks," she said a little shakily. Her tunnel vision wasn't gone, but it was getting better. In another few minutes she would be able to see again.

She felt, rather than saw him raise her head up. "I think I should sit down." She wanted her head down, not up. His moving it made her dizzier. And it was getting darker again...

His lips were warm and gentle. Confusion enveloped her, even as his mouth comforted her in a way she wasn't quite sure she needed.

As suddenly as the warmth was there, it was gone.

"What a touching scene! You do know how to lead the troops, don't you?" a voice sneered.

Vaguely, she registered sarcasm and disgust. It took her several moments to place the voice, but she recognized it much faster after Darren let her go. Of course it was easier to think then, because without Darren's support she grabbed for the car, leaned over and let blood rushed to her head.

She gulped air and tried to convince her stomach to settle completely.

"Maybe you won't mind having a woman along to coddle after all." Chris wasn't finished yet. "Alexia, don't you think you're taking the weak-kneed thing a bit far?"

She could feel him staring at her, but she didn't lift her head. She knew if she did, the ground would start swirling.

It was then that Chris realized something was wrong. His next sentence was short on sarcasm and long on threat. "What did you do to her?"

She knew he stepped forward, but she didn't have time for explanations. She really needed something to eat to get her blood sugar levels up. Determined, but still leaned over, she edged towards the entrance of the main building. There would be food inside her desk. The angry voices faded behind her as she placed one foot carefully in front of the other.

When she reached her office, she invaded her stock of candy bars. All Haven members were required to write down everything they ate as part of the health program so she wrote "Snickers" on the date of her electronic desk calendar. It bleeped, acknowledging the entry.

She chewed and swallowed quickly. She wanted more food and in quantity. The best place for that was at home.

Finishing the candy, she walked carefully out the back way. She was feeling steadier by the moment. She frowned, remembering that she had dropped her package of ammunition. That meant another trip to town.

Yawning, she made her way across the complex. She was very tired. It was past her bedtime.

Halfway up the steps, she realized that the day wasn't quite over. First, she would have to find a way to deal with the glaring beast waiting outside her door.

Chapter 8

Other than pacing impatiently, Chris didn't look any worse for his tangle with Darren. Alexia wondered if Darren was in the hospital since he hadn't also shown up. Of course, if she asked and Darren wasn't hospitalized, Chris wouldn't be pleased.

"Are you okay?" Chris demanded. "Darren told me what happened."

"I'm feeling much better." She waved a hand at her door reader and went in. "It's one of those reaction things. There's nothing really wrong with me."

Chris followed her inside. In the light of her living room, he studied her carefully before glancing at his surroundings. The low level track lighting probably made it hard for him to form much of an opinion about her Southwestern furniture and mismatched decorating.

He turned back to her. "Are you sure you didn't get hurt?" He reached up a hand as though he would pat her shoulder.

His concern was obvious, and Alexia was touched. "I'm okay. Really. I just need to eat and get some sleep."

He finally did touch her, one hand lightly brushing her arm. "I'm sorry. I can't believe I stood there and...let you walk away. I didn't even see you leave!"

She patted his arm. "I was kind of bent over because I was worried I'd pass out. Not that easy to see."

His face reddened alarmingly. To keep him from self-combusting, she repeated around a rather large yawn, "Really, I'm fine."

"Good grief." He closed his eyes and then asked, "Where's the kitchen? The least I can do is fix you dinner."

"I can--"

But he was already making his way to the swinging door at the other end of the living room. She shrugged and sat on the couch. "I was going to order a pizza." Haven didn't support a huge number of restaurants and most of those were health food places that fell in line with the better living theme. She had fully intended to order a real pizza from outside even though it was frowned upon.

She sighed and sat back with her eyes closed. Oh well. Pizzas from Socorro were expensive because no one wanted to drive all the way to Haven to deliver. Maybe whatever Chris cooked would be faster.

Chris came back in and handed her a cup of tea. "You don't appear to have any brandy, so I used milk."

She smiled. "Close enough."

He studied her again and finally looked for the light switch. She could have adjusted it with a voice command, but it was easier to let him set the light where he wanted it. The tea, in any light, was heavenly.

"You didn't get cut or hurt?"

"No," she said, closing her eyes again. "Just tired."

"I'll wake you when dinner is ready."

Alexia didn't think that waking her would be necessary, but a half hour must have passed before she realized it.

Chris brought in a tray. A suspiciously delicious concoction was arranged on a plate.

"Stroganoff?" She squealed with delight, barely believing her luck. "Where did you get it at this time of the night?"

Chris shrugged. "The lady that owns the yogurt shop makes it for me."

"The health food place?" She shoveled in a bite and nearly swooned again. The stuff was delicious!

He nodded. "I provided the recipe. It's hard to find anything worth eating around here. I was complaining about it my second day here and Tracey--the lady that owns the shop--offered to cook."

"Well, why doesn't she serve this in her restaurant?" She didn't look up, but continued eating.

"Come on. Do you know how hard it would be to get into Haven if you said you served stroganoff with real, fattening, life-giving cream? The board wouldn't even take a second look at her application. If they wanted Haven to have all the advantages of the outer world, what would be the point in Haven?"

Alexia paused with the fork halfway to her mouth and laughed. "I think it's supposed to be the other way around, Chris. Here at Haven we're supposed to be the ones with advantages." She took another bite. "However, now that I know the secret, I want an introduction. This is wonderful."

He nodded. "She makes a mean lasagna. Three kinds of cheese, sausage and hamburger."

"Ooh. My heart. My stomach!" She laughed again. "I'm used to driving miles out of my way to get this kind of food."

He grinned. "Yeah, and then you have to report it."

By the time she finished sopping up every last morsel, she was feeling much better. "I hope you already ate?"

He nodded. "I was actually looking for you when...I, uh, ran into you." His voice strangled at the end.

"Oh? Why?"

"The meeting tomorrow."

"What meeting? I must have missed the notice. I was gone this afternoon getting supplies."

"So, you're going to vote for the proposal?"

She frowned. "I assumed that it had already been voted in."

He shook his head and sat back in disgust. "No, Corporate wants a vote from everyone involved. I wasn't certain you were going to support it, because dad said something about resistance from the psychiatrists." He watched her warily.

Alexia curled her legs up on the sofa. "That's strange. I spoke with Ann about the proposal briefly. She didn't seem to approve right off, but she's the only one that I've talked to." She waved her hand. "Don't worry. If it needs more discussion, I'll certainly be there. I think it's a good plan. I'm looking forward to the trip."

"Uh..." Chris looked uncomfortable again. "There was one other area of resistance, although you may have taken care of that."

"What was it?"

"Darren objected strongly to your accompanying us." He was busy looking anywhere but at her. "At least he did earlier today."

"Ah, yes, I heard something to that affect." She shrugged. "I think he has discovered that I can handle myself."

Chris stared at her for a moment too long. He stood, his shoulders rigid. "Can you?"

"Chris--"

He interrupted her as he walked to the door. "I'm glad you're okay. And I hope that you convinced Darren to vote for the proposal tomorrow. The meeting is at one o'clock."

She forced herself off the couch to let him out. He didn't turn back or even look at her. It was probably for the best. She had no idea what to say to him anyway. Really, she didn't owe him an explanation.

Darren and Chris were just colleagues. They all needed to...work together to get the job done. But not too closely. She couldn't do her job if either of them got too close.

Without conscious thought, she entered the lock pattern for the door and dragged herself off to bed. She didn't want to think too hard about what she was getting herself into.

* * *

A full night's rest, plus an extra hour, revived her usual spirits. The New Mexico morning was cool, and she grabbed her favorite black sweater before going out. At the main building, she stopped in the mail room. To her immense surprise, there was a note from a Keith Sandoval, the leader from the night before. Well, well, well. He must have hand delivered it to the complex personally. What might he want that was so important?

She made her way to her office, shrugged out of her sweater, and was about to open the letter, when her least favorite coworker stopped in.

"Got a minute?" Phillip hefted his large frame against her doorway. Surreptitiously, she checked to make sure the support wasn't bending inwards from all the extra weight. Though all the buildings on Haven were temperature controlled, Phillip was sweating.

"If we keep it short." She managed to keep from sighing out loud.

"My office?" he suggested, as she had known he would. He could keep his bulk cool there because his office was never above sixty degrees.

She set the mail on her desk, followed him out and pulled her door closed. As the lock engaged, she changed her mind and pushed on the door, too late. "Let me grab my sweater." Phillip hadn't waited, so she decided not to bother. Since his idea of a discussion was to arrogantly assume everyone agreed with him, she wouldn't be forced to sit in his office long.

He lumbered to his office, where he graciously offered her a chair and held it for her. She knew from past experiences that telling him not to bother was a waste of time.

"Now," he said, taking his own chair and leaning forward across his desk. "We need to prepare our strategy." Beady little eyes surrounded by too much flesh peered malevolently at her from behind his immaculate desk.

"What strategy?"

"Why, to get you out of this silly masquerade! I can't believe that anyone would even pretend that we would sign up to the ludicrous idea of taking the crystal instructions off-site. My psychiatric report clearly states that we should begin an examination of each and every individual at Haven. I'm certain we can ferret out insanity in one individual. I mean, please. It's what I do. Why is it that management is too good to read?"

Poor, trod-upon Phillip. He never considered the fact that his method of delivery was irritating and overbearing. In addition, if he was as good a psychiatrist as he claimed, why hadn't he ever announced that she was the culprit? "I'm voting for the plan," Alexia said, wishing that she had thought to ask what he wanted to chat about before agreeing to come to his office.

He jerked back as though struck. "But--you must be mistaken! You must go before the council and explain that you want nothing to do with this charade!"

She stood. She didn't have time for this. "Sorry, Phillip. I'm voting for the proposal."

He stared at her for a moment and then changed tactics. "Don't expect to win."

It was pretty obvious the psychiatric dissent that Chris was worried about was coming from Phillip. "You have your vote, and I have mine." She tried to make it sound as though it was just a friendly difference of opinion, but probably failed.

Advancing from behind his desk, he wrapped oversized digits around her shoulder and halted her forward momentum. "I will be representing the department vote in the meeting. Our vote will be against this ridiculous plan."

"If I recall correctly, anyone with a concern can attend a council meeting," Alexia said.

"I think it's better if I attend--with one plan."

Alexia shrugged. "I guess that won't be possible."

"You don't seem to understand what I'm saying. I will be voting for the department." His lip curled. "I think you should realize what open defiance means here."

She removed his hulking hand from her shoulder by stepping back.

He followed, standing too close. "You realize you need our approval for your other little projects. You've been anxious to press your new 'human behavior in isolation,' program, haven't you?" He snorted. "We all have to cooperate if we want to accomplish our goals. It isn't wise to force dissent."

She glared at him. "Is that a threat?"

"Threat?" He reached up as though to brush something from her shoulder. His chubby hand pulled her hair, hard. Before she could react, he smirked and stepped back. "Threats are unnecessary and uncivilized. I think we understand each other."

Alexia seethed. He was threatening her, and they both knew it. At Haven, a board of peers generally approved new programs. Phillip could easily have sway over whether her proposals were granted approval. "When hell freezes over," she snarled. She had come to Haven for the freedom to explore ideas, not to exchange one dictator for another. Her back straight, she stalked away. The man had nerve claiming he could ferret out insanity. He was a walking Sybil!

Angry, she detoured downstairs to get a bagel.

By the time she made it back to her office, she wasn't much calmer. Grumbling, she shifted her bagel, placed her finger into the imprint reader and pushed her office door open. She set her breakfast down and picked up her mail.

It took her a minute to locate Keith's letter because it was at the bottom of her mail pile. Taking a hefty bite of bagel, she paused. Hadn't she placed the letter from Keith on top? She had been about to read it when Phillip interrupted. Hadn't she?

She pushed the mail around. It was certainly the only interesting piece in the bunch. How had it gotten to the bottom?

She scanned her office. Nothing else seemed out of place...except...where was her sweater?

She hadn't taken it with her. Who would want her sweater? Her office door had been closed and locked. The only other prints that worked for her door were those for emergency access personnel or security.

Security.

The one unspoken word made her mouth go quite dry. Suddenly the bagel wasn't quite so appetizing. Both Chris and Darren could get into her office should they desire. Both were an integral part of security and if they suspected her...but her sweater?

The print reader would normally flash a message if security had come in for a legitimate reason. In the whole time Alexia had been here, there had only been one entry and that had been to fix an electrical problem.

That left only one other conclusion. If security had come in, they had done so in secret. Or it had been someone else. Her stomach curled.

Had someone else found a way around the fingerprint reader?

It wasn't hard to do, as Alexia had proved the first time security had tried to put the crystals behind a locked door with a reader. She had simply lifted the fingerprints of two individuals that were allowed access. Then she pressed the fingerprints onto a rubber substance that contained an electrical beat that substituted as a heartbeat. When both individuals were out of town, she used one fake set going in and the other to get back out. In theory, the person that entered never left.

Unfortunately, after security figured out how she had done it, the technique was described in several reports, making the method available to anyone.

She tapped her fingers impatiently. There was really no way of knowing who had come in or why. She stared at the envelope. There was, however, a way to figure out whether or not the envelope had actually been opened.

Holding the letter up to the light, she inspected the seal. With the paper inside, it was nearly opaque. She slit the envelope across the top edge, preserving the flap.

It didn't take long to determine that it had been opened once before. Bits of mismatched paper littered the seal. Unless Keith had opened and resealed his own letter, someone, using Alexia's fingerprints, had accessed her office.

Why? And why go through her mail? And take her sweater? Was it like Darren standing outside her window, some sort of spy technique that she didn't know about? Or did Chris have some reason to want it?

Darren was the one more likely to be interested in Keith's letter because he had heard Keith call out his name last night. But what did he really expect to find? A quick scan showed that all Keith had written about was his supposed skill set.

If Darren had been here on legitimate security, why had he glued the letter closed again?

What about Chris? If anyone was smart enough to distrust her, it was Chris. She still shivered whenever she thought about him asking her to step through the laser beams. Had he taken the sweater to see if it reflected lasers? But...it wasn't even part of the same outfit!

She tapped her fingers some more, but the answers didn't appear. No matter. She knew a sure-fire way of tracking how often someone was coming into her office.

Chapter 9

On her way to the meeting after lunch, Alexia ran into Ann. The woman beckoned her to the side of the hallway. "I'm not going to the Corporate meeting this afternoon." She patted her water-wings fretfully. "You know how I feel about the new proposal. Phillip suggested that he represent all of us in the department, and I think one vote should stand for all of us. Otherwise we'd be banding against you, and I'm not sure Phillip's motives are entirely fair."

Alexia's stomach, which had been tying itself in knots, relaxed a bit. "That's really generous of you, Ann. I know you'd rather I stay here, but I think the plan has merits."

Ann sniffed. "The crystals and instructions belong here. No matter what is to be done about all of this, that technology should stay in Haven. We can't go pushing outside the walls, wandering without guidance--" she stopped herself and smoothed her flowered dress across her legs. "Well. Be that as it may, I don't necessarily approve of Phillip's techniques. He has seniority, and one representation from our side is enough."

"I appreciate that." Alexia really didn't want to have to face all of her colleagues down, at least not all at once. "I won't ask you to wish me luck."

Ann didn't smile, but she did wave Alexia onward.

Alexia went on with a small feeling of hope. At least Ann was willing to let Alexia make her own decisions.

The meeting room contained a moving holograph along the entire side of one wall. It depicted an outdoor scene, complete with waterfall, trees and animals. Alexia took a seat so that she could see out the real window and began arranging her notes. There was no way to know exactly who would be here today because Corporate meetings were always open. The ten directors could invite specialists and any individual that wished to attend, could.

Alexia had never met Chris Appleton's father, but she knew him by sight. When he came in, everyone in the room afforded him the instant attention that only an executive garnered. Now that she had met Chris, she could see a family resemblance. His eyes were the exact mirror image of Chris' except that his did not hold a mischievous twinkle.

Chris followed the elder Appleton in and managed to suppress the twinkle, if not the intent. He grinned at her and took the seat by her side. "How are you feeling this afternoon?"

"Fine, thanks." She stiffened involuntarily as Phillip entered. He ignored her, pretending to be busy with his own important thoughts. Then, to Alexia's immense surprise, Dr. Brandon came in. His bright red hair and funny duck-walk normally made her smile, but suspicion of betrayal flashed through her mind. The relief she had felt at Ann staying out of the contest evaporated. Was Dr. Brandon here to vote against her? He had been helping her with her experiments since she had come to Haven. He knew her work better than anyone. Would he align himself with the enemy without consultation?

Darren walked in then and took the last chair, between the environmental director and the finance director. He glanced her way, but gave no other acknowledgment. Alexia was already too confused to try and interpret his actions.

The older Appleton opened the meeting. "I assume you've read the plan. In summary, its intent is to separate the crystals from the instructions. The new security system will be tested by the developer," he gave a truncated nod towards Chris without making eye contact, "and the head of present security, Darren Westmore."

Darren acknowledged the challenge with a cold glance around the room.

"Additionally, there has been a suggestion that one of our psychiatrists accompany the men on their endeavor. She will study the process and actively help implement any ideas she thinks may mimic the mind of the thief." He hesitated. "Frankly, I'm not certain that this last addition is entirely necessary."

Alexia was ready for an argument, but before she could speak, Phillip stood. "Perhaps if we sent someone who could withstand the rigors of the hike?"

Alexia couldn't stop herself from blurting out, "You wouldn't be suggesting yourself?"

Phillip's face flared red, and he glared at her. "Since my theory necessitates the analysis of individuals, I can hardly afford to take time off traipsing about the countryside. I might point out that your own time could be more valuably spent."

Since he didn't mince words, Alexia didn't either, but she didn't bother to attack him. "I think I can be a valuable help in the field. I can make educated guesses as to how our master criminal might proceed. On page twelve there is a discussion on the possibility of making the trek to the secured area on foot versus using a horse. Given the history of the thief, I think it is highly likely he would use both." She knew she was taking risks, but she had to be competent enough to win their votes. Her best defense was to act like her co-workers--show a big ego and act like she knew the mind of the criminal just because she had a degree in psychiatry.

Phillip pounded a fist on the table. "Utterly untrue! I have explicitly pointed out, time after time, that one of the traits of the thief is his obvious insanity! His thefts follow a pattern! Insane people take great comfort in committing crimes over and over using the same tricks to outsmart the opposition."

Dr. Appleton took back the floor. "Whether the thief is insane or not is hardly the issue; let's put the trip to a vote."

Phillip protested, "We've all logged our votes. I checked the tally, and it's quite clear that most of us are against the plan entirely. We certainly have enough votes to at the very least keep Dr. Zimmerman safely at home."

"What do you mean, logged our votes?" Alexia asked. "I think I mentioned that no matter where the department stands overall, I would vote on my own."

Dr. Appleton shook his head. "It seems that some people have changed their votes. The only reason we had this meeting was because we were at deadlock. However, it is readily apparent that Alexia has changed her vote to yes." He looked at her, his gaze quite serious.

"Changed to yes?" she parroted in surprise.

He looked down at a printout. "Are you still against then?"

Confused, Alexia frowned. "I was never against it. I've never voted the matter at all." She looked at Chris. "Unless someone here signed in a vote for me. I was out of the office yesterday afternoon and wasn't even aware of this meeting until last night."

"I did mention that you had changed your vote," Chris said. "When I talked to you last night you indicated support."

"But I hadn't even seen the meeting message! How could I have voted nay earlier?"

Chris stared back at her. His mouth opened and then closed. His father stood and walked a printout over to Alexia.

Sure enough, an "against" vote had been recorded for both the plan and her presence. The time that appeared next to the vote was simply not possible. She had been feeling very sick about that time yesterday. In fact, if she checked her own logs...she hurriedly opened the table console and punched in a sequence. Whoever had logged the vote had done so right after she had entered the Snickers bar. She had been decidedly ill and had left the office right after raiding her private stash of candy.

"This doesn't make sense. I didn't even see the mail message about the meeting!" Come to think of it, she hadn't seen the electronic message this morning either. Which could only mean that her mysterious visitor that read Keith's letter was also a visitor on her electronic mail system. Whoever had voted for her had erased the mail message completely. If she hadn't seen Chris last night, she might have missed the meeting, and her answer would have been recorded as no.

Furious, she glared at Dr. Appleton who happened to be the nearest victim. "My vote is for the proposal."

She turned her malicious gaze on Darren. If he was the cause of her office being broken into again and had the nerve to change her mail-- for that matter, she had already caught both Chris and Darren at her house, staring into her window. Maybe they were both keeping an eye on her, and they had both planned on voting for her.

Chris' eyes widened when she turned her glare towards him. "What? I didn't do it! I suggested you come along in the first place. Why would I vote against my own plan?"

Dr. Appleton took control of the meeting again before an uproar could begin. "We'll have security check into it. Under the circumstances, I think we had all better vote again." He sat back down. "Those for the plan, raise a hand."

She raised her hand. Darren, Chris, Dr. Appleton, and, to her immense relief Dr. Brandon's hand went up. The financial officer and the science director voted yes. The science director was Sam's boss. Alexia had been hoping he would vote with her.

Only Phillip and the environmental director still needed to cast a vote. Quickly, Alexia compared the votes. They had changed in only two places. Her vote, and Darren's were now "for." Previously, both had been marked on the printout as "against." No other votes in the room had changed. It was good to know that Dr. Brandon had been on her side, but she was a bit disgruntled that the environmental director sided with Phillip.

Alexia wasn't positive about why Darren had changed his vote to yes. Was he trying to throw suspicion away from himself or did he really believe she was up to the trip?

Of course, she had no proof against anyone. For certain, someone had retrieved the mail message and logged her vote. Only someone who knew the password should have had access to her mail, but as a thief, she knew it was easy to obtain passwords. She did it often.

Could Darren and Chris have access to all accounts for security reasons? Perhaps they didn't even need a password.

Dr. Appleton nodded as the last hand went down. "The plan is approved. You three will start your journey next week." He verified his assumption by making each of them nod. He didn't linger over any of them, not even his son.

Regardless of the fact that Dr. Appleton would ask security to look into the matter, Alexia decided to bait the guilty party herself. "I've written up a list of how I think the criminal might proceed. I'll provide a copy to all of you right before we leave. It will be interesting to compare results of the actual project with my list after we return." And whoever was so very interested in the project would probably be unable to wait a week to see her ideas. They might try to break into her computer or her office to retrieve it.

Phillip glared across the room. "I will provide a thesis also. Under the circumstances, I think a clear mind will be of immense help."

Alexia ignored his insult. She had more important things to do than spar with Phillip.

Darren caught her arm on the way out. "Good show," he whispered. "You were wonderful!"

"I was?" His enthusiasm caught her by surprise. After the kiss in the parking lot, she not only hadn't seen him, she hadn't even heard from him. The event had no doubt been an aberration. He must have been feeling protective and let it get to his male ego.

He grinned, flashing his perfect teeth. "I had to change my vote after the way you handled those gutter-mongers the other day. You are okay?"

It wasn't really a question, more an assumption. "Yes, I'm fine."

"Good." He looked her up and down, a casual inspection. "You look great. I'm looking forward to going over that list." He patted her shoulder and winked, leaving her at her office door. She watched Darren walk away. He really was a handsome devil.

Shaking her head, she left a bundle of papers stacked on her desk and perused the hallway quickly. It was empty. Everyone had cleared out after the meeting, most likely to develop new arguments. She had never practiced the art of thievery backwards before, but it was high time she did so.

Taking a spool of spider thread, she cut two strips. She held them in place until she closed the door. Neither piece was likely to be noticed by the thief, but if she only left one and it fell, there was always the chance that it had slipped lose. She grinned. If anyone came in, the threads would both fall.

The first thing she did when she got home was change her password and add a retina scan requirement for the email program. Then, she set up a separate system that would collect copies of all her mail. No more would messages disappear without a trace even if someone managed to break into her account.

She wondered again, briefly, about Darren's behavior. Was he trying to patronize her or did he really think she could do the job? Maybe he was hiding the fact that he had logged her vote, but then again, he had kissed her before any of that happened. So...

So nothing. She pulled on a lock of hair and then threw up her hands in frustration. Worrying about it wasn't going to provide any answers. Besides, she had a lot of preparations to complete in one week, starting with going back to town to collect the ammunition she needed.

She paced back and forth for nearly an hour, jotting down things she needed to do before she finally turned the lights off and went to bed.

Chapter 10

The day before Alexia was to start on the journey, the pieces of thread that she faithfully placed there daily, were missing from her office door. Whoever had come in was likely looking for clues about her report or her plans. Unfortunately, that described half the people in the meeting room including Phillip and Darren.

The simple note she had left for the thief on top of her desk was crumpled in a corner of her office. The thief apparently didn't like the message, "No more easy freebies."

She grinned. She only hoped that the rest of her plans would go so smoothly. The crystal thief, if true to her colors, would have to steal the package before the others arrived. She had no idea if she was going to be able to pull it off. If she was sure of anything, it was that Chris hadn't naively described every security device. That was probably the only reason he was bothering to go along. It would be his job to make sure that Darren didn't kill himself by setting off one of the unseen traps and trying to escape in a fury that did him personal harm.

She would have to get away from both men long enough to try and steal the instructions on her own. Failing that, she was going to honestly try and help Darren reach the instructions without appearing too knowledgeable.

Checking the logs for updates, she noted that Chris had returned to Haven early in the morning after placing the instruction chip in a protective, locked case deep in the Gila wilderness mountains. He had used a helicopter. The radar, set to detect any flying vehicles larger than an eagle, had accurately followed the helicopter and reported on progress.

Alexia perused the satellite images again. During the hottest part of the day, the pictures of the area were quite good. Only during night, early morning or sundown was the angle of the clearing wrong.

Overall, she was impressed with the plan. Chris had used technology that wasn't going to be easy to surpass. The theft would have to take place at night, which would require familiarity with the fences and other alarms. From the plans, she had determined that the locked case was probably hidden in a cave or underground site, but she couldn't be sure. Using a remote-controlled robot, unless it looked very much like part of the local fauna, was out of the question.

She was satisfied that she could break through the alarms, but she wasn't absolutely positive. Unless she could be certain of success by the time they reached the site, she wouldn't even try. It would be pointless to risk it, even if she had a good excuse.

Anxious to finish up a few remaining tasks, she shut down her system and carefully put the threads that guarded her door back in place. It would be interesting to see if anyone visited her office while she was gone. She made one stop on her way out.

"Hi Grace," she called out as she entered the lab area in the middle of the building. "Is it ready?"

Grace Chu looked up with a grin. "You realize I shouldn't be helping you with this." Her concern didn't keep her from putting down forceps and removing protective eye wear.

Alexia smiled. She had never bothered with robotics before, but after seeing the setup that Chris had prepared, she wasn't taking any chances. It would be impossible to get to the site, come back to get supplies and then return unnoticed, so she was going to have to take every possible thing she might need. "You know I've been assigned to help test the project. What better way than to take technology with me?"

Grace laughed. "But aren't you cheating a bit?" She finished drying her hands and went over to the lab safe and dialed the combination.

Alexia winced. Once more, people proved her theories. Earn a little trust, and you could get safe combinations, private telephone numbers, anything. The combination lodged itself in her head, whether she wanted to remember it or not.

Grace turned and tossed a light bundle towards her.

Alexia caught the small titanium creature. She looked down and shuddered. "This is really gross."

Laughing again, Grace agreed. "You said you wanted it to blend in, but I assure you it isn't real. The pinchers on your scorpion are much stronger than those of a real one. Watch." She picked up her pocket computer and punched in a command.

"Ow!" Alexia would have dropped the creature, except that its suddenly clinging claws made that impossible. "Leggo!"

Grace relented. "It can only move approximately two pounds and even then might have trouble dragging it over rough surfaces. I couldn't make it entirely of titanium either."

Concerned, Alexia frowned. "Why not?"

"Because you wanted video ability and those parts required glass. Don't worry though. This thing is strong and small enough it's virtually undetectable. I sent you the program for controlling it about half hour ago."

"Let me see," Alexia set down the scorpion and accessed her wrist computer. She found the program, loaded it and played with the menus until a tiny wide-angle lens showed the floor of the lab. She spun the robot around and found Grace's shoes. Quickly, she moved it forward.

"Oh no, you don't," Grace squealed. "That thing looks so real I could barely stand working with it without my tweezers. I never handle the real ones without my longest pair!" She picked up an abnormally long pair of forceps and waved them in the direction of the scuttling arachnid. "I kept having nightmares that a real one had escaped, and I picked it up barehanded by mistake."

Alexia grinned. "Fine. But I still owe you a pinch."

Grace set her tool down and shook her head. "I hope it works. Don't go get yourself into any trouble. Darren is a real stickler for details, and if he finds out you did anything on your own, he isn't going to be pleased. He has a reputation you know."

"So?" Alexia played with the scorpion, testing the controls.

"So, I know he happens to be very attractive, but don't let that put you off your guard. He can be mean and vindictive when someone gets in his way."

"Okay." Alexia retrieved her new pet and looked up at Grace happily.

"You wouldn't be ignoring my free advice again, would you?" Grace asked.

Alexia widened her eyes innocently. "Of course not. I owe you too much to ignore good, free advice."

"You don't owe me anything. I wouldn't even have this job if it weren't for you. I swear, about the time you told me about this job, I was ready to quit my old job and take up haircutting like my mother advised." She rubbed a hand across her short, dark hair, but it didn't even ruffle her Asian hairstyle.

"I was thrilled to sponsor you. It made me look like a genius for recruiting someone of your talents." Alexia glanced around the lab. "Even if that talent is working with crawling creatures." The lab was packed with all sorts of moving creatures, including spiders, snakes, bugs, worms and various kinds of marine crawlers. Grace, petite and beautiful, studied locomotion. That meant studying the things that had the best mobility. To her this translated to studying creatures with lots of legs. Her peers in the regular world, her own mother and anyone she tried to date, usually had a problem with such a career. At least they did until she came to Haven where no one expected her to be normal.

Alexia said, "I gotta run. I'll let you know how it goes when I get back."

Grace called after her, "I'll probably hear about it before then!"

Since Alexia was packed, there was little to do but wait. Resting was out of the question. She felt like she often did before a break-in; calm inside, restless outside. This would be one of the longest expeditions towards a crime scene she had ever tried. Mentally she went over the trip again. If the weather turned out perfect, it would take them a day and a half on horseback to reach the base of Diamond Peak where the instructions were hidden.

Halfway home, Alexia changed directions. Grinning at her overly meticulous preparations, she headed for the stables. The red ranch house where her mare, Speckle, was kept was located near the edge of town.

Instead of finding the stables empty, she was surprised to find Chris, Darren, and Ollern, Darren's second in command, present. The stable owner, Al, was also there. He looked worried.

"What happened?" Alexia's nose told her before anyone could answer. Smoke. Her eyes instinctively checked Speckle's stall. The mare was snorting, rather than neighing her usual quiet greeting. Alexia detoured around the men and went to her distraught friend.

"Someone tried to set the barn on fire," Darren said, pacing along the aisle.

"With the horses inside?" Alexia couldn't believe it, but Chris nodded.

Al made his way along the barn, checking and rechecking the condition of the horses. Al had the veterinary and scientific skills to fix just about anything--except fire in a barn.

"Is your horse all right?" Darren came forward and put his hand on her shoulder. "Let me help."

"That's okay, Darren, I can handle her." No one handled Speckle except herself and occasionally Al. Al might be as big as a lumberjack and look just as wild with his untamed dreadlocks and bushy beard, but he could coax any animal into proper behavior without a single harsh word or action.

Alexia politely closed the stall door behind her, nudging Darren out of the way. It wasn't hard since his attention had switched to watching his agents up in the loft.

"Hey, watch it up there! Don't trample all over everything!" he shouted, startling Speckle. "Ollern, check those guys!"

Ollern, obedient soldier that he was, marched forward.

Shaking her head and watching Speckle's dancing feet, Alexia checked the horse's legs for damage. Ordinarily formidable weapons, Speckle's legs were also delicate enough to break against the hard sides of the stable.

"Is your mare okay?" Chris asked.

Speckle had placed a few new footprints on the back of her stable, but she appeared uninjured. "She seems fine." Alexia checked the lead rope and made sure it was secure. "Poor things. Did you check your horse?" She gave Speckle a quick scratch on her chin.

Chris shrugged. "Al is checking it. I don't own one. I'm only borrowing one for the ride."

"Al's a good guy. He'll take care of them. Who set the fire?"

Her eyes followed his hands as he pointed to the loft. "Group of kids apparently. One of them shot a flaming arrow through to the hay loft."

"Why were the loft doors open?" The doors at the top of the loft swayed freely. "They aren't supposed to be open except when the hay is loaded up there."

Chris shook his head. "It's likely that someone came in and unlatched the door before the group sent the arrow through. But Al swears that if anyone unauthorized had come through an alarm would have gone off. Luckily Al spotted them shooting the arrow and came running. The sprinkler system came on and doused the fire before he even got through the doors."

"Thank God," Alexia murmured. There were fifteen horses in the barn and enough dry hay to start a huge bonfire. "Did he catch any of them?"

Darren chose that minute to reappear. "I've got agents on top of it. I'm sending Ollern into town after those young hoodlums that attacked us. I've been tracking their group since last week."

"How do you know it was them?" Alexia asked.

"It only makes sense. We stop them from violence and they repay."

The logic of his statement, obvious though he may have supposed, was lost on her. "That doesn't make sense." Keith had written her, asking about work. There was no reason for him to turn against them. "How would they know about the horses? Darren?" Darren wasn't listening. He had turned and marched back towards the entrance.

"Check for prints on the latch and on all the stalls. I want this place clean." He turned and bellowed more instructions through the barn door. "Make sure you bring them all in. I want their prints, their records and complete statements."

Ollern saluted before turning smartly and heading away.

Alexia turned to Chris because he was the only one left listening. "Why would those boys try and set the barn on fire? I'm the only one that has a horse, and even though I've been in here with Al to shoe Speckle over the last few days, why would they attack the whole barn? Why not come after Darren or I? Those guys aren't that subtle."

Chris watched her with his careful expression, the one that made her feel like a mouse. "Maybe it wasn't the same group."

"Well, then why is Darren running around like an idiot?" She stomped after said idiot. "Darren!" she yelled. "You'll be lucky to get prints off one lousy latch. The arrow is nearly burned. How are you going to prove--"

"We have an eye-witness. If you've checked your horse, I suggest you clear the area. I've got a lot of work to do before we leave tomorrow."

"Darren--" He wasn't listening.

Throwing up her hands in disgust, she headed for home. Keith had given her his number. If he hadn't been responsible, and she was pretty certain he was not, he might know who was.

Chapter 11

Keith wasn't as easy to communicate with as Alexia hoped. He may have sent her a letter bragging about all of his skills, but like any troubled young person, he mostly had something to prove. The loud, disgusting bar he insisted they meet at was not up to her standards. Not that she was extremely picky, but she had to be able to hear her own questions.

She dragged him outside. "Come on, get in." She ushered him towards the car. "Why is it that you think it makes you tougher and more cool if you hang out in places where no one mops the floor?"

When she started the electric motor, he protested. "Hey! I ain't goin' to no spare parts place! Your fax is short a few transmissions if you think I'm going there!"

Alexia graciously ignored his insults. "Oh, calm down. I have a few questions for you and maybe a job." She took her eyes off the road long enough to glare at him. "But I don't have a lot of time, and I'm not going to waste it. I'll be happy to leave you back there in the dung heap if you don't want to help."

"What makes you think I owe your lily white ass any?" His sentence was interspersed with several other words Alexia chose not to hear. She stopped the car, running it off the road into gravel.

She took a deep breath to help gather her temper. "Keith, if you're going to succeed in life, you're going to have to learn the fine art of networking a little better. Start by leaving out the extra adjectives in your language. You wanted a job. I've got one for you, but I pay the bills. That means you have to play the game."

He jerked away, banging his head on the window in the process. "Maybe I've changed my mind."

"Assuming you have a mind, I'd prefer that you use it, even if it means changing it."

"I hear you do reverse engineering on the brain," he blurted out, tapping his head. "Find out what went in and think you can fix it."

"I'm a doctor."

"Yeah, so? I seen that game. You don't know nothin'. You don't know where it's at."

Alexia gripped the steering wheel in the hopes that it would keep her from yanking out the strands of orange hair that fell across his face. "Yeah, yeah, and your friends back there playing with reality machines certainly know more about real life than I do."

"I ain't talking about the equipment," he said. "I'm talking about real life. I'm talking about takin' the risk."

"The risk? The risk of what? Destroying a future?"

"It don't matter no how, anyhow," he pounded out rhythmically, using her dash as a drum set. "We all gonna die, so the only point is to have the best time gettin' there. You can't get nothin' without risk. You think you can take the computer chip apart," he tapped his head much gentler than he was hitting her car, "but that don't change the program. I ain't gonna be programmed. I can make my own way."

His hand moved to the door handle. She reached out and grabbed it. She knew better than to try logic with him; kids his age had a strange, bizarre outlook on life. Her only hope was to confuse him and outmaneuver him in the process.

"I realize that I'm an old, gas-powered car that can't possibly understand what life is all about. It must be hard to live on the streets and watch your friends die. Of course, you do choose to run around on those streets. I checked. Your parents are educated, they both have jobs, but you run around in the street carrying a weapon."

He had no answer. His hand edged towards the door again.

"Or, is it boredom?" His hand froze on the door lock. "Maybe trying to make something of your life is the biggest risk of all. I'm sure the shrinks in your past listened to your problems, said how terrible your life was and tried to help you 'work' through it. Well, I'm going to give you some better advice. Forget your past. It doesn't matter all that much, and it certainly doesn't matter for this job."

He stared at her without blinking. "Wasn't like I was gonna give you the hard drive to my life."

"Good. Then let's move on to business. What do you know about setting a barn on fire at Haven?"

She had caught him unaware. His eyes shifted before he could stop the motion. "Nothin'."

"Uh-uh. Try again. If you want the job, you have to be honest with me." At his glare, she smiled craftily. "It's a shrink thing. You know how we're always telling you to be honest."

"So, that's the job? I make like a back-up tape and spill everything I know?" He reached for the door release again.

"No, that isn't the job. That's just the information I want right now. The job is spying, but it isn't on your own little buddies, it's on someone at Haven."

"What? How am I gonna do that? I don't hang there."

"No, but I can sponsor you. That would get you in and the rest would be up to you."

"Who do I gotta watch?" he asked suspiciously.

Alexia shrugged. "I don't know."

"What?"

"I don't know. Someone is trying to sabotage a project that I am on, and I want to know who. It will be your job to find out."

The sheer shock on his face was worth the time and the trip.

"How am I supposed to do that?"

"You know how to take care of yourself, don't you?" When he nodded grudgingly, she continued. "I don't know who I am dealing with or what they might do. It isn't normally dangerous in Haven like it is in those places you choose to hang out in. But this is a new problem, and I have an idea I might need your special skills. I'll give you the details, and you tell me what you think."

She waited for him to leave, and when he didn't, she spent the next few minutes telling him about life at Haven, the crystals, the office break-in and the event at the barn.

He didn't say anything, but he paid attention. When she was done, she asked, "Well?"

"There was a rumor that the Twenty-seven's got paid for a hit up there on the hill," he said. "We heard it was a big job, unplugging a guy from the network." He picked at a hole in his jeans. "Maybe they exaggerated."

She nodded. "I guess so. But they did set the barn on fire. Do you know who hired them?"

Keith shook his head. "I could probably find out." Now there was pride in his voice.

Alexia reached over and re-started the car. "I'm not interested in the fire as long as you didn't do it. I don't want you to investigate here, I want you to investigate at Haven. While I'm gone trying to locate the instructions, someone is going to keep doing damage. Or it might be Chris who is causing the trouble, trying to make it harder for us to reach his secure area. Then again, it could be anyone else at Haven that doesn't want the instructions moved off site."

"Makes sense to me," Keith said. "Why take the instructions away?"

"Because we can't guard them at Haven. We don't know if we can guard them anywhere, but we have to try."

"So why not let me find out who hired the Twenty-sevens?"

"Because whoever hired them is smart enough not to leave a trail. I want you to be at Haven to find out the name and the face by catching the person at their next trick--and telling me ahead of time so I can avoid trouble while we're on the way to the site."

"I don't have no contacts there," he pointed out.

"Exactly. You'll have no preconceived notions of who is capable of subterfuge and deceit. I want you to form your own opinions."

"Why can't you figure it out yourself?"

"I know the people, so I see what I expect to see, and I told you, I won't be there. I have to go to Diamond Peak and retrieve the instructions if at all possible."

"Oh."

"Do you want the job?"

He was shrewd enough to ask the next question without answering hers. "What kind of credit does it carry?"

Alexia chuckled. "I knew there was a reason I liked you. I'm going to set it up so that you'll be working for a friend of mine as a technician. So don't worry, there will be money. But I warn you, in order to be a member at Haven, you have to leave all other financial support behind. You can't take money from your parents, or welfare, or any other source. It's one of the requirements because Haven is essentially a new system starting from scratch. You have to make it on your own steam."

He remained quiet while Alexia drove towards Haven. Since he didn't protest, she assumed his cooperation. "There's a six month trial period and if all goes well, there's a board that decides if you have the talent and ability to make contributions. If you do your job well, it shouldn't be a problem." If she had had more time, she might have been kinder, but she was going to be leaving at first light. Besides, like most young people, he insisted he wanted to control his own destiny. So be it.

"This guy I'll be working with is cool?" It was the only indication she was likely to get that he was apprehensive.

"By cool, I take it you mean not guilty?"

He nodded. She shrugged and turned into her own driveway. "I seriously doubt he is involved. He's been looking for someone to assist him for a while now. I'm not telling him anything except that you want the job. Assuming you take the job, that is."

She got out and shut the door. He followed. She hid a grin.

"So, I like, wander around and meet people and ask questions?" He trailed her up the stairs of the porch.

Alexia nodded. "You can do that because you'll be new. It's expected."

"But what about my style?" H pounded himself once in the chest. "My friends? I've got dudes that will worry."

Alexia put her hand on his shoulder and opened the door. "Call your friends. Tell them you're taking a job. Don't tell them what I'm asking you to do because it could get back to someone here." She waved him towards a chair. "The members of the Haven acceptance board will investigate your background, but if they don't have any reason to be suspicious about why you are really here, it shouldn't be a problem. Oh, and call your parents."

She went through the door to the kitchen. When she came back out, she tossed him a can of flavored water. "Sam, your new boss, will introduce you to the reception committee. They will help you find a place to live in Haven and explain the clothing requirements."

A mutinous expression crossed his features, and he ignored the drink. "I ain't gonna dress like you. I be stylin'."

"Sorry, it comes with the job. Only recyclable material allowed. Besides, how do you expect to blend?" She almost laughed at that question; no one blended at Haven. It was the most eclectic bunch of humans on the planet. Perhaps the only thing they did have in common was clothes.

"I ain't changing my hair."

Alexia shrugged and pulled up an extra chair in front of her console. "You want to look like some kind of shredded carrot, so be it. There isn't a law against that here. Just the clothes thing, and that's only because Haven was set up as an environmental project. Even our sewage is completely recycled. Reception committee will show you all that stuff though."

She pointed to the extra chair again. "Sit. I'm going to get you an account. This is how you'll leave messages for me."

"Here?" He looked around her plush living room. His eyes gleamed with sudden plans.

"No." She shut down his hopeful grin. Who in their right mind would leave a teenager in a beautiful home, alone? "Consoles are all over Haven. You'll log into your account using a voice print or fingerprinting if you prefer."

"Yeah, we did that at school." He was unimpressed, but after she set up the account, he activated the account with his fingerprints, a visual of his eye pattern and his voice. Very few people used all three check patterns on their account. Most people assumed no one else was interested--another useful mistake when she was after information.

"Good." His street experience gave him a healthful paranoia. "Now, you and I decide upon a couple of passwords and security features so that only you can leave messages for me. I'll use a different one, one that you decide upon, to leave messages for you. Obviously, we destroy the messages after we read them."

"No listening to them with the voice-a-syzer, huh?"

"You got it." It wouldn't be as easy for him after she left, but he would get by. Hopefully, he would be of some help gathering information.

After they finished setting up the accounts, she stood. "Okay, now I'll introduce you to Sam and show you my office and a few other pertinent places. Sam will make sure you get to the welcoming committee tomorrow."

She walked him over to the complex, showing him the few sights along the way that he might need to know about. Then she showed him the way to Sam's autopsy laboratory, down on the lowest floors of the building.

Sam was delighted to see them and thrilled to have a potential new employee. He had been looking to hire extra help in his lab for some time. For reasons he couldn't fathom, he didn't get a lot of applicants.

Keith wasn't nearly as enthused as Sam when he discovered he would be working on dead bodies. Alexia figured he could use a dose of dealing with the facts of life--and the fact that his too could and would eventually end. If he wanted any meaning in it, he'd better put it there before the dead part.

She showed him around the complex a bit more, gave him a few maps and tips and then walked him back to her place. "You can stay the first night with me, unless you want to take Sam up on his offer to start immediately."

He gave her a look that told her he was thinking of finding a way to make her stay with Sam tonight and not as part of the working team. "You never said--"

"Autopsies aren't your real purpose," she reminded him. "At least not from my point of view. Besides, since we're all going to die anyway you might as well know what you'll have to look forward to. And working for Sam is perfect. No prying eyes so to speak."

"They're dead."

"You'll get used to it. I didn't want you to be overwhelmed with having to act twenty-four hours a day."

"Yeah, thanks." He flopped down on the couch.

"You can sleep there or in the guest room. It doesn't have a bed yet, but it will give you some privacy." When he didn't move, she added, "I'd give you more instructions and advice, but you probably don't need it, right?" She was taking advantage of his attitude, but he was going to have to wear his usual self-confidence around others at Haven, even if he was little more than out of high school. "Oh, and they'll be doing a physical tomorrow morning. You'll have to pass that, but I checked your local records. I don't expect a problem."

He glared at her, but didn't ask how she had managed the feat. Admitting that he didn't know everything would leave him vulnerable, and if he was practiced at anything, it was hiding weakness.

"I'll try not to wake you tomorrow morning, but if I do, you'll get breakfast." She gave him sheets and blankets before walking towards her bedroom. "Goodnight."

Keith didn't answer. Saying good night probably wasn't cool.

Chapter 12

The first two hours of riding the next morning were rough. Alexia was familiar with most of the route because she had hiked and ridden the area before, but high winds sent choking waves of dust their way. A growing thunderstorm to the northwest looked brutal. By ten, the clouds caught them.

Neither Darren nor Chris made the suggestion that was needed. When Alexia spotted a small outcrop of boulders next to a shoulder-high mesquite tree, she finally made the choice.

"We may as well stop. If we get hit by this storm, we aren't going to be able to see. We don't need to have a horse slip before we get halfway there." She reined Speckle back and hopped down. "It'll be easier to erect a canopy before this gets any worse."

"Good idea." Chris stopped quickly and grabbed an open-sided tent structure from his mount. "This rain looks to be coming from the direction we're headed--we may as well let it pass over us rather than swim upstream into it."

Alexia quickly secured one end of the canopy before the whole thing gusted away. Though the boulders weren't much, between the rocks and the mesquite, they had a bit of a wind-break.

"I'll secure this side," Darren shouted. His words were barely intelligible above the thunder.

Chris hesitated, torn between helping Alexia and checking Darren's work.

"Can you expand that pole?" she shouted at him.

Chris did the outer poles and together they arranged a quick shelter. None of the horses would fit underneath so Alexia unsaddled hers to keep the riding equipment as dry as possible. It was already raining before she perched under the canopy.

Darren stayed at the far end, looking up through the mesquite branches.

"What is he looking for?" Chris asked.

"Who knows? Maybe he thinks he can spot hail coming down and warn us early." With nothing better to do, Alexia took off her wrist computer to hold it more comfortably so she could check her email.

The first message was from Keith. It wasn't quite the one she expected.

Did you know that you can kill a person with tiger whiskers just by getting the dude to swallow them?

She signed back, "Yes, and shards of glass, which takes a great deal less effort to obtain, works also. Does this have any bearing on me?"

She might be creating a monster. Keith was supposed to spy, not learn cool methods of murder.

"We should probably move higher," Darren shouted, peering up into the dark storm.

"Won't help now," Chris said. "The only place it isn't raining is back the way we came. We're high enough above the arroyo if it fills with water."

The storm was passing quickly, and they had stayed above the washes and arroyos that crisscrossed the "badlands" known as the Plains of San Agustin. When it wasn't raining, the land looked like a broad, dusty valley with an occasional red-brown mesa making a lonely statement. In reality, it was not a single valley, but a segment of the desert that lacked a full mountain range. It was filled with dried riverbeds, coarse hills and sandy plains decorated sparsely with cacti and tumbleweeds.

Once they crossed this area, they would begin the climb into the foothills of the Black Mountain Range where Chris had hidden the instructions. Alexia was looking forward to the mountains. She was much more at home there than clinging to the side of a boulder on her magnetic bed and typing notes.

The magnetic bed was another invention from Haven. It used the earth's magnetic properties to create a field a few inches above the ground. Originally the technology had been slated for a new type of hover car, but the field didn't support the full weight of a vehicle.

"I'm going to go and look around," Darren called, his head already outside the shelter. "I think it's slowing."

"Try not to get struck by lightning," Alexia warned.

He grinned back at her before facing the elements.

Chris scowled. "Why didn't you mention that blanket thing?"

"The magnetic field simulator? I assumed you guys had one." She scooted over. "Move the saddle and have a seat."

The blanket was more crowded, but at least he wasn't sitting on the ground.

"I understand that women think Darren is handsome," he mumbled, barely loud enough for Alexia to hear.

"Hmm?" She glanced up. "Yeah, he is."

"You really think so?"

"Sure."

"How can you say that? The man is an idiot!" Chris glared at her, rather more fiercely than she thought necessary.

"Him being an idiot has nothing to do with his attractiveness," she said. "Darren is certainly impulsive, and that seems to cause him to make a fool of himself rather too often." She looked outside the tent until she located Darren climbing a boulder and scanning the landscape. "He is good-looking. Very well-built. You're correct, a handsome man." She smiled.

"What's so funny?"

She shrugged. "I don't know. I was just thinking it was a stupid question."

Chris grunted, propped himself against the edge of the canopy and glared out at the weather.

Alexia went back to her email. She scripted another message to Keith. "Go meet people. Live ones. Find out opinions on moving the instructions off-sight. Talk to Sam every now and then about the crystals. If an attempt is made on them, you might not hear about it because you're new. Sam keeps up with important news, at least most of the time."

Darren came back around the protective rock, his hair dripping water. "It's clearing. We can go."

"We can't saddle the horses wet. It would ruin the saddle blankets." Alexia barely glanced up.

"I said we move out," Darren repeated. He clicked his riding staff on the ground and pressed his heels together with the order.

Obviously he wasn't used to anyone counteracting his decisions. She gave him her full attention so that he didn't misunderstand. "Fine. Go." Her horse deserved the best care she could provide and that didn't include giving it saddle sores due to riding it wet.

Darren moved away from the tent. Hearing no one following, he turned back around. "Well? What are you waiting for?"

In addition to being impulsive, he apparently suffered a hearing problem. "I said go. I didn't say I was going anywhere."

His face became the mottled red that she associated with the theft of the crystals. It really did detract from his attractiveness. Shame, too. He had obviously never learned to use his looks to his advantage. He could be much more successful if he practiced the art of charismatic persuasion. Perhaps he would agree to some sessions when they got back.

Darren's outraged rumbling finally brought her back to earth with a clang--literally, since he knocked her off the magnetic field blanket as he grabbed her saddle blanket. "I'm in charge of this operation, and I said move!" He dumped the saddle blanket at her feet, managing to defeat her purpose in waiting because now one side of it was not only wet, but full of muddy sand.

"Don't touch my things." Without meaning to, her voice rose in pitch.

"I'll touch your things any time you disobey! You," he said turning to Chris, who was edging between her and Darren, "get your ass in gear!"

With this last declaration, Darren stomped to his pack and threw it onto his horse. His motions made the other horses shy away and snort.

Alexia stared a death hole in his back. "Bastard." She picked herself up from the ground only because she was afraid that Speckle was going to bolt. Otherwise she would have been content to sit there and let him try to make her get up.

She marched to Speckle and soothed her horse gently. Given the circumstances, it wasn't easy. It wasn't until Darren had completed his preparation and rode off that she truly lost her temper.

He bellowed back at her, "I'll expect you to catch up Dr.. Zimmerman. You said you were up to this task, I expect you to prove it!"

Alexia was left stuttering obscenities. "Pig-eared, callous, son of a---"

"Hmm," Chris said from somewhere behind her.

She spun around to find him five feet away, his arms folded in a disapproving fashion.

"He's so attractive, don't you think?" He threw his own saddle blanket over his horse and went back for his saddle.

"You--" she choked back curse words. "Oh, go. Just because you two chose to be stupid doesn't mean I have to be an idiot." Besides, she could probably track them before nightfall, if they didn't walk off the edge of a plateau or fall into an arroyo and get killed.

"Are you coming?" Chris finally asked when he was ready.

"No."

"He'll say you weren't cut out for the job, you know."

She glared up at him. "And?"

"Hey! Don't take it out on me! I'm just along to make sure nobody gets hurt on one of my protective devices."

"Well, since I'm going to be sitting here waiting for things to dry out, you'd best go watch out for Darren. I can live without your help."

Between gritted teeth he ground out, "That's the only reason I'm going after him and not staying here with you. He's a fool. You, I can at least count on to stay alive." He stared at her for a final moment before turning his mount.

Alexia started to reply, but there was no point. He made it quite clear that he wasn't all that happy about setting off after Darren. He had certainly dropped his happy-go-lucky attitude.

As he rode off, her eyes narrowed in speculation. For a guy who supposedly was renting a horse from the stable, he seemed to understand why she was taking it easy with her mount. Now that she happened to think about it, he rode very well. Better than Darren, in fact. He rode at least as well as she did, handling the terrain as if he had ridden rough ground many times.

"Hmph." Chris had picked the spot for the instructions to be hidden. How had he known a good spot unless he had explored and was capable of handling such explorations? His record had not shown any special interest in scouring the countryside, which is what it would have taken in order to find and build a secure hiding place. No doubt, his record--and his protection plans--had hidden aspects.

To keep busy, she combed some of the water out of Speckle's coat. Speckle tried to walk away. "Stop struggling," she told her horse. Speckle looked back at her as though she had lost her mind. Then she sighed. The horse was right. Who else would stand out in the middle of the desert trying to squeegee out a horse?

Grumbling, she gave up the job and moved Speckle into the sun. She now smelled more like horse than Speckle and was twice as dirty. She took her time packing the shelter and her magnetic bed before saddling the mare. As she finished the cinch, Speckle danced sideways and snorted.

"What now? Are they coming back? Too worried to leave a lone female out here, no doubt."

Speckle, however, did not settle down, and instead of neighing a welcome to other horses, continued to prance nervously.

"Okay, okay, we're leaving," Alexia soothed. When in doubt, go with the animal's instincts. Cocking her head before mounting, she frowned. Was that baying? Out here in the desert?

She listened carefully. Sure enough, it sounded like dogs. Not coyotes, not a cougar, but dogs. Why would anyone have dogs out here?

Not waiting for an answer, she mounted. Speckle had heard the baying long before she had. That could only mean they were getting closer.

Alexia didn't like the implications. The more she thought about it, the more lead rope she gave Speckle. The arroyos were too dangerous to chance in this weather. If it was still raining high in the mountains, the waterways could fill up in an instant, and she and her horse would be caught. That danger was more real than anything chasing her.

Speckle didn't require nudging. The mare hurried along at a quick trot, breathing hard.

At the top of the second ridge, Alexia looked back. They were definitely being trailed by dogs. Big, black ones.

Using her scope she even recognized the breed. Rottweilers were pretty hard to miss.

Was this one of Chris' unwritten traps? If it was, it was pretty stupid. Dogs couldn't roam free in the wilderness and hope to survive. There wasn't enough water and dogs relied upon humans for survival.

It didn't make sense. Unfortunately, Chris wasn't present for the debate. She fired her rifle towards the dogs, once and then again, but they did not slow. She was going to have to shoot to kill if she intended to stop them. Anger bled through her faster than when Darren gave orders. If this was Chris' idea, she might just shoot him. Training animals to track and forcing her to kill them was not her idea of a joke or even a remotely good idea for protecting the instructions.

She lowered her rifle and kicked Speckle in the sides. If she could reach Chris and Darren, she would make him deal with his animals. Darren would no doubt stick to the trail and they were only an hour or so ahead of her. Angry and afraid, she pushed herself and Speckle as fast as she dared.

It was to no avail. The first dog caught her at the base of a canyon and without preamble, attacked.

Luckily for Alexia, the dog went for Speckle's throat first rather than hers. Speckle reared back, kicking the dog away. Regretfully, Alexia raised her gun and aimed. The dog watched dispassionately, barking and snarling, watching for another opening. As it danced around Speckle's hooves, Alexia could tell that the dog had learned its lesson about getting too close to the horse.

Her shot ended up near the dog's feet, a useless attempt to get it to back off.

Before she could make a decision, another vicious animal rounded the corner. At the same time she heard a shout. Chris yelled unintelligibly from the top of the canyon edge.

"Call off your dogs!" she shouted. The second dog kept her and her horse pinned against the edge of the canyon wall.

From somewhere above, a shot came, and the dog backed down. Speckle reared, nearly unseating her, and the second barking animal backed away just enough to provide an opening.

Alexia gave Speckle her head.

She knew she was hunted, but still, they were dogs. Badly trained and attacking, but her heart refused to accept it. Without any other option, she guided Speckle further into the canyon. Water ran at the base. She fervently prayed that it wasn't raining anywhere upstream.

Speckle needed no urging to ride hard. Maybe the dogs would be distracted by Chris and Darren. The water would hide at least some of her scent.

After an hour, she was certain the dogs were no longer following. There had been two more shots and each time, her throat had tightened. How could anyone train dogs to hunt down people? How could Darren and Chris shoot them?

By the time Chris and Darren found her, it was late in the evening. She had tried to go forward out of the canyon and ended up having to backtrack all the way to where she had entered. Seeing them did nothing to make her feel better. Incoherent, she yelled at them both and clutched Chris' collar. "How dare you?"

Neither male seemed to know how to handle the situation, so she solved it for them by screaming at them until her throat was raw.

Finally, out of energy and tears, she turned her back and stomped away. Her hands shook as she unpacked her gear and fed Speckle. "Ssstupid men." She stretched her blanket as far from them as was safe.

Just after she crawled into her hover bed, Chris gently touched her shoulder. "Hey." He waited until she relaxed the instinctive tension out of her shoulders. "I wanted to tell you that we made sure none of them were left out there hurt. It took a while, but we forced them back until you were in the clear. Eventually they lost interest and headed back towards Haven. I followed them partway back."

She could barely see his eyes in the dim light. She took a deep breath and managed to nod.

Still, it was a miserable night.

Chapter 13

Morning brought sunshine, at least to the day. Alexia felt as black as the previous night, but her outburst was over. She approached Chris first thing.

"Were those dogs part of your plan?" Her fists clenched involuntarily.

He looked up slowly from his coffee mug. His eyes were not friendly. "I hope you're joking."

She almost backed down when she saw the hurt in his hostile expression. "No, I'm not." Alexia couldn't hold his stare, and she ended up accusing the dirt at her feet. "Someone owned those animals, someone trained them and sent them after us. I want to know if it was you." She couldn't fathom anyone doing such a thing. It didn't fit what she knew about Chris, but then, there were a lot of things she didn't know about him.

"They were not a part of any of my plans." His voice was devoid of emotion, emptier than the desert. He tossed the dredges from his coffee cup and walked away to inspect his horse.

"We can't ride them today," she said. "Both your horse and Darren's have chafing."

"I'm aware of that."

Alexia closed her eyes. The question about the dogs had burned inside her all night. She had to ask because she had to know. If Chris had trained and sent those dogs…it would change everything. Relief at knowing he hadn't should have made her feel better, but with Chris now angry, she had a different problem.

Chris interrupted her self-centered thoughts with a question. "Was there a particular reason you thought they might be my dogs?"

Alexia offered the only excuse she had. "You set the traps. I thought the dogs might have been part of them."

"You might have noticed that the plans were set up so that no animal would come to harm by any of the protective devices."

She nodded at the ground. "Yes, I noticed. I'm sorry." It was too late for an apology. If the positions were reversed, the accusation would have infuriated her. "It's just that when I had to shoot at them--I'm sorry." She turned back to her bed and sat down, head in her hands. "If they aren't part of the plan, then who sent them?"

"Good question, isn't it? Maybe you should think of legitimate possibilities instead of accusing the closest person at hand!"

She looked up to find his green eyes boring into hers. For the first time that morning, she noticed that Chris and she were alone. "Where's Darren?"

"Thinking of asking him if he sent the dogs?" When she didn't answer, he spun away, scattering rocks and sand beneath his feet. "He knows we can't ride out, but that won't stop him from getting the lay of the land, looking for escape routes, and generally wasting time."

Chris paced back and forth between her and the remains of the camp. "I can't believe you thought it was me."

"I...had to ask." At least Darren hadn't overheard their conversation. "Look, I panicked, okay? I was frightened!"

Chris walked away.

In desperation, she followed and asked, "What do you mean Darren is looking for escape routes?"

"You could have used a better route yesterday, couldn't you?"

"I guess so." Her attempt to keep the conversation going failed. Chris busied himself around the camp for several minutes without saying anything.

She finally tried to eat a scant breakfast. She hadn't unpacked other than her blanket. It didn't take long to roll it up.

She almost didn't hear Chris when he finally asked, "You are all right? They didn't hurt you?"

"I'm fine."

"I wish I knew who was responsible!" He slammed a fist into his palm. "I also would like to know who tried to burn the barn down."

"That was kids," Alexia said. "The idea didn't originate from them, but I never assumed whomever hired them actually told them to burn the barn with the horses inside. Now, I've changed my mind. Maybe they were told to do just that."

He agreed. "The person who sent those dogs could certainly burn a barn full of horses."

"What are we going to do?" Alexia asked.

Chris looked stubborn. "Our job. We won't make it very far on foot leading the horses, but we have a task to undertake, trouble or no. If we don't check the instructions, whoever is trying to stop us may get there first or may convince us not to hide them so well."

Alexia's breath stuck in her throat. "You really think someone is trying to keep us from getting there? But that would mean," her mind raced ahead, "that they have some sort of plan in mind for taking the instructions!" Since she had been the one causing security headaches, she had never really considered the implications of a real thief testing the latest plan.

"It certainly appears that way, doesn't it?"

"I'll pack up. We'd best find out if this plan of yours is going to work as soon as possible.

They caught up to Darren not far ahead. He was diligently scouting the area for any possible danger, real or perceived. Alexia did not ask if he had found anything. She was just grateful that she didn't hear the sound of baying. It was bad enough that every time the wind whistled past her eardrums, she found herself holding her breath.

Since Speckle was the only horse without abrasions, the mare was forced to carry most of the gear. If they had been closer to their goal, Alexia might have done a disappearing act, attempted to complete the break-in and, failure or success, hightailed it back to Haven. As it was, they were still closer to Haven than the site, had no horses to speak of and someone was hunting them down with vicious dogs. The idea of going off alone did not appeal to her.

The rocky ground passed underfoot slowly, forcing them to change the route when the rocks were too jumbled for the horses. As the afternoon wore on, more thunderheads appeared from the west. Winds carried the scent of moisture, and for a while it looked as though they would be stopped again, but within a few hours, the clouds blew over.

As they crossed a saddle-ridge between two mesas, Alexia stopped and looked back. Her hair, turned to straw in the dry wind, whipped across her vision. Clouds boiled across the open space below. There were no mountains to halt the billowing thunderheads as they raced across the plain.

It was hot and Alexia was glad they were headed higher into the mountains. The air would be less dry and tall pines would replace the strangled desert growth. Best of all, they wouldn't be out in the open.

That evening they made camp with less than a day's ride ahead of them. For the first time since they started the trip, the stars were fully out. With the lack of cloud cover, the temperature dropped.

Nevertheless, they cooked with the heating elements and refrained from a warming fire. Alexia was tired, but she checked her messages anyway.

New corpse in from the cities. This place is weird. Hardly anyone carries guns. No gangs. Everyone works. Old Appleton didn't want to talk about his son, by the way. Parents are all the same. My dad gives me the same look. Like a drug trip gone bad and he don't like the vision. Can't blame the drug, can't blame me.

Alexia couldn't believe Keith had somehow managed to get into a conversation with Dr. Appleton. Whatever Dr. Appleton had said, Keith had picked up the same vibes she had. Dr. Appleton didn't fully approve of Chris.

So why was Chris here? And why was he in charge? Had he somehow bullied Dr. Appleton into the position by using parental guilt? That picture didn't fit Chris well, but the bitterness of the father meant that she couldn't afford to rule out the possibility.

Alexia left Keith another list of names, including Phillip Teldman, George, and to be fair Dr. Brandon. She also asked him to look into who might own attack-trained Rottweilers either in town or at Haven.

As soon as she turned off her computer, the heartbeat of the desert rushed in to fill the electronic void. She could hear sand shift in a gully, trickling down, a pebble at a time. Silence then, an eerie quiet broken by the occasional hunter; an owl, a nighthawk, and the lonely baying of a coyote.

A friend of hers had once told her that coyote yipping was the same as listening to city ambulances at night. Like the sirens rising and falling in pitch, the yelps threatened first to come closer, then suddenly were farther away, but always there, all night long.

The sound had the same ring of urgency, of bad news to come.

Chapter 14

Because Speckle always snorted for food early in the morning, Alexia did not bother to roll out of bed quickly. In fact, assuming that the footsteps belonged to Darren or Chris, she didn't even consider reaching for her weapon.

The cocking of a rifle, well, that was a different story.

She grabbed her gun, turned and fired before she even had her eyes half open. She had learned the trick from her father, whose idea of a good joke was to sneak up and shoot tree limbs down over her head when she was camping out.

The tree in this case was a bullet, and her movement caused it to miss. Her return fire kept a second shot from coming.

There was no tent to grab, so she dragged her pack and the blanket with her as she mounted, flinging it around to distract the shooter's aim. Speckle's bridle was in place, and if she lived long enough, she could come back for the saddle.

Darren yelled off to her right. She could not see or hear Chris until she realized he was mounted on his own horse behind her, beating out the same dead run she had easily coaxed into Speckle.

"The other way!" Darren yelled. "East! Go east!"

She registered Darren's instructions and pulled hard to the west. Darren must have found his mount also. Both he and Chris were returning fire rapidly. Chris opted to stay behind her rather than follow Darren.

She looked back. Darren waved and shouted, "Shoot the horses!"

Her mouth fell open. No way. For one, Chris was behind her, blocking any clean shot she might have had. For two, why shoot the horses? They didn't have guns!

"Are you crazy? The horses aren't shooting at us!" Another shot told her that pursuit still followed.

Very quickly, she figured out why Darren had told her to ride the other way. She reined in sharply, forcing Speckle to choke on the bit. The ground ahead disappeared into a yawning canyon. Unfortunately, the path back out was blocked by a rider she could now see. To her right was a tangled mass of giant boulders upon which Speckle could find no footing. Chris must have figured this out at the same time she did.

Ahead of him, she jumped from Speckle's back and took refuge behind a rock. "Stand," she commanded her horse. She was far from being hidden and with Speckle breathing like a steam engine, there was little chance of securing a hiding place, but she could keep the other rider from advancing as soon as Chris was clear.

In the space of a heartbeat, she edged up the side of the rock. In that same instant, she heard a shot as she climbed for a vantage point. Impossibly, Chris had turned his mount and tried to fire back the way they had come one last time.

She started to yell at him to get clear, but the words froze. There was red. Everywhere. Red across his shoulder, red spreading faster than her eye could possibly follow. His weight was shifting away from her too, and she only barely stifled a scream. Time sped up then. He was falling. If he had been a bit closer, he wouldn't have dropped over the side. If his left side had been hit instead of his right, he might have held onto the rocks. If he hadn't been holding his own rifle, he might have been able to hold onto his horse.

But he fell. And his horse moved in the opposite direction in time for her to watch him tumble, soundlessly, over the lip of the canyon.

Chapter 15

There was no time for hesitation, only anger. Alexia ignored the shaking in her hands. She ignored the fact that she couldn't go after Chris until she got rid of the threat. None of her training helped her. No matter how well she understood the human mind, there were certain times that clinical teaching simply did no good. There were times when reaction was the only answer.

She shot. "For a chip. You killed him for a chip."

She didn't aim for the horse. Her rifle snapped back into her shoulder. She ignored the recoil and fired again. And again. She knew she hit the gunman from the way he bent over. She knew he was alive because he didn't fall off his horse. Chasing him to make sure he didn't come back was hardly an option. There wasn't time.

She was off the rock and running desperately, panic taking hold. "Chris." It came out a whisper. Her throat ached on the scream that she held back.

She threw herself at the edge and peered over. "Oh God." She couldn't believe it. Her eyes closed of their own free will. She couldn't stop the blink of horrified disbelief.

"Hold on!" she commanded, not even sure he could hear. What she could see of his head was covered in blood. Only one hand seemed to anchor him in the empty space; the rest of him was dangling off a thin ledge that was twelve feet below her.

"Speckle! Forward!"

She turned and ran, meeting her horse halfway. She had rope from her pack looped within seconds and secured around the mare's neck. It wasn't perfect, but it might work.

She returned, afraid to look, but not daring to hesitate. "Can you grab a rope with your other hand?"

There was no answer. It was almost as if he held there unconscious to everything except his grip. If the gunman came back…she took one final nervous glance behind her.

There was no way she could reach Chris from up here. The ledge that he clung to was at least a body length away.

After dropping her rifle and pack down, she took a deep breath and plunged after it, falling several feet before sliding to a stop just short of the rocky edge. Chris hung just below her. She grabbed the bloody hand that was wrapped around an old gnarled root. With all her strength she held on.

"Chris! Chris, can you get purchase with your legs?"

He groaned then, and she thanked God that he was alive. Logic had told her that he had to be alive in order to hold on, but her emotions dictated otherwise.

Slowly, his head moved. She couldn't see his eyes or most of his face. His head wound was bleeding profusely.

"Please don't let them come back," she prayed. "Please."

By some miracle, she managed to catch the other arm that he flailed in her direction. He didn't let go of the tree root. She panted and heaved and sat on one of his arms so that she could reach the back of his shirt and pull him towards her. He helped by grasping each new inch she bought him.

At last, she held his bleeding head on her lap. Knowing it was crazy and knowing he was probably going to think she had lost her mind, she pulled her emergency candy bar from her pack and chewed as fast as she could. She held him across her knees, her rifle in one hand and the candy bar in the other. She had no other choice. The dizziness had started, and the crisis wasn't even over.

Had there been more than one gunman? Was he coming back?

Shuddering, she tried to pull herself together. Chris was in and out of consciousness. There was no way she could get him back up to the top. Speckle might be able to drag his weight, but without a saddle to tie the rope to, it would be impossible for both him and the horse.

She wiped at the moisture on her cheeks and forced herself to think. The first step was to get him out of here, to get him away from the area in case the gunman came back. If she couldn't go up, that left only one direction.

Chapter 16

She taped Chris up as best she could. With a little tugging on the rope Speckle came forward towards the drop. She cut off as much of the rope as possible and hoped Speckle would run if necessary.

She didn't like her options, but she knew it had to be far easier to get Chris down into the canyon than to pull him back up.

Unfortunately, the path down was a death trap. She needed the rope both to lower the gun down, and to help control their descent. Chris helped sometimes, but just when she thought he was going to make it, his full weight would slump back onto her and they would rake brutally down the rocky incline. She collected more than a few cactus needles across her arms and backside.

The gunshot wound to his arm was superficial, but the blow he had taken on his head when he fell was still bleeding. When they were close to the bottom where the slope leveled out, she re-wrapped both wounds as best she could and dragged him behind some protective rocks. She had no way of knowing whether their pursuer was still looking for them. The rocks and sand had tumbled with them, rattling and pinpointing their location the entire way.

"I'm sorry, Chris. I should have followed Darren."

He moaned. "Why the hell didn't you?"

She didn't meet his blood-crusted eyes. Instead she continued to rebind his arm and apply pressure to his head. It had been pure instinct that had driven her from following Darren's signal. She had been burned once by his impulsiveness, and she was more than happy to be twice shy. "I couldn't trust his judgment."

"Except he was right this time," Chris said, his voice barely audible.

"I know and I'm sorry! I couldn't be certain he was basing his command on real information." She reached over and grabbed his questing hand before he could inspect his forehead. "Leave it alone, you'll only make it start bleeding again."

"Damn bandage is cutting off circulation to my brain, and it's killing me!"

"You're dizzy because you've lost blood, not because your head is being squeezed." She didn't let go of his hand. Instead, she gave it an extra pat and set it gently in her own lap before holding a water bottle to his lips.

After a long drink he asked, "Why do you think we brought Darren along? Security is his business. He's supposed to be an expert at reconnaissance. Why do you think he spends all that extra time walking ahead?"

"I know. But all I could think of was his other mistakes. I know he's good at his job technically, but dammit, he's still basically an idiot!"

Chris peeled back an eyelid. He watched her for a moment and then sighed. "It isn't your fault. You didn't fire the gun."

"Yeah."

Chris roused himself enough to respond to her lack of enthusiasm. "You didn't see me following his lead, did you?"

"If it hadn't been for your protective male instincts--"

"Of which," he said tiredly, "you are not in need." He curled his fingers around her hand and took two deep breaths. "He might be a good tactician, but that doesn't mean he's a good leader, Alexia. Hell, he's made so many bad decisions, he probably couldn't get rats to follow him if he had cheese. All the technical knowledge and experience in the world doesn't make a good leader."

She knew it was true, but it didn't make her feel much better. Lack of leadership was why Darren had to result to bullying his own team. He drilled obedience into them or found men with no self-esteem. It was easier than fixing his own shortcomings.

Chris said, "Now, can I get some rest? My head is killing me."

"You said that already and no, you may not rest. I want you to stay awake for an hour, and then I'm going to wake you every hour after that."

Both eyes opened with that statement. "You're joking."

"No, I'm not. You might have a concussion."

He glared at her. "Since when--" he cut himself off.

"Since when did I become a doctor? A few years ago." This time, she was certain the noise he made was a moan.

"Come now, it won't be so bad. You can tell me all about the traps that you didn't list in the specification while you're delirious."

"Not on your life," he mumbled.

"Pardon?" she asked squeezing his hand until he opened his eyes again.

"Nothing."

"Good. Now, then. We were discussing Darren."

"I don't want to talk about Darren, I want to sleep."

Alexia gave him an encouraging pat on the shoulder. "You only have," she looked at her watch, "fifty-five minutes to go."

Glaring his defeat, he pushed himself up against the rock. He winced when his arm came in sharp contact with the rocky surface. "What do you intend to do once I'm sleeping?"

Alexia shrugged. "First I'm going to go up and find a way to get Speckle down here. With luck, I'll find your horse also."

"Not much chance of that. Hasn't been with me long enough to stay around."

"No, but I'll give it a try."

"And then you'll go get the instructions."

It wasn't a question. She deflected away from the topic. "Someone must have noticed that Darren wasn't a great leader. That's how you ended up on this project, isn't it?"

"I'm here because I wanted a chance to prove to dad that I could keep the crystals safe."

Alexia looked down at him. "Did you keep Darren on until you could be certain that the thief wasn't someone within Darren's organization? Maybe someone taking the crystals to make him look bad? With a such a nasty leader, it's a real possibility. Maybe Darren stepped on some poor sucker's toes one too many times, and that person decided it was time for a payback."

She slapped herself on the forehead. "That's it! Maybe a disgruntled employee is the one who has been pulling the thefts all along!" She forced so much excitement into her voice, she almost believed herself. Actually, after getting to know Darren, it wasn't such a bad idea. If she didn't know better, she would believe it.

Chris wasn't quite as enthusiastic as she would have liked. "Yeah, maybe that person was thinking that he'd be promoted when Darren was ousted." Chris' eyes closed again, so she couldn't glean whether he was actually considering the idea. Not being able to read his expression took half the fun out of lying.

"Well, I think the idea makes perfect sense," she said. "I'm going to write it in my report when we get back. In fact, I think I'm going to start interviewing those who stand to get promoted."

"If we get back."

Alexia bent over and touched his head. "We'll get back Chris. I promise." When he opened his eyes, she put belief and conviction into her voice. Believing was half way there. She had seen it in enough patients to know. "You rest a bit now. I'm going to go get Speckle."

"Now? You don't expect me to force myself to stay awake down here, do you?"

"No, but the doctor says it's okay anyway." He was alert and steady. That was more than she had hoped for earlier. "We can't afford to sit here and wait for things to get better."

He grunted. "Darren isn't likely to stage a rescue. He was mad when we had to go looking for you after the dogs chased you."

"I'm not counting on Darren." She didn't point out the rest of their problems: they had no horses, the instructions were in danger and the enemy was still out there.

Collecting her pack, she took some things out and left them with him. Then, she gave him a final wave.

"Be careful," he warned.

"Absolutely." She gave him a confident smile that belied her nervous heart. She took the first step towards skidding down into the very bottom of the canyon. There had to be an easier way back up to Speckle than the way they had come down.

The morning had faded into the warm, bright sunshine of midday. It had taken a long time to get Chris down into the canyon. She could only hope that Speckle was still patiently waiting.

After two or three false starts, she managed to find a segment of the canyon that allowed her to get about halfway to her goal. From there, every time she started up what looked like a possible path, it became too steep or was breached by large drainage gullies that she couldn't cross.

Chris would be lucky if she got back down by tomorrow.

Thinking of him made her harden her resolve and wedge herself between a crack in the canyon, using the sides to climb up. If she fell...it was imperative that she wake him within no more than a few hours; she hadn't been lying when she said he might be concussed. Grunting, she pulled herself up over a rock and wished she had thought to bring the rope.

Scrapping her way along, she finally managed to reach the spot where she had left Speckle. Her hands were in worse shape than before and most of her fingernails were gone. There wasn't time to look for Chris' horse.

Checking her compass, she quickly rode Speckle back southeast along the ridge of the canyon, searching for sloping ground. When she stopped to retrieve her saddle and other supplies at the camp, she found the tracks left by their attacker. There was nothing distinctive about the tracks, and in a day or so, the wind would blow the loose sand and soil back into place.

She wasted no more time on it.

It took her two hours to get back to Chris. She shook him rudely awake, even though she suspected he had heard her ride up.

"Here. Roll over onto the blanket." She adjusted the magnetic blanket so that he was comfortable. He protested, of course.

"Where will you sleep?"

"Never mind," she replied. Next, she handed him some soup and coffee from her store of supplies. There wasn't time for a fire, even if she had been inclined to give away their location.

After eating, he fell back into slumber. Alexia choked down some of the soup and gathered what she considered the bare necessities for tomorrow. She hiked around the makeshift camp until she had a better lay of the land.

It was too late to start for the instructions, so she woke Chris again, got him to eat a bit more soup and then she left a message for Keith.

Will be going to site alone. Chris is hurt. If you don't hear from me in twenty-four hours, send someone in to get Chris.

Her GPS provided their exact location, and she sent it with the message. The note Keith had left her did nothing to improve her spirits. He had found a possible owner of the dogs. Their lethal habits suddenly made a strange sort of sense.

The doc says George Miller has dogs, and they must have flown the coop because no one has seen them since he got locked in the loony bin. Doc says no visitors allowed so I can't ask him. Keep looking?

The timing was off since technically it had been over a week since George had been admitted. The description fit, however. She had witnessed George's instability. It wouldn't be totally out of the question to find that he owned dogs that were trained to hunt. Keith's message didn't help explain how the dogs had gotten on their trail though.

She penned back another message:

Maybe the dogs were sent to a kennel? Check, but don't be too nosy. Why can't he have visitors?

Unless George had gotten a lot worse, Alexia couldn't understand why George was locked up. She also couldn't imagine why George would put the dogs on their trail. George obviously trusted Darren and Darren was with the group. Had he become so deranged, he no longer trusted his leader? Of course, depending upon the treatment, Dr. Brandon might have suggested to George that Darren was not perfect. That could later have translated into hostile revenge in George's mind.

Sitting around thinking about all the problems wasn't going to solve anything. She had to put her plan into action and get back to safety. She shook Chris awake. He mumbled and complained.

"Squeeze my hand as hard as you can," she ordered. "I won't let you go back to sleep until you do."

She got her wish and then some. "Ow!" She tried to jerk her hand back, but Chris apparently wanted his sleep rather desperately. "Gimme my arm back!"

He finally relented. Even though darkness was falling, she could feel his glare.

Sighing, she pushed aside the blanket that covered him. He was already close to the rock wall. She wedged herself between him and it and then covered them both. He grunted, but didn't say anything. She hoped he wouldn't fall off the other side of the blanket. It really wasn't large enough for two, but the night air was too cold for her to sleep unprotected.

The only good thing about the sleeping arrangement was that it was uncomfortable enough that she wouldn't have any trouble waking up every so often so that she could check on Chris.

Apparently it wasn't comfortable for Chris either. He was awake every time she checked. By morning, she wasn't certain who had more bruises.

Grumbling, she made coffee and threw together a mixture that was a cross between gruel and cream of wheat.

Chris made sure to compliment her efforts. "What the hell is this? Sand?"

She glared at him and tried to remember that he was an invalid. "If you're up to hunting, feel free to bring in some meat."

He looked around as though considering it "I suppose you didn't find Jacket."

"Jacket?"

"My horse. You know, the black and white one that dumped me off the cliff yesterday."

"I didn't know you had named your horse."

He winced as he tried to swallow more of her emergency trail mix. "He had a name. It was on the stall door."

"Oh."

She finished her breakfast in silence, and then slung the pack she had readied the night before onto Speckle's back.

"What are you doing?" he asked, suddenly wide-awake.

"I'm going to go get the instructions." She put her hands firmly on her hips to keep him from seeing that they were shaking. "Then I'm going to come back here and pack you up and go home."

He took his time responding, probably because it took him quite a while to gain his feet. When he did, he looked positively green "I'll go with you."

"Absolutely not. You won't be travel-worthy for at least another day and to top it off, we only have one horse. Meanwhile, whoever took pot shots at us has either gotten there ahead of us, given up, or will be coming back for us. Since you can't travel, it only makes sense that you stay here and recuperate. I'll make the attempt and whether I fail or succeed, I'll come back and get you and we return."

She reached over and helped him sit down. "If we had the horse, maybe. Walking the whole way would be way too slow." For a horrible moment, she saw his body plunging over the side of the rocks again. She took a steadying breath. "I'm really sorry, Chris. I think I can get the instructions on my own. I have all the information that you gave to Darren, and I have the added benefit of not being an idiot."

He closed his eyes. "I know."

She clamped her teeth down hard in order to keep herself from asking, "You know what?" That was part of the secret of not getting caught--never act guilty of anything. Always make light of any answer and never ask questions as though you're afraid someone knows an answer you don't want to hear.

"However," he added, "I think you got more than you bargained for this time." His eyes were still closed. She sucked in a nervous breath and held it.

"The other jobs were clean, and no one was actively trying to stop you. This time someone is more desperate."

"Why are they more desperate this time?" She chose to ignore the warning sign that he suspected her.

"Who knows? Maybe because it's looking like the protection of the crystals is about to be taken more seriously." He opened his eyes. They were a deep emerald green, greener outside against the red rock than she had ever seen them. "It is, however, imperative that you get the instructions if they haven't been stolen already."

"I'll do my best," she pledged. She didn't feel like questioning him right then. She didn't want to commit herself to any action without thinking it over. He could be bluffing. Even if he wasn't, she wasn't sure she wanted to know the consequences of him knowing that she had been the thief. A very big part of her demanded to know how he knew. But that was how thieves got caught. Sometimes you had to accept not knowing until you had the chance to figure out what was really going on.

"Do you think you could help me move to a more secluded spot before you leave?"

She glanced around. The area was fairly open and from the right vantage point it was possible someone might be able to spot him from above.

"I don't know, Chris. How are you feeling?"

He shrugged in answer and rolled back to his feet, slowly. "If I can get partway up this canyon, at least I'll know if anyone is coming."

She had to agree with him. The rocky terrain was covered with fine sandy particles and pebbles. If anyone tried to climb up towards him, he would have some warning. "Okay. Let's get you up a ways."

She packed the equipment she was leaving and hoisted it across her back. She moved it up first and then came back and offered her arm. Chris had already struggled partway, but he wasn't looking very bright or chipper.

"This trip has been like a gold miner in search of a legendary mine that doesn't exist," Chris muttered.

"Well, if this is gold, I'd say forget it," she panted as she pulled on his good arm. "There isn't enough money in the world to make this worthwhile."

He disagreed. "It's worth it to someone."

Silently, she acknowledged the truth in his comment. She should have stayed at Haven and researched who might have the resources to try and get the crystals and instructions instead of pretending she was a superhero thief.

As if reading her mind, Chris stopped and leaned against her. The gash on his head looked darker after his exertions, and she wondered if his scab would hold. He rubbed a tired hand across his eyes and then spoke slowly. "If someone was sent after the instructions, there must be a large amount of money coming into Haven from outside to pay for the job." He shifted his weight slightly and leaned back against a boulder. He was still pale, and if she watched closely she could see an occasional tremor in his hands. "That's the trail you'll need to follow."

"Don't you mean the trail you'll have to follow?"

"Whoever makes it back. I don't think they are after the crystals. I think it is the instructions they want. With those, and a lot of luck, they might be able to manufacture their own crystals--or even more than one set."

"Assuming they don't blow up half a continent trying." Not even the scientists at Haven, who assumed they understood the reaction, had the nerve to attempt a recreation of the freak accident that had resulted in the crystals.

"Exactly. It will be dangerous to obtain the instructions and harder to sell them, but ultimately worth more." Chris reached for the rocks again and pulled himself forward.

"Now that you are involved, I think it only fair that you stick around to solve the mystery." Alexia didn't want him entertaining the thought, not even for a moment, that he wouldn't be making it back.

He didn't turn around or stop struggling forward. "I'm Appleton's son. This was my big chance to prove I belonged at Haven and wasn't just given a spot there because I was his son. Guess I haven't done any better than Darren."

"You're at Haven now, whatever the circumstances. I hardly think your father will throw you out because of one tiny issue."

Without turning around, he responded coolly, "My father is my business."

Alexia had a long day ahead of her, and she didn't feel like wasting her breath on a conversation where she wasn't welcome. After a few more feet, she found a rock with a slight overhang. It would serve to keep him partially hidden as well as dry. It wasn't exactly a cave, but under the circumstances, it was certainly better than where he had been. She dragged the supplies up the rest of the way and set them next to him. "Stay put and rest. You've got the rifle. I'll warn you as I come back. I'll be walking Speckle."

"What if someone is chasing you?"

She rolled her eyes. "If I'm being chased, Chris, I wouldn't come back here. Try not to worry. If I don't check back in another twelve hours, someone will come for you."

She squeezed his hand and headed back down.

Chapter 17

When she reached her horse, she directed Speckle to fly as fast as the sand and rocks would allow. It felt good and right that she head for the target alone. If she couldn't get the instruction chip, it was either gone, or the plan was good enough.

She wondered briefly about Darren, but the nightmare of Chris' body flying over the side of the canyon stilled her inclination to think long in that direction. Darren should have been able to escape, because the gunman had followed her and Chris.

Of course, there might have been more than one gunman. If Darren was still alive, he would head for the site to get the instructions before looking for his comrades.

As long as she only ran into Darren, she would be okay. It was the unknowns out there that scared her.

The mountain terrain took over beneath Speckle's hooves, and the trees thickened enough to hide them both. She spotted a rare frisky fox, but it darted under cover almost before she registered its presence.

Normal. Everything seemed quite normal.

She continued her climb up the hillside, trying to time her arrival within the half-mile radius with dusk. The trees helped protect her from satellite surveillance, but she still planned to do most of the work at night.

As soon as she was up high enough, she stopped and scanned behind her with binoculars.

Uh-oh. There was movement behind her, very close to the path she had traveled.

She held her breath. The binoculars were none too steady given Speckle's shifting. Rather than dismount, she waited, searching harder. Speckle's breathing was too loud. The saddle creaked. The trees whispered. A chipmunk and a bird chattered, probably at each other.

Uneasy, she dismounted. Instead of staying on track, she headed for another spot higher up where she might see better.

The satellites would spot her if she moved too far in the open. Carefully, she peered through the trees.

Whoever was following stayed still.

She moved down again, around Speckle. Three more positions, and she had him!

A lone buck. He rested in the afternoon heat, not moving except to occasionally grab a nearby leaf to chew on.

With a relieved sigh, she returned to Speckled and got moving again.

Deer or no, she checked behind her every time the terrain gave her the opportunity.

Mid-afternoon, her GPS finally indicated she was close. She dismounted and tied Speckle in a thick grove of Ponderosa pines. "Stay quiet," she instructed, placing a bag with bits of grain around the mare's head.

Alexia started out jogging, but covered only about a quarter of a mile that way. The past few days had taken a toll. Resting for a moment, she studied her surroundings. The area didn't match the descriptions Chris had provided, but the location, according to her reading was correct. She checked her compass and map again. Confused, she turned on her computer and looked again at the information.

The coordinates had to be correct. She was within a few yards of the location. The trees, however, showed little signs of clearing. It didn't take a genius to realize that she had been duped.

A small arroyo, perhaps recently formed in a mudslide, was as close to a clearing as the terrain offered. There were no fences, no mysterious boxes to be opened, and from the looks of the trees, no way a satellite could penetrate most of the area.

Chris couldn't have lied completely about the protections. Therefore, he had to have lied about the location. She paced angrily, and then thought better of it because of the noise. Just because she couldn't see motion detectors or cameras didn't mean that they weren't there. She sat down instead and tried to reason her way through the situation.

She wondered if Chris was laughing somewhere out in the desert. "Ha, ha." Some thief she was.

With nothing better to do than explore, she circled the area, making larger and larger turns. Having come from the east, she was comfortable accepting that the location probably wasn't in that direction.

By the time she had made twenty circles, the terrain was rougher and more impassible. The afternoon was turning downright gloomy, with boiling clouds threatening heavy rain. Knowing the clouds would keep satellites from registering her movements, she kept going.

The toughest area forced her to scramble over bushes, cacti and rocks until, panting, she found a stream bed. There was even a trickle in the bottom from the recent rain.

While catching her breath, she looked up. There was certainly enough open space for satellite pictures. If a person came from the north, they could be seen the entire time they followed the stream bed. If they had come from the east as she had, they probably wouldn't have found the stream bed. Of course, there were no fences here either, but Chris was subtle. Why advertise to the thief where you were hiding the package? In fact, she had no idea if the package was actually nearby.

It could be hidden inside a false rock, or under the sand or in a tree. But there had to be some sort of protective devices in place, didn't there?

With nothing else to do, she sat again. There wasn't enough water to bother drinking from the stream, so she uncapped her water bottle and took a long drink.

Splashing sounds from the stream's source echoed through the air. She wondered how far away the waterfall might be and decided to follow the riverbed. With the cloud cover, she still had a window of opportunity to explore without being spotted.

By the time she found the source, she decided that hiding the package under the sand was not a good idea. It had to be hidden behind solid rock. Sand could too easily wash away, leaving the package exposed.

There was plenty of water pooled under the trickling waterfall. Most of it disappeared before creating the small tendril of a stream. She frowned. If the package had been hidden in the stream bed, it had to be watertight. In fact, no matter where it was, it had to be watertight. Since it wasn't protected in a gleaming, steel safe, the best protection was-- something watertight and obvious, but camouflaged.

There were more rocks around than she had time to explore. And if it were in a cave, how was she supposed to find said cave? Sure, with some explosives, she could detonate charges and get a seismic reading. An expert could then tell her where a cave might be. No problem. Except she didn't have explosives and wasn't an expert.

Grumpy, she backtracked to the end of the stream bed. The only saving grace was that the area appeared undisturbed. She hadn't seen signs of anyone else having found the instructions either.

She hadn't a clue. Not a one.

Her stubborn streak screamed as she turned to walk back to Speckle. Her coming had been a complete waste of time. She had accomplished nothing except to leave Chris all alone and vulnerable. She wasn't nearly the thief she had thought. Without specific instructions, she probably couldn't steal a toothbrush. Without a map, she was lucky she had found her way to the end of the damn stream bed.

She took two steps away before she stopped, her foot frozen in midair.

End of the stream bed.

She let her foot fall. She turned back around, her eyes squinting. It was crazy. She was groping at straws. Her own ego had turned her into a lunatic. Still…no.

She pushed forward.

She looked back. Well, she was already here.

Her feet dithered back and forth as if she were inventing a new dance.

Impulsively, she headed back to the source of dripping water. It was far enough away that she wouldn't have heard the water had there been less of it. Of course, the area was a desert and therefore much of the water could be draining through the sandy, rocky soil. But it had rained enough that the water was still running heavily a few feet up stream. Why did it stop when it did?

She checked the pool again, putting her hands into it and guessing the depth. Water seeped over the edges at a healthy rate and ran back to where? She followed it. Her conscious mind registered what her subconscious had already deduced. The water, even for a desert, disappeared too quickly when it reached a particularly rocky area.

It was as if there was a hole underground where the water ran.

She fervently wished that she had a large source of water so that she could test her theory. Lacking a quick means, she crawled on her hands and knees until she spotted what she was looking for. The wet area divided into two small patches, but most of the water was disappearing under a boulder that was roughly the size of a small car.

So now came the tricky part. How could she move the rock to see underneath? If the rock were part of an elaborate place to house the instructions, there would be alarms. Moving the rock would probably set off any protections and rightfully so. If the container with the instructions were uncovered, either by natural means such as a roaring flood or by human hands, the owner would want to know. The rock wasn't a small one either, so the chances of a flood moving it, or a single human such as herself, were nil. It would take purposeful movement and that, she was sure, would trigger some kind of reaction, somewhere.

Of course, there might actually be a real underground cave here and the water was innocently traveling into it.

She groaned and rubbed her eyes. The most probable explanation was that she was insane. She should pack up her stuff and get Chris to civilization and proper medical care.

But what would it hurt to check and see if a cave was under there? It would only take a few minutes, and if she was wrong, no one was here to witness her foolishness.

She reached into her backpack before she could change her mind. Carefully, she extracted her little bug. He would be happy to crawl under the rock that she couldn't lift. He could follow the water.

Of course, the expensive little bug might also get carried away by unknown currents, but what the hell.

Scorpions were not digging creatures, but she set him on the sand and wormed him back and forth across the underside of the rock looking for an opening that wasn't completely filled with water or dirt. From the vantage point of the scorpion, a tiny hole was all that was really needed-- and a where water went, there had to be a hole.

Once the scorpion disappeared from sight, she activated the light and camera and watched the activity on her wrist computer. The rock itself was not hollow, but along where she pushed her little bug, she could see that there were man-made marks. Scratches and dings decorated the rock as if it had been wired to detect movement. She continued her search, moving the little scorpion and digging him through the sand. It wasn't the most efficient maneuver she had ever performed, but she didn't want her own hands digging clumsily through the dirt and setting off an alarm.

At last, poor little scorpion hit pay dirt! Or rather, he hit a pocket of air and fell through onto a bowling-ball-sized boulder tucked under the cover of the larger one. From the camera's vantage point, she could see that the rock sat in a hollowed area. Surrounding the rock, there was a pool of water that slowly drained away to be replaced by the water from above.

She grinned at her success, and then frowned. "How am I going to get the stuff out?" Obviously if the second rock was a fake, it had to be wired so that it couldn't be tampered with. She studied the picture again. There were rough edges that had been covered over by a material that resembled the rock so perfectly, she wouldn't have noticed it had she not been looking at it from the magnified vision of the scorpion's camera.

Of course, her little thief mind chuckled, wires that can be seen can be circumvented.

Alexia carefully directed the scorpion around the rock, looking for the break in the wires. Where the wires connected, the rock had to open.

She found the line soon enough, although it was cleverly disguised. Chris had outdone himself. He had created several secret panels in the rock. That must have been what his instructions hinted at when he mentioned false safes.

From her magnified vision, she could see the outline of an opening. But who would have normally bothered to carry a magnifier with them? She certainly wouldn't have thought of it on purpose. The only reason the scorpion carried such a device was because on such a small electronic creature the camera had to be able to zoom in as well as zoom out. The fact that she could zoom in on tiny details was pure serendipity.

She laughed aloud. "Chris, this is incredible." It was also the most fun she had had in ages. It was better than her first break-in, and infinitely more rewarding than stealing the crystals the first time.

Her mind quickly returned to the task at hand. The most obvious crack was around the circumference of the rock. This was the most likely spot to be tried by someone in a hurry, or someone not thinking. She studied several other pockets around the rock before deciding which one held the instructions. The instructions were stored on a chip no larger than her little fingernail. The safest place would be in the center of the rock.

Once she determined the most probable location, she studied the wiring scheme. In true Victorian style, Chris had secreted the catch to the secret panel in a clever design of the rock. Now all she had to do was figure out the code sequence to open it.

That took the help of her trusty computer. The scorpion sent the data she requested, such as the rock's dimensions. It couldn't give her a weight, but she suspected that the rock was heavier than it looked-- another ploy that might catch a person unaware. The thing probably couldn't be lifted by a normal-sized man.

While the computer crunched numbers and probable combinations based on every piece of information she could glean, she wondered if it was possible to open it at all without setting off an alarm. Of course, she had to take Chris' public specification somewhat seriously. It was quite possible that he had secreted harmful gases in some of the false panels.

The sequence and pressure requirements came through. The model presented was one common to door locks. The space that required pressure was the size of a thumb print. Alexia could only hope that Chris' prints were on the list of acceptable ones. They had to be since he was conducting the study.

At the last minute, she changed her mind. After all, Chris' fingerprints were too obvious. With him along on the trip, his fingerprints were too easily available. Working quickly, she rolled the scorpion out of the hollow and placed the elder Appleton's fingerprints into the scorpion's claws. Then she fervently prayed while she directed the scorpion back into place.

Fingerprints weren't reliable on their own, but they could be a good deterrent, especially if a thief used the wrong person's fingerprints for an attempted authorization. If her attempt failed, she would have to try and override the protective system. In all probability, any failed attempt would be her last.

She held her breath as her little friend applied the print and pressure.

Nothing happened. "Drat."

She tried again, but still nothing.

Then she remembered. Heartbeat! She jerked the controls, forcing the scorpion to release the pressure, checking the time as she did so. It had been just over a second. Probably within milliseconds of an alarm. Luckily Scorpio had more than one appendage.

She tried again, using Scorpios legs to create even pressure and a tapping pincher to fake the beat of a heart.

Like a ray of sunshine across snow, the panel burst open. She couldn't believe it. She would have reached and grabbed the chip had it been revealed in front of her.

Instead, she directed the claws to carefully, ever so slowly, retrieve the chip without applying any pressure to the inside of the panel.

She wondered if pagers and alarms were going off somewhere. Well, too late. If she were a real thief, she could escape into the mountains and then exit the area at her leisure.

Scorpio was out of the dirt within seconds, and the chip was carefully stowed in a special case deep inside her backpack.

She had forgotten only one thing during the whole time she had been sitting there.

Of course, all psychiatrists know that brutal reminders usually only have to be applied once before a victim learns her lesson.

Chapter 18

The boiling clouds hovering over the mountain range were not yet dropping any rain--at least not where she was standing. The wind had picked up, and in the back of her mind she was glad the clouds kept the satellites from detecting her movements. But she had forgotten the danger.

If she had been unfamiliar with the area, she might have kidded herself about the train-like roar. After all, she was sitting in the middle of the stream bed where the water was only trickling.

But rain had probably been falling higher up in the mountains for hours, raising the water table and filling washes and arroyos upstream. When the water in the desert decided to arrive, it came in a flash flood of giant rolling teeth, sucking sand, rocks and everything else underneath its maws.

The sound of that water filled her ears. She looked back, but her legs were already churning. One hand grabbed her pack and the other stuffed the scorpion into her pocket. Knowing that her chances weren't good, she clawed her way frantically up the side of the bank.

The roaring got louder, as did her desperation. The backpack was too heavy across her back, weighing her down. She needed to make high ground. Fast.

The sound of the trickling waterfall was completely lost, and the earth shook its final warning. She grabbed frantically at a thick tree root and heaved herself upward.

Her feet swept out from under her, and she held desperately, pulling herself straight up and pushing herself into the side of the bank.

Climb!

She cursed, knowing suddenly the desperation that had driven Chris to cling to his precarious perch. If strong arms hadn't yanked her shoulders from their sockets and dragged her up, she wouldn't have made it.

"Thank God," she panted. "Darren."

Her words were more of a gasp than a statement, but he answered her anyway. "You're under arrest for the theft of instructions and crystals of Haven." His voice sounded like it came from miles away.

With careless abandon, she shuddered, allowing herself to collapse at his feet. Knowing what was coming, she pleaded, "Do you have anything to eat?"

It was a whisper, but it broke through his list of offenses. "What?"

For the first time, Alexia realized that Darren was holding a gun on her. She stared at it in fascination. "Are you going to shoot me?"

"Do you realize that you have made a complete fool of me?" His tone was one that she had never heard him use. It was quiet and very calm. Very un-Darren-like.

She scooted backwards, carefully. Between the storm and approaching nightfall, it would be pitch black very soon.

His gun followed her motion. "Do you really think I'll let you go?"

"But Darren, I was sent here to get the instructions, you idiot!" Her courage was nearly at its failure point, but unless she could break his calm and get him angry, there was no telling what action he might take. He must have watched her retrieve the chip, even while believing that it was impossible that she had found it. And that, that final theft, was her undoing. After all, what normal psychiatrist came equipped with a small robot and an electrical decoder programs loaded on her mini-computer?

He had made the connection. If she was smart enough to retrieve the chip from a hidden cache in a rock, she was more than clever enough to have overcome his simple traps.

"You did it. All along, it was you."

"I was sent here to retrieve the chip." She wasn't going to admit to anything else. He couldn't prove anything.

That small fact, the truth that he couldn't prove what he now knew, finally took his anger to rage. He cursed and called her names she didn't even recognize. Finally, he pointed the gun again. "You're guilty!"

Alexia was out of words. Not only that, her stomach was about to boil over. The flood waters were rising. She could feel the ground crumpling and falling into the mass of pouring water. Darren was going to shoot her, and all she could think of was a Snickers Ice Cream Bar. "I'm dying."

She put her head on her knees and inched sideways towards the trees. If she had to die, it was going to be like a coward, dammit. She had the right to be spineless. In fact, she might even throw up. She had been chased by dogs, shot at, forced to rescue Chris from the edge of a cliff, and almost been washed away in a flood.

If Darren had been a reasonable man, she would have pleaded for her life. Of course, in the middle of her appeal she would probably throw up on his shoes, but what did any of it matter? He was much too impulsive to give consideration to his own actions. He would worry about justifying the killing later.

She heard a thunk and more curses, but she refused to look up. "Alexia?"

She stubbornly ignored his taunts. She was not going to lift her head so he could shoot her between the eyes. Things were getting a little black anyway. Or was it just dark out?

Then, a scratched and abused hand pulled her head up. A bloody face pushed its way in front of her own. Her vision wasn't completely gone. Otherwise she wouldn't have been able to tell it was Chris and not Darren who was trying to lift her head.

"Do you want a candy bar? You had some in the supplies you left with me."

Alexia stared, nearly blinded by passion. A candy bar? Darling Chris had brought her a candy bar?

She nearly broke his hand in her hurry to snatch it from him. In the remaining light, she could barely see that it was a Milky Way instead of a Snickers, but who cared?

She devoured it with relish. "Thank God."

Chris checked Darren's prone body by beaming a flashlight across it. "You don't have to thank me for saving you from this cretin."

She shook her head and licked her fingers. "No. For the food. You wouldn't happen to have any ice cream, would you?"

He raised his eyebrows and choked back a laugh. "No. Can't say that I do."

Now that she was feeling a bit better, she stood up. Slowly.

"I gathered from what Darren said, you've already retrieved the chip. Under the circumstances, I think we can count my plan as failed." The bloody bandage across his head had slipped. He looked like a cross between a mummy and a pirate.

"Oh. Well. Don't take it personally." She searched for somewhere to look other than at him. Her eyes fell on Darren's still flat body.

"Did you kill him?" Her eyes widened. Truly, Chris would have a reason that any court would find acceptable, but she couldn't believe it.

"No," he grumbled. "Just gave him a few paybacks." He scowled and looked even more piratical.

"How did you get here?"

He shown the light back towards the trees. "Friend of yours."

For the first time, Alexia noticed a scraggly figure propped against a tree. He looked almost as bad as Chris. Two long scratches ran down either side of his face, and he was holding his arm as if it was broken.

"Keith!" Then she looked from him to Chris. "How--what..."

Chris said, "He received a desperate message from you and decided to come and help. He brought two horses; the extra one was for me since you apparently said I was in dire need of rescuing." His tone told her that he didn't appreciate the description.

"Well, you weren't exactly chipper when I left!"

"I'm not exactly chipper now," he replied. "How are we going to get he-man back?" His foot drifted back and forth as if he was considering kicking Darren.

"Doesn't he have a horse?" Alexia asked.

"I don't think so. We found yours, but there was no sign of his."

By this time, "he-man" was coming around.

Darren groaned in unison with Alexia's own sound of despair. Keith edged forward, keeping his eyes mostly on Darren, but occasionally his glance darted wildly from side to side. He skirted the trees carefully, moving from one to the next like a policeman on a raid. When he made it to Alexia's side, she asked, "What is wrong with you?"

He started at her voice. Perhaps he was more injured than he appeared.

"Animals," he whispered hoarsely. "Out there!"

"What kind of animals?" Had someone sent dogs again? She reached for her weapon only to remember that she had left her rifle with Chris. Her knife was in her backpack, but it wouldn't be much protection.

"Relax," Chris said, catching her shoulder before she could back up any further. "Our hero here isn't used to the great outdoors. He had his first experience with a deer this morning."

"A deer?"

Chris grinned while Keith scowled. "Ran across his camp and nearly trampled him from what I could tell. He was shooting up the canyon, yelling like an Indian on a rampage and almost lost both the horses."

She looked at Keith, who, instead of being embarrassed, looked angry. She sighed. How did she get herself into these things? It was time to give up. She was definitely in no shape to deal with this situation. She flopped back down on the ground. "I don't think I can go back with you. I'll have to give you the instructions, and you can go about your merry way."

"What? Why?"

"I can't do it," she said. "I simply cannot go back with three men, one who is trying to kill me," she tried to look at Darren as she said it, but Chris was still blocking her view, "one who is badly injured, and one who blames me for the whole mess!" She waved at Keith with the last statement. She blinked back tears, but one or two escaped.

Keith stared at her. Darren sat up and then froze when he saw her pathetic face in the glare of the flashlight. Chris just stood there.

For a moment, no one said anything at all. Darren managed to stumble to his feet and Keith took a couple of steps backwards. They all began to talk at once.

"I don't exactly blame you," Keith muttered.

"I'll wait to prosecute you," Darren offered generously.

"You're going back with us," Chris said. "I need a nurse." It wasn't exactly comfort, but he did put his arm around her as he urged her to stand.

Darren stepped in front of them blocking the way. "I'll take her."

"Where the hell is she going to run?" Chris pushed Alexia behind him and challenged Darren directly. "There are only miles of desert between her and freedom, and it's a little late to kill her in cold blood."

Alexia peeked around Chris' shoulder. Darren was impulsive, but not stupid. Although Alexia hardly trusted that he wouldn't try to murder her in her sleep, she decided he probably wouldn't kill her at this moment.

She edged out from behind Chris. Picking up her backpack, she found her extra, though smaller, flashlight.

Chris led the way to the horses.

When she reached Speckle, she whispered, "Traitor. You could have told me they were coming."

Without another word to any of them, she tied her backpack on the horse. It was too dark to ride. It was too dark to walk, really.

Darren didn't waste any time dragging his horse from cover. He also retrieved a lantern.

"There's no point in trying to ride back in the dark." Chris went to his own horse. "Let's get away from this arroyo and set camp."

Alexia wasn't about to argue. She was so tired, she felt drunk.

Chris wasted time trying to help Keith--who looked like he had fallen off the horse more than he had ridden it.

Alexia was more than happy to set the pace, walking slowly to safer ground. Darren stayed closer to her than when he had been in "charge" of her safety. Chris seemed just as determined to walk over the top of her from the other side.

None of them dared go more than a couple hundred yards in the dark.

Chris tied his horse and began unpacking. "If it rains, we'll put up shelter. Otherwise, we camp." He tossed her the magnetic blanket.

She protested, but only half-heartedly. "But you're injured!"

"And you're half dead."

Grateful, she set it under some protective branches and hoped it didn't rain. The wind had died down some and under the tree branches, the gusts were tolerable.

Chris handed her the rifle. He had remembered that also.

Too tired to use it, she hugged it close. No one had asked where the instructions were, and she wasn't tired enough to be stupid enough to ask who wanted them.

Chapter 19

Traveling as she was with two confrontational men and a kid more used to sidewalks than rocks, she should have expected the rude awakening at dawn. For some reason however, she couldn't seem to get her wits together. The scene in front of her probably didn't require bullets. She had her gun at the ready, just in case, but she couldn't decide what needed shooting.

Keith, in joyous abandon, appeared to be attacking the ground with a large stick. Chris yelled, and Darren was trying to tackle Keith. Alexia could not for the life of her imagine what could be so important that they had to argue about it at the crack of dawn.

"Stop!" she screamed in her best female screech.

No avail. Keith still hopped about like a mad hatter and stayed just out of reach of Darren. Chris had now taken up his own stick and was either trying to attack Keith or maybe Darren. Alexia really couldn't tell which, because he hit the ground more often than not. Finally, she reached the end of her patience. She had been wrong. The situation did call for bullets.

The firing of the rifle succeeded where feminine screaming had failed. Of course, no one had ever died from a scream, whereas when a woman had a gun, it was wise to pay attention. Even the male brain, in a state of complete chaos, recognized that. Thank God there were a few rules of psychiatry that she could count on.

"Gentlemen. Have you been eating gourds?"

"Snnn," Keith answered.

Normally she wouldn't have been able to understand such a statement, even considering her skills as an analytical psychiatrist. The rattling of a tail, sounding like a low flying helicopter, filled in the blank spots.

Before the men could again begin their bizarre dance, she fired the gun again. "Hold it!" she commanded Chris before he could deliver the killing blow. "I want that snake."

"What?" This question came from all three.

"I want that snake." She struggled away from her blanket, which was still tangled around her feet. "I want it captured."

Keith had reached his limit. He backed away from her, none to carefully. "You're crazy! I knew I never should have gotten involved with you. Missin' a few fax connections, you are."

"Darren," she shouted, "don't let him step on the snake!"

This propelled both Darren and Keith to action. Darren flew through the air towards Keith, who finally realized he had been backing into dangerous territory. The result was not pretty and neither of them were standing at the end.

Meanwhile, Chris used his stick to pin the reptile by its neck. Hissing, rattling and moving, the snack fought for freedom.

Alexia scurried to her leather saddlebag and emptied it. Carefully she moved in behind Chris.

"You're joking!" he gasped as she forced the body of the snake inside.

"Keep the head pinned!"

For a moment, he was too stunned to do anything else. By which time, she succeeded in pushing the snake in and securing the bag.

"I was only holding it to kill it!" Chris moved towards her purposefully. "You can't--"

He stopped. She held between her fingers the reason they were standing on the side of the mountain like fools: a single chip of information, a chip full of instructions that until that moment had only been protected by her person.

Unzipping the edge of the bag the tiniest bit, she dropped the chip in with the snake. Rattling ensued.

"But...but..." Keith stuttered. "What if the snake eats the chip?"

She shrugged. "It's just as safe in the snake's stomach. Besides, rattlesnakes aren't stupid. It recognizes the difference between food and silicon. Just like it will recognize the danger of a human hand reaching inside the bag."

"And it would strike," Chris finished the sentence, finally getting the point. He grinned at her. "Clever. Very clever."

She turned to Darren. "Did you want to carry the bag? No, no, it's better if I do it, I think. Neutral party and all."

He didn't answer her directly. In fact, he was keeping a healthy distance. "It isn't foolproof. I could shoot that bag full of so many holes, that snake wouldn't make a meal."

She shrugged. "You could. And you could also put a hole through the chip if you did that." She draped the bag back over her saddle. "Let's remember that whoever wants the chip, wants it alive."

"You're not gonna ride with it, are you?" Keith gagged on whatever else he might have wanted to say.

"Of course I'm going to ride with it. As long as it's in the bag, it isn't going to bite though the leather."

"Your horse won't like it," Chris said.

"No, probably not. However, I don't see an option. Speckle is going to have to get used to it. We've got a full day ahead of us."

"That's if we make better time going out than we did going in," Darren said. He eyed the bag with distrust.

"I fully intend to. I've had more camping that I can stand."

No one bothered to argue with her. At least in Haven, someone taking pot shots at them in the streets was less likely. As long they were crossing open ranges, they were in danger from the unknown enemy, snake or no snake.

Chapter 20

Haven was not reached during the daylight hours. When it got dark, Alexia didn't stop. "I'm continuing on. You guys can follow or not."

"It's dark." Keith sounded as though he could happily shoot her.

Darren, who had decided he couldn't shoot her and get away with it, pushed his horse closer to hers, causing Speckle to snort and dance away.

Chris was back to being carefree, a state Alexia no longer believed. His plan had failed, she was about to be hung, and they had no way of protecting the instructions from danger. He had no reason on earth to be happy.

Speckle knew the way home without her guidance, even in the dark. They had been through this particular route together before, and once Speckle realized they were headed for a warm and welcoming stable, the mare was all for the plan.

Haven, contrary to the chaos they had been through, was nestled quietly in its valley. As always, lights shone from a few buildings at the research center. No one was out to greet them.

As soon as the first hoof touched the packed street, Daren demanded, "Where do you think you're going?"

"To the stables, Darren, sir." She mocked him was a sloppy salute. "Then I'm going home to bed. You can't arrest me tonight." Technically he probably could, but it was going to take him time to gather evidence. He couldn't accuse her of stealing the instructions this time around. She had specific permission to do just that.

When they reached the stables, lights went on inside the homestead. Alexia yelled out a greeting to forestall a big audience. "Just us returning, Al. We'll check the horses in."

Her reassurance didn't help. Al lumbered out anyway, mumbling about horse thieves. His eyes lit up when he saw them. "You found them!" Al eased over to Chris and Keith's mounts, happily stroking their necks.

Alexia dismounted and nudged Keith. "Why didn't you just rent them?" she hissed.

Keith shrugged. "Like right. Like that dude's gonna take a dig from me."

Alexia wasn't sure if a dig was money or the story Keith would have had to tell in order to convince Al to let him take his horses, but it didn't really matter.

Al checked both horses eagerly. "First the fire, then," he looked up at Chris, "your horse showed up with no rider."

Chris said, "Glad to hear it. Left me lying in the dust. Uh...rattlesnake scared him."

Alexia's eyes grew wide as she wondered how to get the rattlesnake in her bag out of sight without Al noticing. He wouldn't take kindly to the snake being near his horses. The snake wasn't rattling at the moment, but once she moved the horse or the bag, it would probably start up again.

"You're all crazy," Keith announced. He pointed at Alexia. "You can forget our deal. I ain't workin' on no more dead bodies, and I sure as hell ain't keepin' no snakes or going out to get your ass out of the fire again. This place is for lunatics."

With that, he backed out of the stable. Alexia wasn't certain, but she thought he might have left the grounds at a run.

She sighed. One more problem to solve tomorrow.

"What dead bodies?" Al asked. "Did you shoot the horse thieves?"

She shook her head, dashing his hopes. "No, he works for Sam. I guess he didn't like it."

"Oh." Al looked very disappointed.

Alexia eased the saddle bag off her mare and unsaddled Speckle in record time. Darren stood over her the entire time, glowering. He made no move to retrieve the bag or the instructions.

"I don't suppose you're going to bother with your own horse." She wished she could maneuver Speckle to step on him.

"I rented it. Now it's returned. Besides, it's his job," Darren replied.

She knew it wouldn't do her any good to point out that it wouldn't hurt Darren to see to his own mount. Just as it wouldn't have hurt Darren to check on her and Chris after they had been separated. However, he had his own agenda. She had learned the hard way, the same way Haven officials had, that Darren had his own schedule of events.

Chris appeared around the line of tack. "You done?"

She nodded.

"I'll walk you home," he offered. "You and your friend."

Darren stepped between them. "There will be no fraternizing with the prisoner."

Luckily, Alexia had never been the sort to stand around waiting for authoritative figures to get their act together. She slung the saddlebag over one shoulder, her backpack over the other and walked away.

"Halt," Darren commanded. She heard rather than saw him draw his gun. She stopped.

Every muscle she owned, including her brain, demanded that she turn and kick him soundly. The gun in his hand helped her refrain, as did the fact that she was carrying a rattlesnake across her shoulder. Otherwise, no amount of reasoning could have stopped her.

"You can't be serious," Chris said.

Alexia turned around to find Chris forcing Darren's arm down.

"She was escaping," Darren said.

"On foot? I don't think so."

Since the gun was no longer pointed in her direction, Alexia began walking again. Both men followed her and continued arguing. In the background she could hear Al, questioning what all the racket was about. She continued to walk. Darren's only claim to victory was that she was unable to defy him completely and set out at a run. He would shoot her for sure, Chris or no Chris.

By the time she reached her door, they had stopped yelling. She activated the unlocking system and stepped inside. Chris, even without an invite, followed.

"Goodnight, Darren," he said.

"You can't--"

Whatever else he might have said was lost behind the closed door, and the pounding that began afterwards.

Alexia turned in surprise. "You're going to lock him out?"

"Got a better plan?"

She shook her head. "No." Then, for the first time in hours, she grinned. "In fact, I like a man who can shut the door and walk away."

Chris grinned back. "He'll probably sleep on the porch, you know."

That brought an even bigger smile. "Too bad."

"Yeah," Chris laughed. "I can only imagine the look on his face when he realized it had been you all along."

It hadn't been funny. She had been staring at death when Darren figured it out. Still, for some unknown reason, it seemed hilarious now. Without an answer, she sat down on her sofa and laughed.

Finally, Chris interrupted her giggles by asking between guffaws if she was hungry. Since they hadn't stopped, they hadn't eaten. It was well after midnight.

"Starved," she answered.

"Good. I'll fix something quick, and then we can both get some rest. We'll need to get up early."

"And why would that be?"

He didn't stop his trek to the kitchen. "We have to get you out of the mess you are in. We also have to find a better place for the instructions. And we also have a culprit to find."

At the last, he stopped, looked back over his shoulder and waited.

Alexia squirmed. For the first time in her life, she felt guilt well up into a shocking rationalization that it would all be better if she confessed.

Before she could utter a single syllable, Chris turned and disappeared behind her kitchen door. He whistled while he concocted dinner. Ruefully, she acknowledged the clever way he was working on her. He had taken control by walking in without permission. He had kept Darren out. Now he was offering to help. Not accusing her of anything, but offering to help. Not demanding that she confide, but telling her he knew, and then leaving her to think things through and make her own decision. Wow. Almost like he was a psychiatrist himself.

Or maybe a friend, a little rebellious, wishful voice whispered.

She sighed. Picking up the saddlebag, she walked over to a side panel in her living room. As a master of thieves, she also was a master of safes. In her opinion, the best safes had been constructed in the eighteen-hundreds by woodworkers and architects. Put a hiding place in plain view, and no one knew where too look. In addition to secret panels, she had added electronic mechanisms and codes that only she knew. There was no override. If anything happened to her, they would have to take the house apart, brick by brick to get to the bag. After that, they would have to release the snake and recover the chip.

Once the bag was safely stowed, she headed for the shower. Chris was right about one thing. They were definitely going to have to get up early.

By the time she showered, Chris had sandwiches ready. He had managed quite well in her kitchen. She was grateful. He left her to eat her share while he borrowed the shower.

When he returned to the living room, he helped himself to another sandwich. His hair was still wet, but his stubble was gone, and his injuries looked a lot better now that he was cleaned up.

"I thought you ate a sandwich before you showered," she said around a yawn.

"What's that got to do wi' anyfing?" He chewed happily.

She knew exactly how he felt. In another half-hour, she would probably be stuffing her face again if she didn't fall asleep first. "So, do you want to get any of this stuff over with now?"

Chris shook his head and looked around the room. "You've secured the instructions. I'd say that was the top priority. I can probably escape out a window or back door and let you get some rest." He looked down at his feet. His shoulders slumped. Then he peeked up hopefully.

"But how will you get back in tomorrow for our early meeting?" she asked.

He slapped his hand against his forehead, gently. "Oh no. I'd forgotten about that!"

"Right." Her eyes narrowed. "You can sleep on the couch."

He gazed at her, his green eyes all innocence. "Of course."

"You wouldn't have been thinking of anything else."

"Why no!" He placed his hand over his heart.

She stood up. "I'll get you a blanket."

As she walked to the hall closet, she thought she heard him muttering that at least she wasn't making him use the travel blanket.

She returned with a falsely serene smile. "Of course, if you'd prefer, there's always the magnetic--"

He grabbed the blanket before she could finish. "Nonsense. Not when you've brought these."

Shoeless, he curled up on the couch and grimaced the tiniest bit.

She almost felt sorry for him. Almost. Not enough to ask him to share her bed, but--almost. He was, after all, still a potential enemy.

As she found her own bed, her musing turned cynical. Every man, woman and child would forever be a potential enemy because to admit her secret to anyone was to share her secret with the world. Once one person knew, there was no turning back. Once the code of silence was broken, she would never be the thief she had once been. She would never know that kind of freedom again if she talked. Her hobby would have to be given up or she would risk the mocking looks of those around her who would suddenly, one by one, know.

The first person would tell one person. Just to ease the pressure a bit. But it was such a fascinating fact to the listener, that the listener couldn't resist. To be privileged was to have power; the power to amuse, to titillate an audience, to be "accepted."

She groaned quietly. She would have to hold the secret inside in order to keep her freedom and the right to act again, should she need.

Her last thought, almost a fragment of a dream, was that if she never shared her secret, she would also never share the laughter of its success.

Chapter 21

When the dim light of dawn broke, Alexia was not ready. Of course, she was distracted from that thought when she realized that she was staring at another face only a few scant inches from her own. The face was not staring back.

Chris lay on his side, next to her, his eyes closed peacefully. For an uninvited guest, he was breathing far too calmly.

She frowned mightily. Unsure of his sleeping habits, she hardly wanted to risk getting up and waking him too slowly. Might damage him in some way. The glass of water on her bedside table was very tempting, but she didn't want to have to change her bedding later, and, if she spilled it all over him, he probably wasn't going to volunteer.

So, the only alternative was to smother him.

Feeling very sorry for herself for having to perform her duty as a distraught maiden, she couldn't quite keep a grin from forming as she placed a pillow over his head. Gently, of course. One should dream of suffocating before one woke to find it an actuality.

Unfortunately for Alexia, she had forgotten that all of Chris' talents were not duly recorded in his records at Haven.

Her only warning was a single grunt before she found herself thrown halfway across the room and neatly pinned. Chris, not bothering to find out why he was being smothered, was not very careful about tackling her. She therefore landed on her back on the cold floor.

"What the hell are you trying to do to me, kill me? It wasn't close enough when someone took a shot at me?"

Alexia struggled to get her own breath back, which was hard to do considering that his arm was across her throat, and his entire body weight was resting on her lungs. "Reminds me," she squeaked. "You should have that arm looked at. And your head." Although from her current view, she could see the scab on his head was holding.

Noticing her obvious struggle to breathe, he removed his arm. He gazed at her suspiciously. "Since you're so concerned about my health, why kill me in the night?"

"It isn't night anymore." Enough light came in through the window to announce that morning was well on its way.

He grunted. "And that's your idea of a romantic awakening? Why couldn't I have a normal girlfriend, you know, the kind that gives kisses in the morning and rubs up against you naked?"

She stared at him nonplussed. "I'm not your girlfriend!"

"That isn't the point." Rolling slightly to one side, he allowed her to suck in a huge breath of air. "Here. Let me show you the polite way to say good morning."

He leaned down quickly and pressed firm lips on hers. "Morning." Then he looked around the floor as if searching for something. "If we were in bed where we should be, we could now roll over and lie about leisurely." He looked back at her speculatively. "Or whatever."

"Or whatever?"

He grinned. "You know."

"Settle for a shower, why don't you?" She groaned her way to her feet. "I ride for days and days and now this. My backside will never be the same."

Halfway to the shower, she laughed. He had won that round. The tables had so effectively been turned, she had forgotten that he wasn't even supposed to be sleeping in her bed.

By the time Chris had also showered, they were running out of time. It was close to seven o'clock. Darren wasn't likely to wait until noon.

"So." Chris folded his hands on the kitchen table. When she didn't reply, he tapped his fingers impatiently. "I take it you aren't going to confess."

"To what? You believe Darren's accusation that it's been me all along?"

He shook his head. "Of course not."

Before relief could set in, he continued. "I knew it was you before Darren even knew your name. That's why you were invited along. I figured if anyone could find the instructions, it was you. I also thought that if you couldn't find the instructions, they would be safe enough until we figured out who was being paid to steal them."

She frowned. "That doesn't make sense. If you thought I was guilty, why not arrest me?"

Chris waved one of his hands. "You misunderstand. I didn't think you were guilty. At least not of trying to steal the instructions for gain.

You are, however, guilty of the thefts that have taken place over the last year or so." His words were casual, but his eyes were not. If they had been lasers, she would have been cut in half.

"I chose to believe your paper on the matter. I assumed you were taking the crystals to prove that they were not well-protected," he said.

"Interesting theory," she dead-panned.

He watched her. She didn't squirm; she just looked thoughtful. Finally she said, "I still think it might be one of Darren's men, trying to show him up."

His jaw clenched. "You aren't going to tell me, are you?"

"This line of questioning is hardly getting us closer to the answer," she replied.

"What's it like, living in that world you've created for yourself? Ever wonder what it's like to have a real life? One where you have friends? Maybe someone to talk to for longer than a coffee break?"

She started to answer, but couldn't. His line of questioning was too close to her thoughts from the night before. Of course, having thought of it herself, she should be more prepared than she felt.

"That's how I spotted you, you know." His hand reached over and almost touched her face. He held his fingers in front of her as if there were an invisible barrier between them, her on the inside looking out, him trying to reach her, unable to get in.

"I ran profiles through computers for months. It took me all that time to figure out that the person stealing the crystals was not the person preparing to steal them for profit."

"What does that have to do with me?" Her voice was not as steady as she would have liked, but under the circumstances, she felt a quiver or two was justified.

He smiled. "I fell in love with you before I even met you. Here was a woman clever enough to fool every law official, including Darren Westfield, mastermind at catching criminals. But here too," he finally touched her cheek then, "was a woman very alone. Only someone that alone could have pulled the stunts you did."

She knew she was close to breaking, but still she refused to back down. "Why?"

"It was obvious you had to be working alone. Otherwise the thefts wouldn't have worked. It had to be one person performing the tricks. No way could a group stay cohesive enough and of one mind to pull off those thefts over and over."

She stared. He was a mind-reader. That was the only possible explanation. How else could he speak aloud the very thoughts she had held as her talisman all these years?

"Alexia," he addressed the trauma he saw in her face, "there are other people like you all around you. Think about it. Every scientist here has been picked for his special abilities."

She was barely calm enough to ask, "What does that have to do with working alone?"

"All of the scientists are people who work intensely within themselves. Put them together and they've thrived on one another's ideas and made friends. Except for you. Your skills are in understanding the human mind, yet you've remained aloof. You held yourself away because you still felt a need to do so. That need was because of the thefts. Of course, I only recognized it because I'm just like you."

Alexia swallowed hard and squeaked, "You?"

He nodded. "I infiltrate organizations as efficiently as you do a safe or a locked room. I work alone, and I don't reveal methods. That's why it works."

She was mesmerized by his intensity and couldn't pull her eyes away from his. "Yet, if you tell one person, such as me, it isn't a secret anymore. So why are you telling me now?"

"Because, it's the only way this one is going to work! We're trying for the same goals, dammit!"

"Who are you?" She knew that wasn't the issue, but suddenly, she had to know.

He grinned. "I'm Appleton's son. He's tried to get me to Haven for years. I never had a reason to come here."

"The intrigue of the case brought you." For some insane reason, she wished it had been her presence that attracted him to Haven, but that was impossible, because he hadn't even known she existed. It was the crystals and the instructions that brought everyone to Haven. In his case, it was the danger to them that gave him a reason to come.

She looked down at his other hand, resting on top of hers on the table. Was it a seductive ploy to get a confession?

Again, he must have read her mind. "I'm not after you, at least not," he glanced at the part of her body he could see, "not to arrest you."

She rolled her eyes. "Great. That brings me solid peace of mind."

"You never were my immediate target, although I couldn't believe it when my computer found you. It wasn't until I saw you standing in the room where the crystals had been with your reflective suit that I actually believed you existed." He grinned at her look of horror. "I didn't think it was possible for anyone to cover their tracks like you do. You show absolutely no guilt complex. The only type of criminal that ever has such a clear conscious is a killer who has no morals."

It came out in the tone of a compliment, but she could hardly take it that way. "Thanks. Being compared to a murderer with no morals is very flattering."

His boyish grin faded. "I didn't mean it like that! I meant that I kept expecting you to look over your shoulder or bare your soul, or break down. You never batted an eye."

"What would be the point? I'm not guilty of anything, so why should I appear guilty?" She wasn't arguing her lack of thievery, she was arguing the philosophical point, and he knew it.

"Exactly. That was the beauty of it. You were a criminal with no record and no real crimes. You've gotten so used to feeling that way, you have no guilt complex. And I suppose, you really shouldn't have one. You haven't done anything wrong."

She smiled again, and the tenseness went out of her body. "No, I haven't." He wasn't trying to wring a confession from her at all. They had sat and discussed the entire situation, and he had never once forced her to admit to her follies. He had the self-confidence of knowing he was right. He didn't require her support. Her secret felt strangely safe. He knew, but she had never confessed.

The thought made her bubbly. She probably would have laughed, but a solid sounding knock interrupted her joy.

"Damn." They both said it simultaneously.

"We need more time," Chris said. "We need to figure out who is really after the crystals. There's a money trail here somewhere."

"Not to mention we need to find out who sent the dogs."

"He can't hold you." Chris squeezed her hand. "He can question you, however. Can you hold up?"

"Of course." She smiled. "I've done nothing wrong." There was freedom in the statement. She had never quite thought of it the way Chris phrased it.

When she answered the door, Darren stood outside, flanked by Ollern and two other burly men. They were army men, men of military, men who would obey orders.

"You'll need to come with me, Alexia," Darren said.

"Let me get my sweater."

He nodded and followed her in. From his bright-eyed look, she surmised that he had not personally kept guard last night.

He frowned when he saw Chris. "I heard you didn't leave."

Chris smiled. "My job is to keep the instructions protected."

With that reminder, Darren looked around the empty room. "Where are they?"

"Sorry," Chris replied. "Privileged knowledge. I'm still officially in charge."

The look of hostility that comment earned could have roasted a pigeon. "Now that I've caught the person responsible, I'll see that changed." Darren jerked his head her way. "Cuff her."

Alexia shot Chris a look of disgust. If he hadn't angered Darren, she might have gotten away with keeping him in his fatherly role. Now that he felt his authority was threatened, he had to show some muscle.

"There's no need for cuffs," Alexia said.

Darren yanked her towards Ollern. Ollern cuffed her efficiently. He may as well have been cuffing a tree limb rather than handling a human being.

"I'll be back for the instructions," Darren promised Chris on his way out.

"Fine."

Since Chris didn't follow them out, Alexia wondered exactly what he intended to do. He had certainly made himself at home. She frowned. She didn't like leaving him alone with the instructions. No safe was foolproof. Of course, if Chris was really the culprit out to get the instructions for his own use, the whole task they had run was useless. He would have done better to let Darren shoot her in cold blood, grab the instructions and leave.

Unfortunately, as they walked towards the laboratory building, she couldn't help but think that Chris was one of the few individuals that was clever enough to actually make off with the instructions. If that had been his plan from the start, what better way to do it than become part of the team?

She shook her head. It couldn't be Chris. It just couldn't.

Chapter 22

Alexia assumed the questioning was going to be, if not easy, tolerable. She had not counted on the multiple personalities of her captor.

Darren started out with the persona of a shunned, but still caring, friend. He apologized for pointing a gun at her. He told her he understood what it must be like trying to prove herself over and over.

"I found the instructions by pure luck," she said for the tenth time. "Luck, Darren, that's all there was too it."

Predictably he lost his temper. "That was more than luck out there. You walked that place like you'd been there!"

"I've been out hiking in the desert for years, Darren. Hiking experience is what clued me into the fact that water should have traveled better in the stream bed." The lie detector attached to her wrist verified the truth in her statements. "If the river had been running or had been completely dry or had been in any other condition except the one I found, I never would have recovered the instructions!"

Darren didn't listen. In fact, she wasn't even sure he was recording her responses, other than to check the devices that, in his opinion, should have been indicating lies.

When they brought in tapes of the last theft, she sighed in relief. He showed her the camera shots of the blank room. "How did you get into the room without your picture showing? What did you do to the camera?"

"I did not fool with the camera." She had fooled with the picture, not the camera.

"Dammit!" He whirled away and then back again. "You're a smart woman. You tell me how you got in this room without the camera noticing!" He pointed to the tape. "Look at it. How did you get around this machine?"

Obligingly she looked. Then she sat up straight. The monitors attached to her wrist sent shooting pulses to the machines, and they beeped.

"Aha!" Darren crowed in triumph, pointing to the beeping monitors. Ollern actually moved a hand to his gun.

"Aha, what?" Her face flushed. He was an idiot. She went back to staring at the camera shot, not believing what she was seeing. "Is that a roach on the wall?"

"What?" He was shouting so close to her face, she could feel his hot breath on her chin. "Where?" He faced the picture himself.

"Can you get a close up?" She couldn't believe what she was seeing. Roaches lived in wet climates like Louisiana and Alabama. They weren't all that common in the desert, not only because of the lack of food, but because of the lack of a constant water supply.

What was a roach doing in a clean building where the instructions had been kept? There were plenty of other places that a roach could make a more comfortable living. The instructions weren't near food. She had never seen a roach in Haven.

"I asked you a question," Darren said.

"I don't like roaches." Not only had Darren been unable to figure out how she had gotten around the cameras, he wasn't even looking at the right section of film. Whoever had analyzed the pictures had totally missed the fact that for several minutes there was no real feed into the camera.

How could someone miss that? She had long since expected them to discover her little trick. Maybe they lacked ingenuity or imagination. Darren gave so many orders, maybe no one had an original thought.

Thankfully, her musings took her mind off of Darren, who continued to scream at her. He went over other tricks, well-known ones such as the fingerprint placements. He wanted to know her whereabouts, he wanted to know how much she weighed, how much she ate and how often.

Finally, weary beyond belief, when she had endured more that she thought possible, the door opened. Dr. Appleton, a very grim look on his face, entered.

"I asked not to be disturbed, sir," Darren said.

"You're getting nowhere, Westmore. Let her go. You've no more proof than when you walked in here. Until you do, it's over." Dr. Appleton helped Alexia up from her chair.

With the activity of the last few days, she didn't mind the extra the support.

"I'll walk her back," Dr. Appleton said.

Darren clamped his mouth shut. Ever the faithful soldier, he took his orders.

Alexia was surprised to find that it was dark outside. "What time is it? No wonder I'm hungry."

"We can stop and eat before I deliver you to your door." Being in charge of Haven had not given him the arrogance that she expected.

"That's okay. I keep plenty of provisions." She didn't even care if she ate at the moment. She was too tired.

He didn't insist, but he did walk her home. Chris was waiting for them in the doorway.

"Hey, I thought you must have escaped and run into the desert."

Dr. Appleton eyed his son with disfavor. "She hasn't eaten."

Chris nodded. "I made sandwiches."

"Good night, Dr. Zimmerman." For a moment longer he stared at his son as if he would say more, but, thinking better of it, he retreated.

Just before he shut the garden gate, Alexia's sluggish mind thought of a question. "Sir?"

"Yes?"

"Where did Chris grow up?"

"Mostly in Europe, I'm afraid. Didn't see much of the states until college."

"Where was college?"

"Supposed to be Harvard, but I think the majority of it was spent in Fort Lauderdale."

"Thanks." She ignored Chris' look of reproach and went in past him. He shut the door and folded his arms. Sandwiches awaited her on the coffee table.

"Still don't trust me?"

She could tell from his tone that he was hurt that she had asked his father questions. "Of course, I do. I let you stay here, didn't I?" She collapsed on the couch without bothering to pick up any food.

He sat down next to her and put a sandwich in her hand. "Eat. What's with the forty questions you asked dad?"

She took a bite and chewed before answering. "He does seem to be your father. Not a very approving one. I like that he doesn't look at you as if you're perfect."

"Yeah. And?"

"I'm going to go to bed. I'm not hungry."

He stared at the sandwich she handed back. "What's wrong?"

She stopped halfway to the bedroom. "Don't leave it on the table.

Might get roaches."

She looked back to catch the expression on his face. Gotcha. Fort Lauderdale had roaches. And if he had used a small camera in the past, why not make it nearly invisible by fitting it into expected surroundings, just as she had chosen to do with the scorpion? Roaches were everywhere, they were small enough to hide in crevices and they were usually ignored.

Except, some got seen. Or stepped on. And some roaches turned up in rare places. But that roach explained exactly how he had known it was she who stole the crystals and instructions.

Telling her he was just like her indeed. Acting as if he had figured out that she was guilty from studying her profile, acting smarter than everyone else.

She giggled, unable to help herself. The trouble was, by playing innocent and not coming completely clean, he was more like her than he had admitted. For some strange reason, she found great comfort in that thought.

Rolled up in her thoughts, she slept the sleep of the innocent and exhausted.

Chapter 23

Alexia should have suspected that she would wake with an arm draped casually across her body. Carefully, trying not to startle him, she turned over. It was a useless gesture. Chris was awake and busy looking innocent.

"I thought I'd make sure you didn't fall on the floor this time," he explained raising his arm and then letting it drop back protectively. "I don't know how you managed before I showed up."

She rubber her eyes. "It was quite horrible waking up on the floor every morning. It's a miracle I survived." Knowing he wouldn't attack her since he appeared in possession of his waking facilities, she decided to get up and shower. It was easier than facing the intimacy of a bed partner she wasn't sure how to deal with.

Chris was waiting in the kitchen when she reappeared with a towel around her head. He had not started breakfast.

She stared around the spotless kitchen before making her way to the fridge. "Let me guess, oh wonder gourmet. You only know how to make sandwiches."

He lowered his head humbly. "They are good sandwiches, though. I didn't want them to go to waste."

Since she had just nabbed one of the leftovers and was busy eating it she could hardly argue.

"So." He slapped his hands together and rubbed them enthusiastically. "What are the big plans for the day?"

She shrugged and opened a carton of milk. "I thought I'd cook. For the week."

"For what week?"

"The one coming up. I always do that."

"Oh."

"Besides, I'm too worn out to do much else."

He stretched and then slouched into a kitchen chair. "How did you find out about the roach?

"It was on the film Darren showed me yesterday of the entry room where the crystals were stored." She took another bite of her chicken sandwich. She took out a pen and paper and started scribbling. "Can you go to the store for me?"

The list was almost complete when she realized he hadn't answered. She looked up to find him staring in fascination at his fingernails. "Can you go to the grocery or not?"

"Uh, well...no." He didn't look up. "I'm not leaving the premises unless the instructions go with me."

She stared at his bent head. "Not safe with me, is that it?" He still didn't trust her. After all they'd been through and the things he'd said...she should have known better.

"It isn't you I'm worried about." He talked faster when she threatened to spill the remaining milk over his head. "Honest! We've got a satellite taking pictures of your house, we've got the rattlesnake still living in the bag, and no one knows about your safe except you."

"And? Don't tell me you didn't take this place apart, stone by stone trying to find it!'"

He looked a little sheepish.

"Oh, I'm sure you found it." It still made her angry. "Don't bother to play up to my feelings. You're here until the chip leaves, and you obviously don't dare trust me. You can't decide to trust someone anymore than you can decide to like someone. You either do or you don't."

His woeful expression disappeared. "I do trust you."

"How much?" She took out a spatula and a pan. "It's going to have to be enough to leave me here in your stead on occasion. Otherwise, who is going to find out who sent those dogs after us? Who is going to find the money? You can't sit here like some housekeeper, and I am not going to let you do the cooking if all you know how to cook is canned chicken sandwiches!"

He stared at her and blinked. She pushed the sliding turbaned towel out of her eyes. "Well?"

"Uh..."

"You can use my computer to do some of your tracking. But how are you going to find out anything else cooped up in here?"

"Dad could provide information."

"Or you could go find yourself somewhere else to work. Either trust me or don't, Chris. You were the one telling me that I had to learn to trust sooner or later, all the while keeping your little vermin camera a secret." The towel fell off her head, but she ignored it. "And no, your dad cannot move in. I don't want him here. You can take the instructions and go protect them. Go, goodbye, good riddance."

She picked up her towel and flung it over her shoulder. What did she need with the responsibility anyway?

He watched her warily while she banged pans around. Finally, he sighed in resignation. "You're right. One of us has to stay here, and it can't always be me."

"I can't stay here twenty-four hours a day either," she said as she slapped frozen hamburger in a skillet. "There are some things only I can check."

He shook his head. "I can get into any record--"

She waved her hand impatiently. "I wasn't talking about records, I was talking about people. You aren't completely accepted here. Besides, everyone knows that you're Appleton's son and on the security force. It isn't as though you're going to be able to sneak around infiltrating and gathering information."

A muscle ticked in his cheek. "I hate working on the side of the law."

She took a much-needed deep breath. "I'm not exactly used to it either. Maybe there's a better place for the instructions than my safe? Maybe then you wouldn't have to worry about trusting me." She busied herself with her cooking again so that she didn't have time to think too hard about how trust was a two-way street. She tossed precut veggies into a pot.

"You call what you're doing cooking?" he asked.

"What would you call it?" She took a bite out of a carrot. "It's a lot better than the trail mix I've been eating."

"Most of which you brought."

"I'd been planning on using a campfire at the very least." She stirred more ingredients in a bowl, getting flour on the front of her t-shirt. She set the bowl under a mixer and retrieved an oblong cooking pan from the cupboard. "But we were chased by dogs and couldn't even do that."

"I'm the one that ended up getting shot!"

The trusting part was bothering him at least as much as it was her. Neither leopard was willing to change its spots. She finished pouring the mixture into the pan and punched instructions on the oven. "Yes, I call it cooking. I bet even you could learn."

"Well, if I hadn't spent most of my life tracking down criminals like--" he stopped abruptly.

She froze in place, her hand over the start button. "Like me," she finished, her heart missing a beat. The whispers, the ones she knew would find her, had begun.

"That wasn't what I was going to say. You know it isn't." When she would have walked past him, he reached out and snagged her hand. "You're a psychiatrist, use your head. I didn't mean that, I was just... whining." When she didn't respond he added, "I don't want to trust you because...because."

She pulled away and was halfway down the hall to the bedroom before she stopped. She had to know. "Because why?"

"Because I care, you stupid female! I'm doing my damnedest not to let it affect my judgment, and it isn't working."

For some reason, a ridiculous little smile spread across her face. "Really?"

There was a grudgingly long pause before he said, "Really."

Her eyes narrowed with another thought, but she didn't turn around. "You mean like you're part of security, and you don't want to see me hurt?"

"That too."

Her grin got wider. Too? He liked her! Even though she was a thief, he liked her anyway! "Oh. Well, as a psychiatrist, I'd advise you to not count on your own facilities at all then. Caring can do strange things to people, you know." She peeked around behind her, but his eyes were closed, and he looked like he was trying to pull his hair out by its roots. He was positively adorable.

"No," she said in her best doctor voice, "can't count on your own judgment at all." She retreated to the bedroom to comb out her hair.

The smile didn't leave her face when she heard the back door slam.

She skipped back into the kitchen, humming. He had taken the shopping list with him. Good. She needed her supplies replenished, and if Chris was staying all week, she was definitely going to need more food.

Chapter 24

Alexia cursed. She had thought returning to work was going to be easy, but it appeared that Sally, the ward clerk, was in one of her joking moods. "What do you mean, only George's doctor is allowed to see him?"

"Sorry, Dr. Zimmerman. Dr. Reven ordered it. She said that George tends towards extreme aggressive behavior."

Alexia curbed the urge to become violent herself. "George? He wasn't even aggressive when we brought him in!"

The brunette waggled her pencil. "I honestly don't know. Dr. Reven put him in room twelve down the hall and gave us a key. We aren't to use it unless we suspect a medical emergency."

"Dr. Reven? Ann? I thought Dr. Brandon was looking after George."

"Dr. Reven took over after Dr. Brandon had his accident. You know. He fell off his bike."

Curse Haven and its exercise program. Alexia apparently had some catching up to do. "When did this happen?"

Sally teased, "You only lasted one day. Then Dr. Brandon made it about a week."

Alexia sighed impatiently. "I leave for a few days and the world goes to hell."

Sally agreed. "The nurse isn't even administering his medication. When it comes up from pharmacy with the other medications, we keep it locked up until Dr. Reven comes in. Then there's a lot of yelling and coaxing while Dr. Reven sings to George about how it's "one little blue pill for you and let us pray and then I'll go away." Sally sang to the tune of "rain, rain go away," and patted the sides of her head, pretending to check non-existence water-wing curls. "The way it's been going, she better change him to some sort of shots so she can give the medication from a distance. A looong distance."

"I still want to see him," Alexia said.

Sally reached into the desk drawer for the key to the medicine cabinet. "Doc Brandon hasn't been too thrilled with life either. That man walked funny as it is, and you should see him now." As she got up to go to the cabinet, she did a little duck walk with a limp.

"You're awful," Alexia chided, trying not to smile.

Sally, not chastised in the least, extracted a square badge key from inside the cabinet. "You sure about this? Doc Reven is the only one that has been in there for days. It doesn't sound that great when she goes. George makes it quite clear that doesn't like taking his little blue pill, and he doesn't like visitors."

Alexia took the key. "I can't believe that Ann locked up one of her patients. Whatever happened to her forgiving nature?" Without waiting for an answer, Alexia marched down the white hallway. Haven didn't have a special mental ward, and it certainly didn't require an area for that sole purpose. In order for him to be enclosed in a locked room, Ann had taken over one of the smaller laboratories usually reserved for bacteria isolation. Maybe the hospital built a church chamber in room twelve, and Ann couldn't resist locking a patient inside.

Although she was in a hurry, Alexia wasn't stupid. Ann must have had a good reason to lock George up. She used the video display to make initial contact. "George, it's Dr. Zimmerman. You may remember me. I'm here to visit."

She waited patiently for him to turn on his monitor and answer. When he finally responded, he did not turn on the picture.

"It isn't time for my appointment."

The single statement was made without any voice inflection. It was as unemotional as Alexia's kitchen mixer.

"No, but it is visiting hours." She kept her voice light, happy.

"I haven't had any visitors."

"I just got back from a trip or I would have come sooner. We were taking the instructions off-site to try and protect them. They are back now. The plan didn't work, but we were able to keep them safe." She knew the crystals represented something to George. He had once devoted his sanity to their safekeeping.

"Dr. Reven says the crystals don't matter. Only salvation matters."

Alexia moved her head away from the video screen and rolled her eyes. "Okay. But the crystals are powering your comfortable little room and this conversation as well. Can I come in?"

There was a weighty silence, one that she didn't think he would break. She waited a moment or two and then inserted the key on her side and punched in her identification number.

George was backed away from the door. He waited in a defensive, fighting position, swaying unsteadily on his feet. A small amount of spittle dripped from one side of his mouth.

"There's no threat here, George. I'm not here to hurt you or threaten Haven in any way."

He did not relax. His eyes were unfocused.

Alexia left the door very open. "How do you feel?"

"Headache."

"Is there something you would like? Maybe something from your home?"

He shook his head and looked confused. "I don't know."

"Do you miss your dogs?"

At the mention of his dogs, his body began to shake and his eyes search frantically, either for them, a weapon or for escape.

"Did you train the dogs yourself?"

He nodded vaguely. "Protect the crystals. Train them to protect the crystals." The shaking got worse. "Can't see them." His voice rose in pitch, but he still didn't move. "Dogs!" The shrillness of the last word made the hair on the back of Alexia's neck rise.

She had seen more than one certifiably insane person during her training years. George was past even a classical example.

"Crystals...Dogs!" Each word was punctuated with a deep breath. "Feed them. Four-fifty-seven. Seven minutes."

He held up seven fingers. With that movement, he seemed to realize that he had the ability to move other parts of his body. Before he could slide his first step forward, Alexia hit the floor and rolled. She got her foot behind the door and slammed it shut before his brain had time to send the command to his other leg. She sucked in a large breath of air.

A two-yard sprint shouldn't leave a person winded. But then, how often did one have to do two yards with George behind them?

The intercom emitted a howl that George's dogs, had they heard, would have been proud to call their own. She shivered. She reached up and turned the sound off.

After settling down, she stood and turned the video picture off. She only wished that she could tell George not to worry about his dogs. Pressing the intercom to speak, she yelled, "George!" She could only hope that he could hear her over his own yowling. "George, who is taking care of the dogs?"

Sudden silence.

"Someone must be taking care of them for you. Haven is a good place. Did Dr. Ann promise to watch the dogs?"

"Me!" he shouted back. "Meee!"

"George, no one could take care of the dogs like you could--"

"Me, me, ME!"

Alexia turned off the sound. George was no help. It didn't matter to him who was watching the dogs. It wasn't him and in all probability, it hadn't been him a week ago.

She made her way slowly back to the desk. Sally was still there. She shook her head in a, "I told you so" way. "Any other keys, doctor? He needs another blue pill, maybe?"

"Why did Dr. Brandon drop him?" Dr. Brandon wasn't one to give up a challenge.

Sally reached for the record. "I wasn't kidding about the limp. He's kind of a klutz, and I'm thinking with good old George being...a little resistant to therapy, Doc Brandon wasn't too keen on trying to run away from him if it became necessary."

"Here, let me look at something." Obligingly, Sally moved out of the way, and Alexia entered a few commands on the desk console. The screen answered. Dr. Brandon had left the case due to a broken ankle and head concussion that had occurred the day after Alexia left. Dr. Brandon had been working on easing George off the calming drugs.

There were no helpful clues there. "Thanks, Sally. Tell Ann I was by in case she doesn't look at the logs."

"Sure, no problem."

Rather than make any calls from the hospital, Alexia walked back home. Of course, she had forgotten that Chris was using her equipment. From the scattered papers and hand-helds, it was obvious he intended to hog her entire desk.

He paid no attention to her at all, even when she read from his screen, "First Bank of Haven." He was obviously hot on the trail of someone's bank account. If he was hoping to find bizarre activity, he was looking in the right place. No one in Haven was normal.

She paused on her way back out the door. "Chris?"

"Hah?" He didn't look up.

"Never mind." Alexia wasn't sure what to ask him anyway.

The entire walk to her office she worried about George. Sure, he had been in trouble, but what had caused him to retreat into such a corner?

Once at the complex, she checked, but unfortunately, Dr.

Brandon's office door was closed. On the other hand, both Ann and Phillip's doors were open. She could just go in and ask Ann about George being locked up. Of course, if she questioned Ann about George, Ann might take it personally and assume Alexia was criticizing the treatment plan. Alexia would then have to listen to an hour-long lecture.

She went into her office and checked her email.

By the third message, she wished she hadn't come to the complex at all. Phillip had sent his opinion about the failure to protect the instruction chip by taking it off-site. His lengthy commentary detailed what he determined were her failures--as a psychiatrist and as part of the desert team. He spitefully requested that she be removed from any team working with the safety of the crystals until "a fuller evaluation can be made of her tendency to follow egotistical leanings at the expense of the crystal's safety."

Great. She had Darren convinced she was a master thief. At least one of her colleagues was attacking her competence as a doctor. It was a good thing she hadn't questioned Ann about George's treatment. The last thing she needed was alienate anyone else. At this rate, she would be lucky if Haven didn't throw her out.

Thinking of the world outside reminded her that she still had not dealt with another small, nagging problem. Keith.

The rest of her paperwork could wait. It was close to one o'clock and Sam might be in. She headed downstairs to his lab, hoping that she could explain to Sam why his employee had disappeared.

When she walked into the lab, it appeared that her luck had changed. Keith was in the lab with Sam, working away. "Hi."

Neither looked up. Both had their hands inside something, a something that was mercifully covered with a sheet.

"Uh, I thought you were leaving?" she directed her question at Keith, who at the moment, appeared almost as content as Sam.

He finally looked up and realized Alexia was addressing him. "Oh, hi! I've got an idea for your chip. Monkshood!"

"Monkshood?"

"Yeah." He pulled his hands out of whatever he was delving in. They were covered with a suspiciously dark pink substance.

"Ugghh."

Keith ignored her horror. "Look at this guy." He flipped back part of the sheet.

She did not glance that way, instinctive reaction or not. She studied the floor with a passion she usually reserved for her best chocolates.

"That's okay, Keith really."

"No, look, it's perfect for you! It grows in New Mexico and we have a jar of the stuff right here. You smear it on whatever you're trying to protect and wham! The guy who steals it gets it on his skin and then next thing he knows, he's in here."

Alexia managed to look up at this point. His hands were cleaner. Keith had stripped the bloody gloves off. He was holding his prize, a plain white jar, high in the air.

"Monkshood?" she guessed.

"Monkshood!"

"It has a toxicity of six," Sam said, still buried in the corpse. "Come over here and hold this tissue back."

Keith obeyed, re-donning gloves, but didn't give up on his mission. "You can get rid of the snake. It's only got a toxicity of four. This other stuff is way stronger."

"Works better if the victim eats the stuff," Sam said. "This guy rubbed it over most of his body. Herbal treatments. Caused paralysis of his muscles." Sam stripped off his gloves. "Clear-cut." He frowned. "Who are you wanting to kill? This boy's been asking more death questions than a police investigator."

Alexia felt like she had fallen down a rabbit hole. "No one." She backed away from the flailing gloves.

"What's this about a rattlesnake?" Sam continued to stalk her, undeterred by her lack of enthusiasm.

"Pet," she whispered, glaring at Keith. Had he gone bonkers? She had told him these things were supposed to be a secret!

Keith said, "Aw, don't worry about Sam. He's okay. If he wanted the crystals, he coulda poisoned the whole joint. Put something lethal in the air ducts."

She had taken an innocent child and created a monster. "I thought you liked guns."

"Well sure. But it's all the same. It's the risk. This other stuff is more subtle."

"A pet?" Sam interrupted with a roar, setting Alexia back another few steps. "My God, woman! Snakes aren't meant to be pets! Do you know how many times people get killed by such pets?"

Alexia had never noticed that when Sam frowned, he did not have two eyebrows. The single gray line dipped dangerously in the middle of his forehead as he advanced upon her.

"People get eaten whole in the jungles by pythons the size of trees!"

"I'll get rid of it right away!" It was quite obvious that Keith had no intention of leaving Haven and was doing fine. He was mentally unstable, but fine.

Sam's long arm reached out to snag her. "Snakes?" He shook his head. "I don't believe it. You get rid of it."

Alexia was pretty certain she should be angry with Keith for causing Sam to lose faith in her, but she wasn't going to be able to make that point right now. Keith was once again inspecting the corpse with complete concentration.

Defeated, she beat a hasty retreat. Her brain knew that Sam was trying to save lives, but her stomach was having none of it. His examinations helped determine the diseases and ailments that claimed victims, but by God, did he have to find it so fascinating?

And she had brought Keith into it. Apparently it was a good fit. A completely unintentional match made in heaven.

Shaking her head, she made her way back to her small, once peaceful house.

Chris was standing in the doorway. "I've got to go on an errand. Can you stay for a while?"

It was politely phrased, but an order nevertheless. Since Alexia needed a nap in the worst way, she was hardly going to argue.

"Absolutely."

He was out the door before she finished the word. She barely made it to her bed before collapsing.

Her dreams were not good. Within an hour she was sweating, breathing rapidly and sitting up in bed. In her dream, snakes crawled out of disemboweled bodies. She bolted for the bathroom and splashed water on her face.

Keith was wrong. A real snake was a better deterrent than invisible cream. The snake was staying. In fact, she had better put some poor hapless mouse inside the safe to feed the damn thing.

Now then, where was she going to find a live rat?

Well, were else but the institute? What kind of science community could function without little white rats?

Chris had not returned, but Alexia hardly thought that either of them were true protection for the chip anyway. Their best ploy was to act normal. Only she, Chris, Darren and Keith knew the instructions were in her home. Darren or Chris had obviously told Dr. Appleton, and if they had let the cat out of the bag to anyone else, well, that was their problem.

She wasn't going to make it obvious for anyone watching that she and Chris were guarding the house.

Even with all her logic, she hurried. Luckily, Grace was able to help her so it didn't take long to retrieve the subject.

Alexia felt very sorry for the little creature as she shut it in the safe. She unzipped the saddlebag enough for the rattlesnake to worm its way out, and then quickly slammed the door shut. Sam was right. Damn thing would definitely bite the hand that fed it.

Everything was back in place.

By the time she finished dinner, a weary Chris returned. He was not talkative. From that, she deduced that he had not had a very productive day. "You know," she said, "there really is no need for you to stay here."

"Don't start."

She took one look at his hard face and left it alone. If he had felt comfortable elsewhere, he probably would be there. If he thought his presence was somehow keeping the instructions safe, more power to him.

"I got a rat today after you left. Fed the snake."

"You left the place open?"

"I locked up like I normally do and went about my business."

"You have that much faith in your safe? It only took me a day to find it." His voice rose with each word.

"Yes, but you didn't kill the snake, so you must not have taken the instructions. Since the snake was still there when I put the rat in, I figured that no one else took the chip either." She picked up his dirty dishes and stacked them in the cleaner. "You know what they say about hiding something out in the open?"

He didn't answer, but his mouth worked in an attempt to hold back an explosion.

"By acting like we've nothing to protect, we might fool them a little longer."

His mouth finally formed a word. "Them?"

She shrugged. "Whoever is after the instructions."

He stood up, his chair rolling back into the wall. "It may fool them for a while, but for how long?"

"Chris, there probably isn't a trap we can build that someone won't eventually be able to break into. It's been a constant race of mankind since the beginning of time." She picked up a knife. "Knives, then guns." She put the knife down since he was eying her nervously. "It's the same with safes. We built banks with thick walls. The walls get thicker and thicker, but the enemy keeps finding holes."

"And that doesn't concern you?"

"Why should it? It is our nature to be competitive, to beat the other guy, to have what he doesn't have."

"Is that why you became, uh, you broke into things?"

Her chin lifted. "I've never stolen a thing in my life."

They stared at each other for a long moment. Alexia felt her heart beat a little harder. Trust. She took the plunge. "I broke into buildings because I thirsted for knowledge. Then, it became a challenge. Before I knew it, I worked around the system instead of with it."

His hand touched her shoulder. "And now?"

"And now, it's time to work with the system. To try and make it work against the other guy."

"What if we fail?"

"We can't afford to, can we? We can't keep building better hiding places, better safes. We have to stop them!"

He suddenly grinned. "That's my job."

When things got challenging, Chris was at his best. Just when things didn't appear to be working, like when they returned from the desert, Chris got more determined. And determination made him a happy man. Alexia sighed. "Do you have to enjoy it so darn much?"

He laughed. "Do you have to enjoy breaking and entering?"

She couldn't deny it. There was a thrill to it. As she got older, she had to be good at something. People that never found a talent usually ended up seeing professionals like Alexia. They were searching for a way to slow the clock of time, the thief that was stealing their potential. Some people even found a talent, but it wasn't enough. Those were the dangerous ones.

Chris was staring at her and Alexia blushed, realizing she had been speaking aloud.

"I never thought of it like that. What am I? What is my talent?"

"You're not smart enough for a talent," she muttered.

"What?" He laughed. "What the hell does that mean?"

"It means you're the third type. You're the type that's too busy living life to worry about talent. You'll wake up old one day, and it won't matter. You'll be too busy grinning about some personal joke or small deed you managed to pull off."

He chuckled again, loud and hard. "I like that. I like it a lot."

She didn't resist when his teasing eyes got closer, and his lips lowered to touch her own. She didn't even protest when he deepened the kiss. Her feelings were bordering on a complete haze when he murmured softly in her ear, "Now this, this is living."

She pulled away and smacked his arm playfully. "We have a job to do." Her voice was more breathless than she intended.

He shrugged and smiled innocently before reaching for her again. "Too busy living to worry much about it."

She would have protested, but he was rather convincing.

Haven was all about experiments. It couldn't hurt to research his way of doing things for a little while.

Chapter 25

The next morning, Alexia fretted. She worried about the instructions, she worried about George, and she worried about the information Chris was pounding out of the computer. Sooner or later, they had to figure out who was after the instructions, or that someone was going to steal them.

Since Chris was using her desk console, she used her wrist computer to check messages. As expected, the debriefing was scheduled for tomorrow. She had approximately a day and a half to come up with a plan. Throwing up her hands, she declared, "We'll have to tell everyone that the instructions weren't found. That will give us time to come up with a new place for them."

Chris threw cold water on that idea in a hurry. "Darren can't wait to retrieve his post. He isn't going to go for that. The only reason Darren is leaving you alone now is because dad ordered it."

"But he has no proof--"

"Darren's silence doesn't mean he isn't going to drag all kinds of accusations up during the meeting." Chris scooted his chair closer to the desk console. "At the very least, Darren is going to demand his post back based on the fact that taking the instructions off-site failed utterly."

Alexia knew Chris was right. Darren wouldn't sit by and wait for the crime to be solved. Of course, knowing Darren, he probably thought the crime was solved. Thankfully, the council wouldn't judge on his opinion alone, or Alexia would have been drawn and quartered already.

She sighed. Not only did they need to find the thief, she needed to find a way to convince everyone that she couldn't be the thief. Now there was a challenge. "I'm going to the office."

Chris, busy at her computer, grunted a non-answer.

She made her way across the complex to the main building. Once there, she finished the main body of her report. Before she could decide what to do next, Ann's wheelchair rolled into her doorway.

"Heard you made it back safely," Ann greeted her from the

doorway. "Was glad to hear it. I prayed every day. Not a good place for a young lady."

"No, it really wasn't. How are things here?"

Ann's shoulders moved as she filled her lungs with air. "It's been rough. I had to take on George Miller. Poor soul."

Alexia was happy that the opportunity to discuss George's condition had come up. "How is he doing? I stopped in to see him, but it didn't look good."

"This one is out of my hands, it truly is." She gave a sad shake of her water-winged head. "It's like my old legs here. Have to learn to function with whatever you have."

"I don't think George is going to learn to function with what he had when I saw him last." The man hadn't been short just a few cards; he appeared to be missing most of the deck.

"No, no, of course not. I mean that all that's left is prayer."

"You aren't going to continue drug therapy?"

Ann bobbed her water-wing curls in the affirmative. "Of course, I am, dear. But really, what chance does he have?"

"What about his dogs? Maybe you could use them in therapy. You know how pets often sooth their owners when a trauma has occurred." Alexia felt that confessing now was in her favor. "When I stopped by to try and speak with him, I mentioned the dogs."

"Oh dear. He probably wasn't ready for that."

"No, he wasn't. But then I'm not sure he was ready for a discussion of any kind."

"I have no idea what happened to his dogs," Ann said. "He mentioned them once. They may have escaped and gone off to fend for themselves. I was hardly able to go running around searching for them."

"Of course not." Ann rarely mentioned her disability, but it was obvious she had limits. Alexia wouldn't expect her to go sprinting around after animals, especially these particular ones. "Someone must know what happened to the dogs. Even if they escaped, didn't anyone report a disturbance?"

"What kind of disturbance?"

"If they were hungry and trying to get out, someone must have heard them. If they escaped, surely someone saw them."

Ann shrugged. "Once he mentioned the dogs, I had someone check his house. There weren't any dogs in his house or in the yard. I can't imagine where they would have gone, but I suppose they will be fine."

"Was there someone that knew George that might have been taking care of them? Maybe he mentioned someone?"

"Only Darren. George was one of his men you know. Darren seemed to be his only friend."

Before Alexia could ask more questions, her console beeped, indicating a call.

Ann waved a hand. "You go ahead and get that. I'm looking forward to your report, dear, and hearing about the instructions." She rolled herself backwards. "I really am glad they are back here. It's where they belong."

The console beeped again. "They're back here?" Alexia called after Ann, her longtime practice in innocence standing true.

Ann must not have heard because she didn't answer. Or she already knew the answer and didn't deem it worth arguing about.

Alexia hit the receive button. "Hello?"

"Hi, Brandon here." His freckled face and bright read hair appeared on the monitor.

"Hey friend, how many races you running these days?"

"All this technology and it still takes six weeks for a bone to mend." Wild red strands of hair infused the monitor as he shook his head, forlornly.

"Sorry to hear about your leg. Poor George must think he can't keep a doctor around."

Brandon nodded. "Checked on him a few days ago myself, but he's gotten worse, instead of better. He was suffering from paranoia. I expected him to recover when he realized that the crystals were safe. Planned on the usual anti-stress, change career, find something he could handle."

"I saw from his chart, he's being treated with a low dose of Haloperidol now, right?" While he nodded agreement, she called up the medical records. "Haldol," she read the brand name which contained the active medication haloperidol. Nothing appeared unusual except the fact that he hadn't shown any sign of improvement. They still knew so little about the human mind.

"How was the trip?" Brandon asked.

"Fine. I'm still tired. I had hoped that George would be better. It would be nice if we could talk to him about some things." She told Brandon about the dogs and asked if he had any idea when and how they might have gotten out.

"That's terrible." Brandon was horrified. "He mentioned the dogs during treatment when we went over his various duties. I was working towards trying to separate his person from his job. He was in charge of feeding them in the evenings right at the end of his shift. There were several others on the security team that looked after them too. I wonder how they got out?"

"You mean someone on George's team was helping take care of the dogs? Do you know who?"

Dr. Brandon shook his head. "From what I gathered, the dogs belonged to Haven security. They are guard dogs being trained for use around the complex. Part of his duty was to feed them right as his shift ended."

Alexia's mouth dropped open. "They weren't his personal dogs?"

"No, no. Do you think they were neglected after he was hospitalized? Surely someone looked after them."

She blinked, but couldn't answer. Darren had to have known when they were attacked exactly where the dogs had come from. He had never uttered a single word. Her face turned as red as Dr. Brandon's hair. "Well, someone took care of them enough to send them on our trail." When next she saw Darren she would take a large chunk out of his hide for not confessing that the dogs belonged to his security team.

Dr. Brandon tapped his fingers against his console. "We're going to have to spend some time considering alternate treatments. George wasn't responding that well to the discussions we were having, but he has gone further downhill in a hurry. There must be some way to reach him."

Brandon, for all his odd looks, was an excellent doctor. Working with him was like talking to a huge kewpie doll. He was weird looking, but comforting. Maybe his patients were consoled knowing that at least they didn't look like Brandon.

"I'll give it my attention also." One of them would break through the barrier eventually. She waved and signed off.

As long as the records were up, she delved in again. George's chart showed that Ann had prescribed reasonable amounts of Haldol, two milligrams upped from half that when he hadn't responded. The only abnormality was the half-hour of prayer that Ann listed in place of a psychological exam.

Well, maybe it was time that some cold, hard psychology be applied.

First, she wanted to check in with Chris--and tell him about the dogs. She still felt guilty about accusing him. At least now she could tell him that she should have asked Darren.

She went back home, but Chris was gone. The program he had been running was still cranking through bank accounts. She watched it for a while, hoping he would come back.

She grinned as she realized what he had done. The program was searching accounts randomly without repeating any one person's name. From the flashing numbers she deduced that he didn't access the accounts long enough to be detected. Every few seconds it would exit into another file and insert a line. The lines consisted of a person's name and deposit.

It seemed like a difficult way to track unusual activity, but since the program was doing most of the work, it wouldn't hinder him from looking at other things while it was running.

On her way out the door, she frowned. Why had he left the console running, in plain sight? Granted, she had said that the best way to keep the secret was to act as if there was no secret, but that didn't mean he had to make it too obvious.

She walked back over to the console. He could have at least brought up a dummy program to run. She sat and started one that appeared to be researching cases on patients with similar symptoms as George. With luck, the program might actually find something. It didn't take long to enter his symptoms: confusion, depression, unsteadiness and psychosis. She entered his vital signs as close as she could recall them. His heartbeat had been rapid, but she had attributed that to her visit since the readings on his chart had shown abnormally low blood pressure.

She watched a few lines scroll and smiled, satisfied, when the drugs of choice appeared. They were doing everything they could for George. She still felt bad that her theft had played a part in his pain, but now, perhaps they could truly help him.

Her self-satisfied smile wavered as she read through the drug list. There were several other drugs they could try, of course, but that wasn't what bothered her.

She read down the list.

Haldol dose: 1mg yellow; 2mg pink; 5mg green; 10mg aqua; 20mg salmon.

Next to the two lines were pictures. It was the pictures that caught and held her attention. She bit her lip and tried to think. "Rain, rain...go away...." What had Sally said? "A pill for you...a prayer..." She racked her brains.

Before she could remember the elusive thought, a sound penetrated her heavy thinking. Even as she tried to ignore the rattle in favor of what she knew was an important thought, the hypnotic sound caught her attention.

Rattling? Rattling. In her house. Under the desk.

Her hands jerked before she could stop them, and she almost jumped up.

Moving would be fatal. Rattlesnakes didn't see well, but they smelled with their tongues and sensed temperature. And motion, motion was what helped them hone in.

She peeked under the desk.

The snake was coiled at the back of the desk and ready to strike.

She stopped breathing. It might not wait for her to move, but on the other hand, her best defense was to at least try to hold still.

There was nothing of use on the tabletop. She cursed the day that books had become outdated. A heavy volume would have gone a long way right now. She needed something big, but the console area was of no use. The computer was part of the tabletop, and the lights shown from cavities in the wall. The age of technology had taken away such messy things as lamps with their bulky, bothersome cords.

In her panic, she almost missed the obvious. She might have sat there the entire afternoon waiting for the snake to strike if it hadn't occurred to her that humans still used desk drawers to store meaningless paraphernalia.

Moving as carefully as possible, she extracted the drawer furthest away from the snake. The body of the desk kept the snake from seeing her move.

There was no room to maneuver the drawer, but she fixed that easily enough. Thank God Haven believed in natural materials. The drawer was made from wood, and she was able to pull the side free without letting her vulnerable legs move even an inch.

Now. To strike at the snake and hope it went for the threat. She took a deep breath. Not too deep.

Alexia could think of many other creatures she would rather fight. In no battle would she choose the limited area in which she was presently cramped.

She threw the board, shoving it forward and down with all her might under the desk.

She snatched her hands away, hopped up onto the seat, leaped over the back of the chair and then fell in a heap when her leg caught the edge of the chair. She rolled and then crawled to the couch. The rattling stopped. She gulped and looked down at her legs.

Did they hurt anywhere? She couldn't even get enough air past her choking throat to figure out if she felt pain.

Was that a jab of poison?

Realizing that she was getting light-headed from holding her breath, she forced herself to breathe. "Come on, Alexia. No one dies of rattlesnake bites these days."

She patted her legs carefully. There was no horrifying pain. She ran her palms around her ankles and up her calves.

Intact.

Her nerves barely had time to register her safety when a very cold, horrible thought entered her mind. There was only one place from which the snake could have come.

And Chris wasn't here.

Blind panic made her miss the safe combination three times before she calmed down enough to open it.

The bag was gone. So was the snake, but then, she knew where it was. At least she had. She spun around and stared at the now empty spot under the desk. Sure enough, sir serpent had slithered elsewhere. "Oh God. I'm an idiot."

Where was Chris? Who had taken the instructions?

Suddenly it became transparently clear why Chris had left the console on. He had been interrupted, and whoever had interrupted him had taken the instructions. Since Chris was no longer present, they had also taken Chris.

Again, her breathing failed. The pounding of her blood was worse than when Keith and his gang had attacked, but this time, there was no immediate way out.

She stood. It was no good. She was as bad as George. She couldn't think.

George.

She stared at the screen. The Haldol facts she had been looking at stared right back. She took two steps forward and shook her head. With a gasp and sudden clarity, her brain made the connection. The revelation helped blood into her face.

It wasn't possible. Sally had to be mistaken.

Alexia, the snake forgotten, ran to the console. Her adrenalin was still running high, but she grabbed a pack of M&Ms from the pile of things she had removed from the desk drawer. While she crammed the candy into her mouth, she read the screen.

There it was in full color. But had the clerk been wrong? Sally said that every day Ann gave George a little blue pill. The dose for Haldol came in several colors in pill form. The closest was aqua but it was ten mg, not two milligrams. Had Sally just been simplifying things by saying blue--but blue was too high a dose. The correct color should have been pink and maybe given a couple of times a day. If Ann had upped the dose to avoid having to give the pills more than once a day, the chart should clearly show that.

Alexia closed her eyes and pictured the scene. Sally had been rhyming and singing. "Rain, rain, go away, pill for you...what was it?" The only color that rhymed with "you" was "blue." Or had she been rhyming something with George? No, it had been something about a pill for you. "Or was it a prayer for you?"

A nurse might have noticed and questioned the dose, but Sally handled administrative and logistics tasks, not actual medication. If Ann was giving the pills herself, there would be no one else to verify what was written on the chart. The aqua pill was ten milligrams. Why wasn't Ann using the smaller dose that was entered in the chart?

"Tell me I'm wrong." She had to be wrong. Ann wouldn't do anything like that. But...George had gotten worse instead of better.

Sam. Sam would be able to verify.

Not for the first time, Alexia found herself running to the lab. By the time she reached it, she had a painful stitch in her side. It was after three. She thanked her lucky stars. Sam and Keith were both there.

"Sam," she managed to gasp out.

They both turned and stared.

"What...what are the doses of Haldol?"

Sam's forehead crinkled in a frown. "Why didn't you look it up?"

He turned to his own console, but by now, Alexia had made it across the span of sparkling white floor and grabbed his arm.

"I did, I did. But it is never in a blue pill at two milligrams, so what is?"

He did not try to disengage her death-grip on his arm. "Matter of life or death, I see."

She nodded. He finished punching keys and followed the list with his free fingers, the ones not restrained by Alexia's clutch.

"No, no," he muttered. "No blue pill. An aqua one though."

"What is in a blue pill form?" She realized she was asking a stupid question. He wouldn't know every pill by color either. "It isn't Haldol. So, what is it? What is she giving George? Thorazine? Lithium?" Most of the psychotomimetic agents would cause psychotic effects in a person that didn't require treatment. She tried to shove the pieces into a coherent picture, but the puzzle didn't make sense.

George hadn't shown such severe symptoms when she first checked him in. Alexia had expected to treat mild paranoia and possibly stress. Even Dr. Brandon had seemed surprised at the quick decline of the patient. "Could it be? Would Ann do something like that? Why?"

She held up her hand to forestall questions, and with military precision snapped through her paces across the floor. She could be wrong. Sally could have meant aqua. But the dose was still wrong! Had Ann forgotten to update the chart?

Sam refused to stay quiet and let her think. "George Miller? The man who collapsed after caring for the crystals?"

She nodded. "We haven't got time! We've got to find out for certain if he was given Haldol or something else. If I get you a blood sample, can you diagnose what is in it?"

He nodded. "Of course. But it will take time. Always does when I don't know what I'm looking for. I can tell you quite quickly whether it is Haldol, though."

"Okay," she said. "It has to be something like it--possibly one of the other drugs used to treat a psychological disorder. Given when there are no real symptoms, they can cause what they are supposed to prevent: anxiety, manic behavior and hallucinations." Maybe Sally had noticed something else that would give them a clue.

It was still possible that she was wrong. Sally could have been making a silly remark and said blue when she hadn't even seen the pill. "Keith," she grabbed his arm and held him still when he tried to escape. She was acting unhinged, but she didn't have much time. A man was possibly being drugged incorrectly, and the best way to save him was for Sam to find out what drug he was being given. "I need you to do me a favor."

"But..."he stuttered, "I'm working and--"

Sam interrupted. "Alexia needs a favor, we fit it in." His eyes were focused and clear, and instead of the involved scientific stupor Alexia was used to seeing, he looked vividly alive. He smiled at the surprised expression on her face. He waved a careless hand around his lab. "Just because I work with dead bodies doesn't mean I don't know the difference between the dead ones and the live ones. I'd rather not have another one brought in here and tell you after the fact what it was."

Alexia's heart fill with gladness. Sometimes she forgot how human these people were underneath their experiments. "Thanks." Turning to Keith, she said, "I need you to rescue George. Get him out of the hospital and keep him safe. He's confused and shaky and...potentially dangerous."

Sam nodded for Keith. "I think we can handle that." He slapped Keith across the back. "What do you say?"

Keith wasn't quite as ready to jump at the opportunity, but some final words from Sam decided him. "It's the live ones that are important, lad. I do this to keep the next one alive, not just to find out why they died."

Alexia said, "He's in a locked laboratory, room twelve, at the hospital. We've got to get him where he's safe and can't hurt himself or anyone." She took a deep breath. "I could be wrong."

Sam backed her slipping courage. "Testing his blood won't hurt him. We'll take care of him, but what about you?"

Alexia turned to the door. "I've got to find someone else that went missing." Her voice shook, and for a moment, she was almost overwhelmed because even if she were wrong about George, she knew she wasn't wrong about Chris. The instruction chip and he with it--were gone. And she had only one vague clue as to who might be responsible.

Chapter 26

Alexia started her search in Ann's office. Of course, if she was wrong about George and the medication, Ann might roll her chair in any minute and demand to know why Alexia was searching through her things. But if Ann wasn't responsible, that left Alexia with no one. That thought was untenable. If she couldn't figure out who had taken Chris, who would?

She searched every crevice in the woman's office to find a clue, anything that would tie Ann to the crystals, but other than an extra wheelchair and a neatly ordered desk, Ann didn't have much in her office. Alexia had always assumed Ann's office was sparsely furnished so that Ann could maneuver easily. Almost empty drawers seemed a bit odd, but there was no actual proof of anything untoward.

Hands on her hips, staring blankly around, she remembered what Chris had told her. Bank accounts. He had been going through bank accounts. Had he found proof? Had he confronted her?

No, that didn't make sense. Whoever had approached Chris had come to her home. Nothing had been disturbed there, but the instructions had been taken. Whoever it was must have ordered him to retrieve the instructions, and then forced Chris to depart. He had certainly left a large clue--he hadn't bothered to turn off the computer. She headed home as quickly as her legs could travel.

Halfway across the courtyard, she met Keith and Sam. They were rolling a gurney with a casket on top. She stopped and stared.

"He's not--tell me you don't have him in there!" Eyes popping out of her head, she mouthed other words but no sound came out. Sam passed her with a smile. His gray hair blew wildly, caught by the wind. He had never looked happier.

"Well my dear, who is going to disrespect the dead? And it locks, too, so he can't escape and cause himself harm." He flipped a final wave her direction as they disappeared through the lower door.

She stared after them, aghast. That hadn't been anything like what she had had in mind. Poor George.

Well, he was secure. The casket looked pretty heavy, and if they put it in Sam's lab, no one was going to go around opening the boxes hoping to find a live person. "Oh boy."

Before she could progress forward, to her great frustration, Darren hailed her.

"Argh!" she yelled and sprinted away. She didn't have time for Darren right now.

Of course, his legs were longer, and he wasn't under stress.

"Wait!" he commanded, dragging her to a halt.

She glared at him, panting. He looked almost apologetic. The last time he had bothered to apologize, he had been after a confession. She wanted none of it and no more of his accusations. There was a thief on the loose and said thief had Chris. "Lemme go. Appleton said you can't detain me without proof!"

"I'm not trying to detain you. I'm looking for Appleton. Chris."

"Oh." She stopped struggling. "I don't know where he is."

"He's staying with you, is he not?" Darren's beetled brows bore down towards her.

"He was. He isn't anymore, and I don't know where he went." She desperately wanted to ask Darren for assistance, but admitting that Chris had disappeared along with the instructions wasn't likely to elicit a supportive response. Darren, in his characteristic way, would probably seal the compound, shout instructions and with military precision find everyone except Chris.

"We can resolve things much quicker if you would cooperate and be forthcoming with useful information." It was a command, not a suggestion.

"Forthcoming?" He nodded while she ripped his fingers off her shoulder. "Just like you so quickly confessed that the dogs that chased me were part of your security team?"

He let go of her abruptly. "Well. It was obvious they weren't properly trained. I couldn't be sure they were our dogs, and I have already looked into it."

"I'll bet you did. And did you find out who had gotten overzealous in training them and sent them after us?"

Darren rubbed his forehead impatiently. "They escaped. George was originally helping care for them. He was part of the team that was training them. Perhaps with him not following his normal routine, the dogs got out of control. They escaped shortly after we left."

"Escaped?"

He nodded. "Such careless training won't be tolerated again. Now, will you tell me where Chris is?"

At any other time, she might have stuck around to give him an even fuller opinion of his dog training, but she didn't have time. "No. I don't know where he is, and you are not walking me home."

She turned to go, working into a run.

Darren snatched at her, nearly tearing her shirt in the process. She yanked free and kept running. He stayed behind her, but she didn't stop. Having learned the technique from Chris, she slammed the door in Darren's face and rushed to the computer. She sat before she remembered the snake. Quickly she eyeballed the underside of the desk. Thankfully, it had not returned. Someday she was going to have to track it.

Chris' program was still running. He had to have been sorting the information into a file. Since the program was running, he must have been caught by surprise.

It didn't take long for her to find the file since it was her computer. He had kept his stuff in a new directory. Four names with transactions appeared in the file, but Alexia already knew the one she was most interested in.

Ann Reven. The entire account had been reconstructed, piece-by-piece.

Alexia had absolutely no idea what might have pointed Chris towards Ann. Unfortunately, there were no unusual deposits from what she could see. Her salary and disability payments were the only two deposits. Neither looked overly large.

She shook her head. The program couldn't have accessed Ann's account long enough to trigger a warning to Ann either. So why had she attacked? Ann had been hiding relatively secure for a long time. There was no reason to blow her cover unless she suspected that someone was on her trail.

Chris had to have done something--called the bank, checked her salary figure with payroll and discovered that it was too large or something. The problem was, Alexia didn't know what the something was. All the proof she had was a clerk who described a medication that George might not have needed. Alexia could be following a false trail while Chris' life was in danger.

With nothing more than her instinct and the evidence of a stupid rhyme, Alexia tried the only other place she could think of.

Like the thief that she was, she went to Ann's home.

She had never been there before, but she prepared as she would have for any other break-in. The sun was close to setting, so she chose black. As she dressed, a shaky smile came to her lips. Chris had probably gone through her wardrobe. That alone would have told him that she was a thief. Who else had a black Ninja outfit, complete with hood?

She grinned, thinking of the arguments they would have when she explained that she was in karate and that's why she owned the outfit. Good excuse, but Chris wouldn't buy the story. She only hoped that she could find him in time to try it out.

The smile disappeared faster than the tools of her trade into the hidden pockets of her suit. She would be safer if she waited until dark, but there wasn't time.

Hesitating at the last minute, she sent two messages. One was to Dr. Appleton, Chris' father. He could decode it if necessary. The other message she sent to Grace, knowing the scorpion designer would be as tenacious in chasing down an enemy as a genuine scorpion was in real life.

If I disappear, tell security (even if it is Darren). Tell him I was investigating Ann Reven. The instructions have been taken.

That should at least get someone started in the right place.

Alexia left casually, her hood hidden inside the jumper. She walked towards the gymnasium as if she were going for practice. Instead of entering the building, she walked around back, all the while doing stretching exercises, which might be necessary anyway, and acting as though she intended to use the jogging track.

She jogged half the stretch and then headed for the hills. If anyone were watching, they would know that it wasn't uncommon for her to hike; it was recorded in numerous places that long walks were one of her favorite pastimes.

Slowly, she doubled back. It wasn't quite dusk when she reached Ann's stucco house. The house was white, a fact that didn't surprise Alexia any. Ann was always discussing the light and the way. How Ann could be a thief and discuss God in the next breath was beyond Alexia, but then, people were rarely simple.

The first problem Alexia encountered was that Ann's house had no doors. Not a one. Two ramps led down, one in the front and one in the back. They ended at blank walls. Alexia noted this from well outside

Ann's yard.

Even though Ann's house was a single story, the windows were higher than normal and all in the shapes of circles with crosses. Again, the design was in total keeping with Ann's personality. Of course, it also made for a great hide-a-way that no one could enter. The shape and size of the windows made it impossible for Alexia to fit through.

The longer Alexia studied the setup, the more suspicious she became. From her second vantage point in the back, this time a sturdy pine tree, she noticed a vertical split at the end of the ramp. The ramps no doubt opened into some kind of elevator platforms.

There was one small problem. How to activate the platforms?

She shrugged mentally. It couldn't be any worse than a locked door, now could it?

She reached inside her pocket and extracted Scorpio. Scuttling along like he good pet he was, he scrambled along the rocks until he reached the end of the ramp. The walls presented no problem for Scorpio, but they didn't provide any openings either. From the camera's vantage point, she determined that the doors were most likely activated much like her own doors--with a proper code, they would slide sideways rather than in or out.

Normally, coded entries didn't present a problem for Alexia, but if Ann was inside, there was no way she could activate the elevator without Ann noticing. Even if the mechanism were noiseless, which she doubted, there had to be air displacement.

She sent Scorpio to the windows. Maybe if she could scout the inside, she would get a better idea of how to deactivate any alarms or find another plan for entering the place.

Scorpio was not nearly the help she needed. He had been made for small crevice work, and the windows were sealed and opaque. Even with the largest panoramic view, details inside were fuzzy and undecipherable. She worked him around the house. The stucco revealed a few cracks, but none penetrated far enough.

Next, she tried the ventilation outlets, but, to her surprise, they were covered with fine wiring.

She could have climbed up the walls herself now that it was fully dark, but a better plan formed in her mind. At least she hoped it was a better plan.

George was Ann's patient. Who better to tell about his disappearance?

With a smile, she walked back from the house a ways and placed a link call to Ann's office. She hadn't expected an answer and was relieved when she didn't get one.

She hurried forward towards the house again and placed another call.

Ann was at home. It was a good thing Alexia hadn't tried to climb up to the windows.

"Ann? Alexia, here. I've just come from the hospital. Have you moved George?"

"Moved him?"

"I went to check on him, and he was gone. I thought perhaps he had begun responding to treatment, and you moved him out to the regular ward, but his records didn't show any such movement."

"Of course I didn't move him! Good heavens, the man is ill. There must be some mistake."

Alexia made it to the elevator lift where she rang a bell. "I hope I'm not imposing. I headed this way after leaving the hospital." She put the concern she felt for Chris into her voice since she knew that George was actually as safe as he could be at the moment. "I hope nothing has happened to George. Do you think he managed to get out of the room?"

Ann's outside viewer came on, but she didn't invite Alexia inside. "Why didn't you notify security?"

"His chart didn't have anything special on it, but the lab door didn't look forced. I thought you had decided to run a different treatment and must have moved him. Then when I called your office and didn't get an answer, I thought I'd try here."

The elevator was making noise at last, but it wasn't to let Alexia in, it was to let Ann out.

"We must find him, right away." Ann rolled forward, obviously agitated. "He is a sick man."

And might not remain sick if he doesn't get his regular dose of medication. "Are you sure no one else would have taken him somewhere? Did he maybe have a relative coming to see? Or perhaps Dr. Brandon?"

"Nonsense!" Ann pushed a button on her chair. The door behind her rolled shut. At the same time, she activated the wheels, and they carried her up the ramp.

It was enough for Alexia to form a plan in her mind. She wrinkled her forehead. Ann was going to look bad, even without a statement from Alexia, if George showed up in better condition than when he disappeared.

"I'm going to go find Darren," Alexia said. "He'll know what to do."

Ann's chair was already moving towards the hospital. "Have you asked the clerk? The other nurses?"

Alexia shook her head with a woebegone expression and decided to keep Ann busy for as long as possible. "I thought I better check with you first. I'm terribly sorry. We've got to find him before he hurts someone."

If the older woman answered, Alexia didn't hear. Alexia was already dashing towards the complex. She smiled. All she needed was Ann's spare wheelchair. The electronics were bound to be the same. The chair was like having a key to Ann's house.

Chapter 27

The halls in the complex were down to only auxiliary lighting, but that didn't stop Alexia from running full speed. She had already searched Ann's office and knew there was nothing of interest besides the chair.

It took less than four seconds for her to get inside the office. Inspecting the control panel on the chair, she found, much to her surprise, that the entire sleeve on the armrest, including what appeared to be the door activation button, could be rolled off. The sleeve was made of a slick silicon that matched the chair's color.

Now why would Ann make it removable? To put on the other wheelchair? The other chair was equipped with its own. Of course if the chair malfunctioned, she would still need her computer and remote control commands, especially to get into her house.

Alexia grabbed a roll of opaque tape from the top drawer, tucked the sleeve into her pocket and headed back to Ann's house. She had no idea how much time she had before Ann returned. Thankfully, George really was gone, and if Ann spent any amount of time searching for him, Alexia would have time to break into the house and find Chris or at least a clue to his whereabouts.

Halfway across the complex, she ran into Keith. Literally. He took the brunt of the damage since she was sprinting, and he was walking.

"What--"

Alexia didn't stop to explain. "Ann's looking for George now," she called back to him. She continued her mad dash. If anyone saw her, they would think she was crazed. Keith already believed it, so she wasn't losing ground there.

As she jogged back, she opened her communications application and searched through the directory. Dr. Appleton's number was readily available. By the time she placed the call, she had made her decision. The man deserved to know.

"Dr. Appleton? This is Alexia." She hesitated, wondering how to phrase it. Finally, she blurted out, "Ann Reven has your son."

The image staring back at her closed his eyes. "Is he alive?"

The awful truth of why Dr. Appleton seemed to disapprove of his son dawned on her. Here was a man who had helped create one of the most amazing places on earth. He should be happy and fulfilled. Instead, he sat at his desk, in his powerful office and waited for The Call.

The call about his renegade offspring who had to do things his way; the son who was constantly pursuing criminals instead of busying himself with a scientific venture. A son who was now in danger of making nightmarish worries a reality.

"I think so." What must it be like to love a person who constantly disappeared? A person whose challenge in life was to outsmart minds that were devious and, at least in Ann's case, sick enough to knowingly administer drugs that made a patient worse instead of better?

"I'm not completely certain it is Ann, but I have some evidence that it may be." She filled him in on the details of the pill. Her theory sounded shakier when she spoke her suspicions out loud. In sheer desperation she mentioned that Chris had obviously suspected Ann also and explained about the computer program running on her console.

"What did it show?"

She shook her head, feeling defeated. "Nothing substantial, I'm afraid. It listed bank accounts, credit card activity, disability payments and salary. No large cash influxes that I could see. But sir, it has to be her!" How could she tell him that she knew? There wasn't time to explain her instincts, but she was positive.

"Disability payments?" he asked.

"Yes. I don't know what Chris found, but her name was on a list of only four people. Perhaps her credit wasn't being used enough, and he felt she must have been using cash from some other source to survive. I didn't have time to go through everything completely."

"It's the disability payments. She has to be the one. Chris would have known."

Alexia didn't understand. "What?"

"When anyone comes to Haven, they leave behind any lawsuit compensation, worker compensation, even social security payments. Of course, you're not old enough to worry about that."

Alexia felt like smacking herself. It seemed trivial, but of course. Disability was against the experiment of surviving in Haven without outside help. Stupid, stupid, stupid! She had even told Keith that he couldn't get support from his parents!

"I'll find Darren and send him to the hospital," Dr. Appleton said.

"We're short on time. If she knows that Chris discovered her guilt, it's only a matter of time before she makes her next move. If she isn't at home, we'll have to get in and get Chris out. I don't want a hostage situation." Even as he said it, his face paled further.

She nodded into the screen. "I'll get him out."

She started to sign off, but Dr. Appleton got out one final command. "You come first, Alexia. If there's danger, get out and leave Chris. That's an order."

He closed the communication before she could answer.

What was the use anyway? It wasn't in human nature to know what sacrifices one was willing to make until the situation presented itself.

Riiiight. Like she could walk away and leave Chris to die. Not likely.

She moved quickly, arriving back at Ann's house to find it quiet and still. There were few night noises in Haven; no gas cars and very few animals. Alexia could hear her own breathing. Her heartbeat was loud enough to wake the dead and make them think their own hearts were beating again.

Assuming that the last fingerprint reading to press the activation button on Ann's chair sleeve belonged to Ann, Alexia put tape across the controls to preserve Ann's prints. She pushed on the button.

It took three very long heartbeats for the door to roll open. She breathed a quick thankful sigh of relief.

Her thief instincts warred with her now, but she tamped them down. Normally, she would take more time sizing up the job, checking for other security measures. Unfortunately, she was dealing with a person who had no respect for life or sanity. If Chris was still alive, she didn't have time to fool around.

Before pulling her mask over her face, she yelled up the dark cavern, "Ann? Are you there?"

No answer, but it never hurt to try.

Her foot was in the air, ready to step forward, when she heard a sound. She froze in place.

Thump.

It came from beneath the floor where she was about to step. Metal on metal? Or metal on concrete? How could it be coming from beneath Ann's house? And more importantly, why?

She withdrew her foot and scooted backwards. The sound continued. "Chris?"

The sound came twice more then stopped.

"Are you down there?"

Two more rings against something hard.

If it was Chris, she hoped he was using a sequence of two rings for yes.

If two rings was yes, one must be no. She racked her brain for an obvious question. It wasn't too hard considering the circumstances. "Can you get out?"

The ring of metal occurred once and was louder than before, signaling his irritation. Alexia couldn't help but grin. After all, if Chris could get out, why would he be clunking a metal object against the floorboard?

She chuckled. She couldn't help it. The situation was far from funny. Chris was obviously in dire straits.

"Can I get in?"

The sound was a quick and definite, "No!"

He didn't want her to try.

Right. She should just sit and yell down at the floorboard until Ann came back.

"Can I get to you through the house?"

One ring. No again and emphatically.

That made no sense. If Chris was beneath Ann's house, how else had he gotten there except through the house?

"A tunnel?" she asked without much hope. If it was a tunnel, she could search the hills for days before finding it. Besides, how had a woman in a wheelchair created a tunnel?

Her hopelessness had been correct. This time his answer was no, but it didn't sound so desperate.

So. He didn't want her to go through the house, and there wasn't a tunnel.

Now what?

She reached inside her sleeve and retrieved Scorpio. She sent him scurrying across the floor, looking for cracks or openings or any type of clue. How had Chris gotten down there?

Alexia didn't question the why of it. That part, given the missing instructions, was apparent. Ann had put him down there. How much time did Alexia have to get him out?

The banging started again.

"I'm here, I'm here," she yelled. "I'm trying to find a way in!"

No! Emphatically.

"I can't just leave you there!"

Yes!

More frantic banging as though he were sending panicked thoughts. Only one thing would cause him to react so badly. The answer clicked into place as suddenly as her lock pick into a keyhole. "Ann is coming back."

Yes!

"Uh-oh." Alexia stood and searched frantically for the close button on the sleeve. Her heart skipped a beat. A small red light was illuminated. Worse, there wasn't any other button available that might close the door.

She pressed the same button she had seen Ann press that had caused the door to operate. Nothing happened. The door remained a looming opening of darkness. "Bad. Bad."

Alexia was smart enough not to use the ramp to escape. Her hood in place she grabbed the outside wall of the ramp and pulled herself out of the hole. Without standing, she edged towards the trees. If Ann was waiting outside to see who had entered her house, she might, just might miss the darkness of Alexia's shadow creeping into the brush.

With nary a sound, and many sweat-drenched moments later, Alexia crawled into the cover of the trees.

Since no one had shot her yet, she stood and let out a deep breath. There must be some other code that the system expected after the door was opened. When that hadn't happened, the door had locked open and probably sent a message to Ann. Or maybe she had somehow set off some other alarm.

With the patience of a thief, Alexia waited. If Ann was coming back, she wasn't hurrying--unless she too was watching from afar, waiting for Alexia to make a move. Occasionally, Alexia checked the light on the sleeve. It stayed on. If it hadn't been for the red light, Alexia would have gone back and tried to find out more.

A full fifteen minutes later, Ann rolled through the pathway. She was moving slowly. For the first time, Alexia noticed that Ann's wheel chair was noiseless.

Ann moved to the top of the ramp and turned on a light.

Alexia didn't know what she might be looking at because when she had scrambled out of the hole, there had been nothing to see.

Whatever the scene, Ann changed it. Abruptly, the light on the sleeve flashed. Alexia heard a resounding clank and the sound of a sliding panel.

Ann waited at the top of the ramp, still looking down.

Alexia's eyes were glued to the scene or she would have missed the faraway, almost dreamy smile on Ann's face when Chris yelled.

"Let me out!"

Ann actually waved. Like a mother saying good-bye to a child getting on the school bus, she waved tenderly, almost sadly.

Chris continued to yell, but was drowned out by the panel sliding shut again.

Alexia, for the first time since the craziness had started, believed, with all her heart, that Ann was guilty. Not only was she guilty, she was capable of killing, of sending dogs and murderers on their trail and of dosing a patient with the wrong medication. Ann, the woman who spouted forgiveness and healing, was after Haven's secrets and would stop at nothing, including Chris' life.

Up until now, some part of her believed that if Ann were involved, she wouldn't really hurt Chris. Oh sure, someone had sent the threats after them, and Ann had possibly drugged George, but the two personalities had not merged in Alexia's mind until this moment.

She ground her teeth together. She was supposed to be a psychiatrist and couldn't spot a loon two doors down. It was no wonder Keith thought she was a quack.

The next noise Alexia heard was so unexpected, she nearly fell out of the tree and lost the gamble entirely.

It came from her own mini-computer on her wrist. It was Chris' voice.

"Does this damn thing have ears?"

Alexia was so startled she answered the question. "What?" Realizing her mistake, she bit her lip hard enough to draw blood. Ann's head swiveled, listening.

With a sick foreboding, Alexia jumped from the tree and ran. She worried less about noise and more about speed. She almost made it.

When the floodlights hit, depending upon where Ann was looking, Alexia might have been seen. Of course, in her dark clothes, Ann might not know who it was, and the trees may have blocked her vision.

A gunshot answered the question, but Alexia didn't stop moving. Once Alexia was outside the floodlit area, Ann could shoot for a very long time before hitting a target.

The good news was that Alexia now had even more proof that Ann was the guilty party. Of course, Ann could deny the whole thing and say she was merely defending her property, but how was she going to explain Chris locked in some sort of hole below her elevator?

That was assuming that Alexia could get him out and make it far enough away to tell anyone. Still running, she decided her first priority was making certain that someone knew what was going on.

Chris spoke again, but this time it sounded more like radio hissing. She stopped and looked down at her computer. The image was fuzzy due to distance and some kind of interference. Scorpio had been designed for nearby operation.

Still, she could see a face peering back at her. The mouth was moving. She turned the volume up.

The static was too loud for her to make out Chris' words, but when she got back, she had a way to reach Chris. Chris didn't appear relieved. She could have sworn from the expression on his face and his motions, he was shouting at her.

She took a deep breath of fresh air. What if Ann had hit her instead of missed? Would the struggle to breathe be over, or would she be fighting still? She wished desperately for a candy bar, but there wasn't any time. Thank God she still had adrenalin to keep her going.

Fingers shaking, she punched Appleton's office number again, but there was no answer. He was elsewhere gathering the troops. Fine. She left a message with the barest of details. Chris in the basement. Ann taking shots at her.

In the distance, the floodlights went off. She ended her recording and called Ann's number.

No answer. That didn't mean that Ann wasn't inside, it just meant she wasn't communicating.

Alexia edged back towards Ann's house, hoping help was on the way. From the trees, she watched the dark house for a few moments before turning Scorpio's monitor back on.

Chris was no longer speaking to the device. In fact, the viewfinder was almost dark, which made no sense since she had activated the light on Scorpio's claws. She moved Scorpio forward and was richly rewarded.

"Aaagh!" The viewfinder spun wildly for a moment and then settled on a segment of a shoe.

"Alexia?"

She started to answer and then groaned silently. Grace had made the scorpion capable of picking up audio signals, but the arachnid was supposed to be for exploration, not communication. Grace hadn't bothered to put output on Chris' end.

It took her second to think of copying Chris' idea, but when she did, she directed her pet to wave its stinger. Twice.

Since he was staring right at it, he couldn't miss it. Besides, a scorpion's stinger was its most attention-worthy part.

"Alexia?" His voice was hoarse.

She waved again.

"You can't talk?"

Technically speaking, she could; it was Scorpio that couldn't. She settled for a quick "no" wave.

Chris reached down and picked up Scorpio, sending images too quickly for the panning camera to filter. Alexia blinked rapidly before one of Chris' large pupils came into focus.

"I'm under Ann's house. Not sure how long the oxygen will last."

She would have dropped her computer had it not been attached to her wrist. She waved the stinger incoherently.

"Yes, I'm afraid so. Some gets in, but not much unless Ann goes in or out. I get pretty lightheaded."

She waved the tail frantically. How do I get the door to you to open?

Chris' eyeball moved as he talked. "I can't get out. I don't know exactly how the platform operates."

Alexia could hardly afford to approach the house until Ann was in custody. Not unless she could get the door open without setting off any alarms. She bit her lip, and then cursed when she realized she had drawn blood again.

It wasn't fair. She was a thief and a good one, but she had never been up against this kind of time limit. Frustrated, she began walking back towards Ann's house.

There was still no sign of life from the house. She could try.

She punched Dr. Appleton's number again. He didn't answer. Neither did Darren when she tried his number.

So, she was on her own. She knew how to get the door open, but she didn't know how to activate the floor below. She also didn't know what set the alarm off when she had opened the door before. Her only clue was the wheelchair. If the chairs were exact duplicates, then something on the chair had to...the wheels!

She didn't bother to wave the tail at Chris before heading back to the lab. He might have been talking to her the entire time she was thinking. She hadn't noticed.

As she ran, the insane thought that she had over-exercised this week popped into her head. If she logged the trips back and forth from the lab to Ann's tonight, the person looking at her chart would record her as having over-exerted herself. The thought didn't slow her down, however. She ran full-out towards Ann's office.

The chair had to work. It had to be the answer. It was the only thing that made sense.

She reached Ann's office, retrieved the chair and returned outside. The clouds had cleared. A three-quarter moon lent its eerie light to the path. Alexia plopped herself in the wheelchair, put it in gear and let it spray gravel behind her as she pushed it to its highest speed.

She didn't bother with quiet. For one, Ann had to know the game was up. For two, sneaking up on the house with the wheelchair would be impossible. Alexia fully intended to activate the door regardless of the consequences.

In the near distance, coyotes began howling. Their yapping was maniacal laughter, daring her to complete the task. She shrugged. Indians believed the coyote was a thief and a very talented one at that. Surely, it was a sign of luck.

The inside of the house was no longer dark. The game was up. Ann was watching, either from inside or from the grounds. In her shoes, Alexia would have chosen the house. The view was better and, if the outside of the building was any indication, the house had probably been built with high security in mind.

Ann might be in her own territory, but she wasn't untouchable. Alexia let her mind pass from emotional worry to business. From a safe distance, she shot out four of the floodlights. Several others could have been reached with a rifle and done the job better, but she didn't have time to complain. The wheelchair didn't handle areas off the path until Alexia found the magnetic switch.

She should have known. The magnetic field worked well when it came to lifting the weight of approximately one human being. When she activated it, the chair lifted a few inches off the ground. A spoke attached to the center of each wheel elongated until it reached the ground outside the field. The mechanics that normally powered the wheels moved the "legs," to propel the chair smoothly forward through the air, much like a skateboarder would propel himself.

Alexia allowed herself a single link back to her emotional side, just long enough for a prayer for luck.

As she got closer to the house, she could hear Chris through Scorpio demanding to know what was going on.

She didn't answer him. He would no doubt heartily disapprove of her plans.

Alexia didn't bother with stealth. She drove the wheelchair up to the door, pressed the button and when the door opened, she rolled the chair in and held her breath.

By riding the elevator into the house, Chris would get air into the chamber below. She didn't know how else to make the platform move upwards, and she was only going to get one chance at this.

As the elevator moved, she turned the audio and controls for Scorpio off. She didn't need Chris' voice distracting her. The light that had flashed red before remained quiet. The elevator platform moved within the walls until the walls ended. She sat flush with a living area.

At least she had been right about one thing. The chair itself was part of the security system. If the sensors didn't receive the input of the chair, it activated the alarm. No one but a person in one of Ann's wheelchairs could enter without permission.

Alexia wasn't prepared for Ann even though she expected her inside the house. But then, really, what prepares even a psychiatrist for insanity?

Ann waited patiently, a crucifix in one hand, a gun in the other. Her eyes were clear and focused, unlike the drug-induced insanity she had caused in George. "I knew you'd come. Stand up, my dear. I don't want you to get too comfortable. Take off your wrist computer and leave it on the chair. Empty your pockets."

"Gosh, thanks." Alexia would have liked to think that she had her back to the door, but technically it was beneath her feet. She wasn't certain she knew how to get back out either. As slowly as possible, she removed her mini-computer watch and pushed herself out of the wheelchair as ordered. She kept her body partially in front of the chair and emptied her pockets one at a time. She made sure to take out all the large, obvious objects and set them behind her on the chair.

"You've been a worthy adversary." Ann's voice was as prominent and brassy as ever. Her coiled hair was neatly in place. The only sign of wear was her red lipstick, which had thinned to a severe pencil line. "Kick the chair backwards now."

Alexia did so, happily. With it went Alexia's gun, knife, extra computer, lock picks and other tools. More importantly, the arm of the chair was further from Ann's inspection.

"You were an evangelist before you came to Haven, weren't you?" Alexia asked. "I'll bet if I checked your degree, I'd find that you never even studied psychiatry."

"I don't bother to tell lies, child. I am more qualified than you ever were to enter the human mind."

"And destroy it?" Alexia needed to keep her talking. Surely someone would be able to rescue them if she wasted enough time.

The first sign of rage flitted across Ann's face. "If need be."

"Killing someone is a contradiction to the Lord's work. So is stealing."

"I'm not stealing."

"No? You took the chip. It doesn't belong to you."

"Power belongs to the Lord, not to the people. We must depend upon him."

If Alexia could convince Ann that her god didn't want the crystals...she frowned and started to bite her lip. Pain reminded her that it wasn't a good idea.

Was Ann stealing for her god and keeping the money in her other fist? Could Alexia appeal to any remaining logic? "The chip doesn't belong to you. Neither do the crystals."

"I have the chip, thanks to you." The gun rose to point at Alexia's head. From ten feet away, she could hardly miss. "I have been after the crystals for over a year. Almost two years while you waltzed in ahead of us before we could break through the ridiculous attempts to protect them. Had I any idea it was you, I would have shot you long ago. Now, you will bring the crystals to me."

"You would ask me to sin? To steal?" The hypocrisy of that statement almost made Alexia smile, but she doggedly followed what she saw as her only chance. "You're one of god's messenger's. I'm not. I shouldn't sin."

"I'll be sure and forgive it as part of the greater good."

Anger replaced Alexia's better judgment. "Do I get half your cash, when I'm done?"

Ann threw her head back and laughed. "Absolutely not."

"Why not?"

"It is mine."

Alexia had enough experience to know when a patient substituted stubbornness for logic. "How will your god forgive such a thing?"

Ann smiled. "My god won't mind. Trust me."

With incipient dread, Alexia realized a harsh truth. Her stomach hit bottom hard enough that Chris must have heard it land. She held her breath, but the truth glittered from hostile eyes. Ann was no religious zealot. Her constant preaching was merely a front. Just as Alexia used her skills to blend in, Ann used an annoying personality to make sure no one stuck around very long. The woman could clear a room with the start of one of her tiresome lectures. She had effectively isolated herself and afforded herself the freedom she needed to accomplish her real goals.

"You sent the dogs." It wasn't a question. "You already tried to kill all three of us."

Ann smiled. "My dear, we tried to keep you here and out of our way. If the barn had burned, there would have been no need to turn the dogs out. But as usual, you had to interfere. George did a beautiful job on their training. It wasn't hard to convince them to go after you. You never even missed your sweater, did you?"

"You're the one that took my sweater?"

Ann laughed. "The smell of it proved crucial in getting the dogs to hate you. A day or so of training them to follow horses and your scent, and it was easy to set them loose to hunt." She pointed the gun at Alexia's middle. "I don't really need you to obtain the crystals. I have Chris." The thought made her laugh. "Appleton's own son. What better bargaining chip?"

Alexia took her eyes off the weapon that Ann aimed. She sucked in air, preparing to roll. Determined to give herself a chance, she dove forward, but she was too late. With nary a sound, the floor dropped out from under her. Trying to throw herself away from a bullet, she ended up doing nothing more than falling through the floor.

She hit the tallest object in the small chamber below her feet. At least it broke her fall.

She bounced off Chris and fell onto the floor. He was less happy about her luck than she was. The momentum knocked him over. Chris pressed himself against the wall of the five by five foot chamber as she tried to stand up. She stepped on his foot.

Alexia looked up in time to see the floor gliding back across the opening. She sighed as the last sign of freedom disappeared.

Chapter 28

Glancing about her new quarters, she was unimpressed. The chamber was probably required in case the elevator needed maintenance. Chris had no doubt tried to pull away the panels to get to any machinery, but other than Scorpio, he had no tools.

The next thing she noticed was Chris' face. "Hi!" she said cheerfully.

He grabbed her shoulders and shook her. She could hear his teeth grinding. "I told you not to come in the house."

From a clinical point of view, he was moderating his voice quite well. However, the clenching of his jaw was a dead giveaway. So too, was the pressure on her arms. He was furious with her. He couldn't hide it.

She grinned widely. "I'm glad you're okay." She would have hugged him had he not had such a tight grip on her arms.

"This is a death trap! There's very little oxygen!" He was now shouting.

"Your dad knows where we are. He's working with Darren."

"Darren? Oh, that's a big relief." He glared at her, releasing her at last. "That's great news. No doubt we'll be rescued in a flash. He'll probably decide to burn her out. Kill her and get the prize. Fabulous."

Alexia returned his glare with a brilliant smile. "Then we'll have to extradite ourselves before he gets here and burns the house down."

Chris was unable to respond to that statement with anything more than an outraged sputter. He closed his eyes and took a deep breath of their precious oxygen.

Alexia rubbed her hands together, picked up Scorpio from the floor and put the bug in her pocket. "We had best get started."

Chris ground his teeth together again. "Does it occur to you that I may have tried escaping?"

"Well sure. But you didn't have me."

"We're going to die."

"Nonsense." Frankly, his attitude surprised her. Surely, in his line of work, he had been in dire straits before. "This can't be the first time you've found yourself in a sealed cavern."

He didn't respond for a moment. Alexia was busy studying the walls when his reply finally came. "It's the first time I've been hopelessly trapped with a smiling--" With obvious effort, he swallowed whatever word he had been about to use. "With you," he finished lamely.

"Exactly. But that's a good thing."

The agony on his face didn't go away. "Has it never occurred to you that this trap might be too good, even for you?"

"Nope." She stood in the middle of the chamber and reached inside her sleeve. "Voila," she mouthed, having no idea whether or not Ann could hear what went on inside the room.

Chris wasn't as worried about being overheard. "What the hell is that supposed to be?"

"Door opener," she mouthed, showing him the buttons. "It's a tiny pocketknife," she said aloud, hoping Ann wouldn't think the idea of a knife very effective. If Ann happened to change wheelchairs or notice that the sleeve was missing, they were in a world of trouble.

His eyes narrowed thoughtfully. "It can't be that easy. You can't just pry open the door."

Alexia shrugged. "Why not?" Her grin was finally catching. He grabbed her arms and this time instead of shaking her, he kissed her.

As a psychiatrist, Alexia had always believed that transferring anger to another emotion was healthy. So of course with his medical interests in mind, she felt she should encourage him. Heartily. Besides, they had to at least try and wait until Ann left the house.

The pleasant interlude lasted until they were both out of breath. Chris pulled away slightly and rested his forehead against hers. "At this rate, it's going to be hard to tell when the oxygen runs low."

"Yeah," she sighed back. "Don't want to waste it, though."

"No way." They reached for each other with equal enthusiasm. Alexia forgot the medical reasons behind the embrace. In fact, by the time they pulled apart again, Alexia was having a hard time remembering why they wanted to escape.

"I don't suppose that bug of yours can slip through the cracks?" Chris asked between gulps of air.

Alexia shook her head. "She has my computer controls." If worst came to worst and the oxygen got low, they would have to activate the door and run like hell. Alexia had shot out as many of the floodlights as possible before she entered. She hoped that someone outside would help them if they managed to get out of the house. "She's going to negotiate with your father for the crystals."

With that one statement, Chris went from amorous to dangerous. "Using what to bargain?"

Alexia nodded her head, indicating that he had guessed correctly. "What else? I'm sure your father wouldn't willingly let you die."

"And now she's got two of us."

Alexia recognized the dangerous quality of his voice, and she moved to stop him before he could complete his intentions. "No." She yanked the sleeve away from him.

"He cannot be allowed to suffer!" His voice sounded like chunks of concrete in a disposal unit.

"No? Do you imagine that he doesn't suffer daily, wondering where you are, and what you're getting yourself into? At least this time he knows where you are. Maybe he even has the power to help you. I told him before I came here where you were. I outlined the situation. For once in his life, he can actually make a difference instead of sitting by the phone waiting for the call that it's too late."

Chris' eyes flickered. "What is that supposed to mean?"

"It means that he has already been suffering for a long time worrying about you and the risks you take. We owe it to him to let Ann make the next move. It gives us--you-- the best chance of getting out of this alive. Don't be selfish."

His eyes widened in disbelief. "You're telling me that by getting out of here, I'm being selfish?"

"Exactly. You're suffering because you know he's suffering. So you want to relieve your guilt by busting out of here and putting an end to it. You end his suffering and yours stops. However, I prefer to keep you alive, so I vote we stay until our chances are better."

He stared at her without making a sound for a minute. Finally, he shook his head. "That's the craziest thing I've ever heard. I will not be used as a bargaining chip against my father."

"Yes, you will." She moved the sleeve carefully behind her and backed up against the wall. Chris was going to have to take it from her, and she didn't think he would. "It's the least you can do. You can suffer for your father for a little while. You can wonder what is happening to him, to the crystals, to the fate of Haven and find out what it feels like to be in doubt about the safety of someone you love."

"This isn't fair."

"That he has to worry?"

"No dammit." He swung away from her. "That you had to point out that he does."

The smooth sliding of machinery reached both their ears at the same time.

Chris spun towards her anxiously. He reached out for the sleeve.

"Wait," she whispered. "She said she wanted the crystals. I expected her to demand delivery here, but she can't stay here after she gets them. She has to be out in the open where she can make her escape. Maybe she's leaving."

The wheels of Ann's wheelchair were too quiet for them to discern, but the ceiling floated back down. They felt the vibrations of the outer door slide open and then shut, but neither could tell whether she had actually left.

"We wait five minutes," Chris whispered in her ear. "If we don't hear anything, we make a run for it."

"If she clears out, I would expect your father to send someone to help us get out."

"He knows we are down here?"

She nodded again and sat down to begin the wait.

It didn't take long until they were both pacing the small chamber and growling at each other every pass. After five minutes, they had heard no sounds from inside the house or out.

Chris put his hand out for the sleeve.

Alexia handed it over. "Let me get on your shoulders first. I want to be able to spring out quickly in case the door slides shut again."

He agreed and helped her onto his shoulders.

"How do you know which button it is?" He grunted as he lifted her. Alexia had to bend her head in order to keep from bumping it on the ceiling. He staggered a couple of steps. She pulled his hair.

"Ow!"

"Well, quit acting like you're having to carry the Leaning Tower of Pisa."

"Why is it women think they're light as air and that we should be able to endure their weight gladly?"

She yanked his hair again. "Because. We are dainty."

"Right," he groaned. "The button?"

"The very end one will open the outside door. Then press twice on the inside button to open the top panel."

"How'd you figure that out?" He sounded impressed. "Lemme guess. Great thief that you are, you learned it by being in the same room with the owner of the buttons."

"Of course." She had stopped watching the gun and kept an eye on Ann's other hand instead. If Ann chose to shoot her, watching the gun wasn't going to stop it from going off, while watching the other hand had paid off handsomely.

For a reply, Chris pretended to stumble again. "The weight of your head is going to topple us both over."

"I'm light as a feather." Alexia was finding it rather hard to be dignified while clutching his head as he careened around the room. "Will you try the buttons already?"

He pressed the first one and they both heard the door slid open. "Ready to jump?"

"Yes!"

He pressed the sequence as she instructed.

Alexia couldn't suppress the joyous grin that spread across her face. She straightened and leapt in one movement, catching the edge of the wall and heaving herself onto the space outside the door. Chris' head may have suffered marginally by a wayward foot, but he didn't waste time complaining.

He was out before the panel had finished sliding all the way open. Of course, he managed to land partially on top of her and then squashed her completely by rolling a bit.

"Hey!"

"Shh," he instructed. "You want to get shot?"

"Is that why you're smashing me? In that case, rest easy. There's only one vantage point that Ann can use too look down here, and that's from the top of the ramp. I already checked. She isn't waiting for us."

"Oh." He grinned down at her. "Then in that case, I'm just paying you back for kicking me in the head."

"Off." He grinned again and gave her a quick kiss.

"Let's go. We have a thief to find."

Alexia barely had time to get a breath before Chris helped her into a low crouch.

"We separate at the top of the ramp." He pointed to her and indicated she go left.

"I'll circle towards you." At the last second, she reached inside her sleeve and extracted a knife and handed it to him wordlessly. He rolled his eyes, but he accepted the weapon.

Alexia carefully palmed another knife. Most likely, neither knife would do any good. The knives weren't balanced for throwing because

Alexia chose them specifically for breaking and entering, not protection. But if worst came to worst, a blade was better than nothing.

They moved to the top of the ramp together.

Alexia rolled one direction and scampered towards the trees as quickly as possible. Her ears ached with the strain of listening for the first shot. For some weird reason, she prayed it would hit her rather than Chris.

Thankfully, she didn't have time to analyze her feelings. A shadow, low to the ground, hissed at her out of the darkness. "What are you doing? Waiting for an invitation? I didn't mean to stay as close as possible to the house!"

"I was waiting for you." She jumped up to follow him. He took off at a dead run, one that she had trouble keeping up with.

"Where are we going?" Noting the direction they were headed, she answered her own question. "Why the complex?"

"The crystals are there. Run faster," he whispered.

Alexia tripped instead and startled an owl into flight. Had she a gun, she would have fired instinctively. The thought forced her to accept that she was running in a blind panic.

The main complex, contrary to the habits of its usual occupants, was completely dark. Even Sam's office. "Oh no," she whispered.

"No doubt Ann told dad she'd release us after picking up the crystals. She can't know that you already told dad where we were."

Alexia didn't reply. She sincerely hoped that Sam and Keith weren't in any trouble.

"The crystals are in dad's office," Chris said, moving stealthily ahead.

"Why?"

"Quit asking questions and come on." He unlocked the fire-escape door with a key and completely ignored the palm reader and other identification devices. Since Alexia had never bothered to break into the complex from this door, she hadn't known that the security devices were dummies. "Hmph."

False security devices often worked better than real ones, but the fact that she hadn't even guessed disgruntled her. From personal experience she knew that a thief could go to a great deal of trouble trying to disarm devices whose only purpose was to discourage and perhaps stump a thief completely. After all, it was hard to tell when you had successfully bypassed a security device that wasn't turned on in the first place.

Without warning, he stopped. She ran straight into his back. "Umph." She froze, barely breathing. She muttered under her breath as he began moving again. She didn't like going into dark alleys without first checking them out.

With minimal trouble, they reached the top floor where the executive offices were located. There were still no lights.

"Dad will be guarding the crystals. He won't have been caught unprepared," Chris murmured in her ear.

Alexia was pretty sure the elder Appleton was no longer in his office. He had left to help find Chris. She shook her head, but it was too late.

The hallway lights went on all at once, catching them in the open. Chris reached for her before rolling. Her head smacked against his on the way to the ground.

"Ow!"

"Hush."

"I think we've been spotted, Chris." She could clearly see Ann's drawn and tired face around Chris' shoulder.

"Shoot them." What was left of Ann's lipstick was cracked. Her rouge stood out across cheeks covered in base that had dried to an unbecoming paste.

"Ann, are you hurt?" Alexia did her best to sound concerned. Chris chose that moment to roll over, leaving her exposed for a moment, before settling back on top of her.

"It doesn't matter," Ann replied.

But Ann's voice was strained, and Alexia had seen bright red blood across the woman's lap in the brief roll. Alexia looked around Chris, into barrel of a gun. The face at the other end was familiar, but her jaw still dropped. "Ollern?" She could barely breathe with the shock of it. That or Chris was getting heavier. "Let me guess. You thought you'd get Darren's job when he failed. And you didn't."

"I don't need his job." His chiseled face showed no strain. "I have a better one. Three countries are waiting for me to secure the crystals. I can pick and chose."

"Guess it's a good thing you rode the other way when you did," Chris said looking down at Alexia. "He would have known exactly which way Darren would go."

Ollern snarled and for a moment his military precision cracked. "I assumed you would at least go where there was an out. Only a fool would have gone where you did." He snorted in disgust. "It doesn't matter.

We're here now."

Alexia pushed futility against Chris' chest, trying to move him away from her. He wouldn't budge.

"The little woman wants to stand on her own again." Ollern pointed the barrel of his rifle at Chris and ordered, "Let her up."

Chris glared at him for several tense seconds before rolling away. There was only Ann and Ollern to deal with and one long hallway, in either direction. None of the doors were open in the corridor, leaving them nowhere to run and hide even if Ann or Ollern could be distracted.

"Open it." Ollern pointed to Dr. Appleton's office door.

Alexia let her mouth gape. "Me?"

For her trouble, she got the barrel of the rifle shoved under her chin. "We didn't know it was you until Darren told us you recovered the chip in the desert. I should have shot you when I had the chance and left you for the carrion."

But instead, Alexia had injured him, and he had returned to Haven. He had plenty of time for Ann to treat him before the rest of the group got back.

Ann rolled her chair further away, carefully keeping herself out of Ollern's way. "You caused us a great deal of trouble."

Alexia felt an immediate need to do something, even if it was wrong. If she could stall long enough, maybe Ann's injury would give them an advantage. It had better. Chris stood ready to pounce, the tension obvious in every line of his body. Ollern moved back out of reach, more than willing to callously shoot either of them.

"Why didn't you want us to test Chris' plan?" Alexia blurted out. "Too many live people in the way?"

Ollern laughed. "Don't be stupider than you have to be, Alexia. I had no problem killing all of you as long as I had the crystals and the instructions. Since I doubted you had the talent to break through Chris' defense plan, I didn't even care if you reached the site. The dogs had been eating pieces of your sweater for over a week. If they had succeeded in getting rid of you, Darren would have recovered the instructions, and I could have talked Darren into getting rid of Chris." He shrugged. "Then there would have only been Darren left."

Chris said, "And Darren trusted you enough that you could have disposed of him at any time."

"He trusted me enough that I always had access to the security plans. That would have been enough except for you." He pointed the gun at Alexia. "You kept getting to the instructions before we could make our move. This time, we didn't wait."

Ann's lips trembled. "Exactly. We have the instructions, and now that you're here," she pointed at Alexia, "are going to open the door and get the crystals."

"Why should I?" Alexia crossed her arms.

Ollern pointed the rifle at Chris. "Your choice, sweetheart. Death can be painful, or death can be quick."

Alexia swallowed hard.

He smiled. "Go ahead. Get them."

The only thing that kept Alexia from screaming hysterically was that Chris' fate rested in her hands. She glanced between Ann and Ollern. There was no escape. She moved towards Dr. Appleton's door.

Chris didn't protest. He must have known it wouldn't do any good. Alexia was hardly going to stand by and let Ollern shoot off body parts until Chris either died of blood loss, shock or both.

"It doesn't matter if you set off the alarms, dear," Ann said. She turned to Chris. "They know where we are. Your dad must be so proud. I'm certain it was his bullet that caught my leg, but I can't feel anything in my legs so it doesn't matter."

"He would have helped you," Chris said.

She shook her head. "He shot me. He had no intention of letting me finish my job and take my share of the reward. What I've been paid until now is peanuts compared to what we'll get for the final sale. I have the cards this time. You are my safe ticket out of here."

Alexia shivered. Facing the door was better than watching Ann. She forced her concentration towards the lock, blocking out the threats. It appeared to be an ordinary lock, just like the one at the fire escape. She turned to Chris. "Key," she said, palm out. After all, why would Dr. Appleton give Chris the key to the fire escape and not to the office?

The look he gave her could have peeled layers off an onion. "It wouldn't take me more than five or so minutes to get it open on my own anyway." She didn't mention that she had been in his father's office before, just for the challenge.

"So why waste any time." Ollern motioned Chris with the rifle.

Sooner or later, Alexia was going to have to make a move. It was the only way at least one of them would make it out alive. Unfortunately, she didn't know how to signal Chris and thus far, neither Ann nor Ollern had dropped their guard.

When Chris handed her the key and a coded badge, she unlocked the door.

It opened soundlessly. Ollern nudged her forward with the end of the gun. "Bring the crystals out."

Ann said, "Go in with her. She could find her way out of there. We'd end up stuck with only one hostage."

Ollern curled his face into a snarl, and Alexia thought he might shoot. Unfortunately, he was smarter than Ann when it came to tactics. He knew that with Ann wounded, the odds weren't heavily in their favor. "Thirty seconds."

"No way," Alexia protested. "Well, unless you send Chris. I don't know where they are! I didn't even know they were in here."

"You've been watching them since you came to Haven. You don't have time for any more excuses. Thirty seconds." He didn't even spare a glance at his watch.

Alexia was desperate. She didn't know where the crystals were. "But I didn't have to figure out the location before because I always had the specs. How tough could it be?"

Ollern waved the rifle. "You've been holed up with daddy's boy for days. You know."

Her voice shook badly when she answered. "No, I don't and if you kill him, I still won't know where they are!"

"Fine," he snarled. He shoved her into the room. Even if she hadn't meant to fall and roll, the push would have forced her.

Expecting to roll and rise quickly, she only got as far as the roll before a body pinned her to the ground. Before she could discern what was happening, a shot was fired. It came from within the room.

"Chris," she yelled, trying to squirm her way out from under whomever was sitting on her. It couldn't be Chris. Not even he, with his penchant for constantly smashing her, could move that fast.

"Don't move again." Ann's authoritative rasp echoed through the doorway. Then she called out for her partner. "Ollern, dear?"

To Alexia's immense relief, Ollern didn't answer. "Lights," Alexia said. "Will someone turn on the damn lights?"

Expecting Chris' father and company, Alexia nearly fainted when the lights when on. She decided to cry instead. If it had been possible, she would have put her head in hands and never looked up. She could not face the motley crew that surrounded her. The holes in their heads were only outnumbered by the holes they sported in their pants.

"What are you doing?" she yelled at the only face she knew, the one attached to the body sitting on her.

Keith smiled. "We got your back." Keith and his ragamuffin, bored friends, plus one addition, filled the room. The addition was the young lady from the alley. She held a gun on Ollern. He was lying on the floor not moving. One of Keith's friends had retrieved Ollern's rifle.

"Should we kill him?" Keith asked.

"Oh God." Now Alexia was going to be responsible for the deaths of several people, not just Chris. When she got to the gates of heaven, she didn't want to sign the tally. Several patients cured. Oh, several deaths? Slam. The gates would close forever.

The girl with long black hair looked at Alexia. Alexia shook her head. "No, don't kill him." She hoped the girl would listen.

Ann's voice broke the short respite. "It turns out that I'm not feeling particularly well, dear. I'll allow you another full minute to hand over the crystals."

The black-haired girl turned her gun towards the part of the wall where Ann's voice registered.

"Don't bother." Alexia pushed against Keith to get him off of her legs. "The walls have fiber-casings woven in. They're bullet-proof."

The girl nodded understanding and threw one of Keith's friends something that resembled plastic string. "Hold him."

"Thirty-seconds," Ann's sweet voice called out.

Before Alexia could think of stopping her, the girl stepped into the doorway. "Your draw, bitch."

Now, Alexia forced Keith aside by poking him hard in the ribs and rolling away. She didn't get much further than standing since the black-haired girl was blocking the door, but she could see what was about to happen.

Ann must have known that the girl was going to pull the trigger, but she too was desperate. "There's no point in me walking out of here alive unless I have the crystals." She turned her gun purposefully away from Chris towards the girl.

Before Ann had a chance to aim, the girl fired. Alexia saw Chris roll and then crawl away as quickly as his knees would carry him, but it didn't matter. Only the one shot was fired. The bullet caught Ann at the top of her shoulder and pushed her chair backwards. The gun Ann had been holding crashed to the floor. She was left screaming, trying to hold the gushing wound.

Chapter 29

The next several hours were filled with running footsteps. Authorities burst through the door yelling orders. Someone yanked Alexia out into the corridor to supposed safety. More people ran back out carrying Ollern's tussled form.

Dr. Appleton's office was bugged, allowing the watching army some idea of what was happening. They rushed in, but Alexia wasn't certain it was an improvement. In the mist of the chaos, she happened to hear the nearly soundless footsteps that were fast fading down the corridor. Her eyes caught those of the black-haired girl right before the young woman disappeared down the fire escape. She mouthed a single word at Alexia before she was gone. "Payback."

Alexia turned to the walls around her and noted an officer splayed on the floor. She worked up the energy to crawl over and find a pulse. Good. The girl hadn't killed him. She had given him a bruised chin and tarnished ego, but he was otherwise unharmed.

Then, the walking back and forth from office to office began. She insisted on a candy bar, refusing to talk until she had sugar. After telling her side of the story, she needed another one.

Alexia couldn't tell them everything. For one, she didn't know everything and for two, the people that had guessed her secret had been incarcerated. She wasn't about to admit to more than absolutely necessary.

She did know someone who had some answers though. As soon as the officials were done with him, she headed Keith off before he could escape. "Who was she?"

Keith looked quite innocent. He had had plenty of practice with the officials. "Dunno. She showed up after I called my buddy Pete."

"Why did you call Pete in the first place?" She tried hard to maintain her calm. It would be easier if she could forget that they had all nearly been killed.

Keith tossed her a cocky grin. "Looked like things were getting dirty. Stuff I'm a little more familiar with than you." He pounded his chest with a fist. "I figured someone would be after the crystals."

Dr. Appleton chose that moment to make his presence known. "Which brings up another question, young man. How did you know where the crystals were, and how did you get into my office?"

Keith, with the daring of youth, refused to be intimidated. "Where else would they be? It's the best guarded place around here."

"How do you know that?"

"Because. When Alexia asked me to check around, it was the only place I couldn't get into without a lot more time."

Dr. Appleton stared at Alexia who was old enough and smart enough to be intimidated. She squirmed until he redirected his attention to Keith.

Under his cold stare, Keith decided to take things a little more seriously. "So, I asked Pete to come up here."

"And who is Pete?"

"My bud."

Alexia sighed at the depth of his answer. "Pete would be the one that held Darren at knife point that day in town?"

"We let him go," Keith mumbled.

"Does Pete know the girl with black hair?" Now that Alexia thought about Pete's features, there might have been a resemblance between the two.

Keith shrugged. "She just came along."

Dr. Appleton paced in front of Keith. "How did you know the crystals were in imminent danger?"

Keith, unaware of the rather frantic look on Alexia's face, began explaining. "Well, after we put George in the coffin--"

"He's dead then?" Dr. Appleton whirled to face Alexia. "We were too late?"

"Uh..."

"Oh no," Keith said. "We got him out of the hospital, like Alexia asked. He's down in the lab. Sam's figuring out what was poisoning him. I wanted to stay and help, but Sam told me to go make sure Alexia was okay."

Alexia wished for a hole to crawl into. "Why didn't you look for me? Why did you come here?"

From his next statement it was apparent that he did not recognize danger. "I figured you'd be coming after the crystals eventually since that's why you hired me in the first place. Coming here was the fastest way to find out who was trying to mess with you."

Dr. Appleton turned very slowly towards Alexia. "You hired a--" he stopped short of calling Keith a child. From the look on Keith's face, it was apparent that Keith guessed what Dr. Appleton had been about to say.

Alexia avoided the question completely. If Dr. Appleton wasn't going to finish it, she wasn't going to pretend she heard it. Instead, she took out her discomfort on Keith. "Next time, maybe you could find me first."

"I would have told you when you ran into me, but you took off."

Alexia decided that keeping her mouth shut was the smartest thing she could do.

Dr. Appleton said, "As soon as I alerted Darren that the instructions had been taken, he assigned Ollern to my office area along with several men to guard the crystals. I'm guessing your friend here got inside before they arrived." He shook his head at Keith.

"I didn't know to warn you about Ollern," Alexia said. "I had only figured out Ann's part in things."

"The only good news was that Ollern had to wait a while before he pretended that orders came to reassign the guys with him. He didn't have time to start searching for the crystals. When Ann left her house without you two, we thought we had her. She kept us back by threatening to blow her house up with you in it."

Alexia swallowed hard. It was completely possible that Ann had her house rigged with explosives. Had they really been trapped there...

"We followed her here, but still didn't know Ollern was guilty. We hadn't even had a chance to assign anyone to get the two of you free when we saw you and Chris open the fire escape door." Dr. Appleton's voice trailed off. He closed his eyes as if searching for a peace he never expected to find. With that gesture, Alexia suddenly noticed that someone was missing. Her heart skipped a beat.

"Where's Chris?"

Dr. Appleton opened his eyes. "He gave his report."

"But where is he?"

He looked at her rather strangely. "I have no idea. He's his own man."

Alexia felt suddenly cold. She refused to believe what Dr. Appleton was implying. "He left?"

At her stricken look, Dr. Appleton seemed to realize he wasn't the only one that cared about his son. He managed to come out of his own bitterness long enough to explain. "He said something about needing a new identity. His old one was too well-known." He hesitated before adding sympathetically, "I'm sure he didn't mean to hurt your feelings."

Anger boiled like an eruption from deep underground. "Hurt my feelings?" Chris could probably hear even if he had managed to make it to the other side of the planet. "I nearly get killed trying to rescue him from a room without oxygen, flattened several times, shot at, bitten by a snake, and he just leaves?" She stared at Chris' father, aghast. "I'll kill him myself."

"The snake bit you?" Keith did some sort of hand signal thing. He looked impressed. "Where? Did you kill it?"

She glared at him. "No, it didn't bite me, no thanks to Chris who left it roaming freely in my house. It'll probably get me yet." Seeing no point in staying, she turned towards the door.

"Thank you for your help in keeping the crystals safe, Alexia," Dr. Appleton called after her. "Although, I think it might be prudent to discuss a few of your actions in private. I realize that Haven is unconventional, but I have to question your judgment in allowing certain parties to get involved." He didn't have to look at Keith to get his meaning across.

"Yeah. Big deal," she muttered. "Getting him killed here has got to be better than him getting shot on the streets, which is where I found him."

"What?"

"Nothing." Dr. Appleton was right. There was no excuse for involving Keith. Not, she argued in her own defense, that she had known he was going to collect his buddies from town. She certainly never would have advised it, even if it did so happen that they had saved the day.

Her final stopping place that night--rather morning--was Sam's laboratory.

"Hello, Sam." She called out a greeting even though Sam wasn't the jumpy type.

He turned with a wide grin on his face. "He'll make it!" He pointed to his computer. "It was Halcion."

"Halcion." She went to the console. An overdose would absolutely cause several symptoms, including confusion, drooling, exacerbation of psychosis and psychotic reactions in those not previously crazy.

"He's going to be okay?"

"I'm treating him carefully," Sam said. "I don't want him to suffer from withdrawal, so we must take him off slowly."

She nodded.

Sam caught her second yawn. "Not used to these hours, are you? Why don't you go home? We can transfer him back to the hospital tomorrow."

"Thanks."

"No problem." He waved off her gratitude. "I trust everything turned out okay?"

"Mostly."

"You must tell me about it." He stared down at a peacefully sleeping George, his attention already elsewhere.

She smiled and felt as if her face would crack. The strain of the last twelve hours had more than caught up. "I suspect that Keith will be wanting to tell most of the tale."

He turned back to face her with a chuckle. "The lad is quite bright. Glad you brought him here."

"So am I." Even if he hadn't used good judgment, he had pulled her butt out of the fire. If it hadn't been for him, she or Chris might have been hurt or killed.

With thoughts of Chris, she scowled again.

She glared at Sam's back and then sighed, taking her leave. It certainly wasn't Sam's fault.

Chapter 30

It wasn't until three days later that the picture of events became any clearer. Once again, Keith was responsible. He and Pete showed up on her doorstep late in the evening.

"Hi." They both waited expectantly.

"Would you like to come in?" She backed away from the door to give them room to enter.

Keith shook his head. "Not me, man. I gotta go to work." He waved and jumped down the steps. Pete wiped his hands on his jeans and tried to smile. It looked he had swallowed monkshood.

"Well, don't just stand there. Come on in." Knowing little about kids and probably less about kids that weren't really kids anymore, she stuck to a neutral subject. "Hungry?"

Pete brightened immediately. "Yeah, guess so."

From the way he ate when she brought out sandwiches, she decided "guess so," was a euphemism for "the brink of starvation."

"So," she said picking at the crust on her sandwich, "what brings you my way?"

"Keith said you wanted to know about Lee, and that even though you're from the hill, I mean Haven, you're okay. Crazy, but okay," he added in case there was any doubt that he might count her fully normal.

"I see. Lee would be the girl with dark hair."

He nodded and helped himself to a second sandwich. Alexia surreptitiously put her other half back on the plate.

"Lee is with the Seventeens," he told her.

"I assume the Seventeens is a local gang, not a sorority."

Pete looked back at her as though he might bolt. She stifled a groan at his lack of humor and switched to a more serious question. "Why did she come here?"

Now, Pete looked wary. "That lady, the one in the wheelchair. She bought it, right?"

Alexia shook her head. "She can't use her right arm or legs, but she is alive." She didn't chastise him for his look of disappointment. Alexia wasn't too certain how she felt about Ann's survival.

"What about the other dude, the one you didn't want us to kill?"

Alexia rolled her eyes. Surely there had been some other memorable element to Ollern besides her command that he be left alive. "Don't worry. He won't be going anywhere."

Pete looked stubborn. "Keith says, like, it's different on the inside. He says you won't let the dude walk."

Alexia hesitated, but knew she needed to be honest. "I don't know what will happen to him, exactly. But he won't be set free."

"You gonna make him into a rat?"

"You mean, are we going to try to make him confess?"

He shook his head and studied the tabletop. "No, I mean, like them white rats."

It dawned on her that Pete thought they might use Ollern for human experiments. Rumors outside Haven were definitely getting out of hand. "No. Contrary to what you may have heard, Haven is not a huge laboratory where we all undergo experiments on ourselves." After thinking about what she said, she changed her mind. "Well, not experiments like you're referring to, anyway. We aren't going to try and take his brain apart."

"He won't get out?" When she nodded, he continued. As he talked, he picked up the half sandwich she had set down. "Lee, she figured she owed you."

"Because of the alley rescue?"

Pete nodded. "Yeah." Pete finished the half sandwich and licked his fingers. "She owed you. She pays her dues."

"I see." Pete was a street kid, and from the looks of things, not from a family as well off as Keith's family. He was already nervous about being here; jumping down his throat and demanding information was not going to gain his cooperation. She tried to be approchable rather than forceful. "Do you suppose she might come back here and talk to me?"

Pete stared at his hands until Alexia asked, "Well?"

He lifted his scrawny shoulders. "Don't know."

"I have to find her."

"Why?" Pete watched her as though she were the lost rattlesnake.

"Because." That in-depth answer was bound to gain his instant cooperation. She tried again. "I want to talk to her."

"She'll come around if she wants. Sometimes she calls Keith."

"She does?"

He pulled on his ear and avoided her eyes. "We came up here to help because Keith called in the favor on Lee. I'm part of the Seventeen's. So was Keith. But then he left. See, the only reason we let you go was you helped Lee."

Alexia would have liked to believe her bravery played a role. Apparently her act had been for nothing. "If Keith isn't part of your gang anymore, why did you bother to show up in Haven when Keith asked for help? Or are you just crazy?"

Pete grinned. "Keith said he was in the know here. He got a message to us. We came to help. This morning, he told me you wanted to know about Lee, so I came to explain."

"That little double-dealing, conniving...so he endangered you because of one little rescue?"

"We was gonna help you once before. He told me you were being chased by mad dogs, and he was gonna settle the debt. But when he got back, I dunno. He said the debt wasn't paid. We were too late."

There was no telling exactly what Keith had planned. She might be a psychiatrist, but teenagers apparently weren't her strong point.

She still wanted to find the girl. Keith might help, but then again, he might not. If he'd wanted to come clean, he would be here now. Alexia sighed and sat back down. "So. Now what?"

Pete immediately looked uncomfortable. "Wha'dya mean?"

"I mean what are you going to do now?"

He shrugged and stood up. "Guess I'll go home."

He didn't move towards the door.

Alexia read all she needed to know on his face. Hmm. Maybe there was help to be found here after all. "I'd still like you to get a message to Lee. But besides that, we have at least two vacancies in our security. Are you interested?"

His eyes lit up. "How much does it pay?"

"Finding Lee? Not much. The security job, I'm not sure about. The job will last though because the vacancies are permanent. George won't be coming back into the ranks. Ollern isn't coming back for certain. Darren is an idiot, and I don't know if he'll be forced out or not. You might have to work for him, but maybe you can keep your brain from rotting like the rest of his troops." Pete was without direction, just as Keith had been. If Chris had hung around and taken the job of replacing Darren and his security team, she wouldn't have worried about sending Pete into the security job.

For the last three days she had tried to forget Chris' face. For three days, every task she thought about seemed a natural for Chris.

"You mean work at Haven?" The high-pitched crack in his voice could have been fear, but she suspected it was eagerness.

Alexia deduced that he had come and offered the information on Lee hoping something like this would result. She stood. "I'll get the application. If you need help filling it out, Keith can help. How well can you read?" She went to her desk computer. Since she had just accessed the application files recently it only took about four clicks to print it.

When she turned with the paper, he snatched it from her hand. "I can read."

"Hey. Some of our scientists can't. They use voice-activated computers." She smiled blandly and didn't mention that both scientists were blind.

"No kiddin'?"

"Sure. Of course, you can learn or get better at it if you want. It'll probably make things easier. But, like I said, for now, get Keith to help. He filled out his not long ago."

After another moment he seemed to digest the information. "Yeah. Yeah, maybe that'd be a good idea."

"Great. You staying with Keith?"

He nodded happily. "Yeah. He said you might--" He stopped, chagrined.

"Good. Fill it out, get it back to me and tell Keith to set up a physical."

At the door, Pete turned again. "Thanks." He shuffled his feet. "Keith said you might sponsor me."

Alexia felt right for the first time in days when she replied, "I'm not sponsoring you." Before his face could fall, she added, "Keith is."

His head lifted. "He can do that? He ain't been here long."

"No time like the present. Haven isn't about paying dues. It's about taking on as much as you're ready to take on and setting your own boundaries. Keith didn't know he could sponsor you. But I know he'll want to."

Pete matched her grin. "Wow. I'll find Lee for you! Just wait and see. I'll tell'er you wanna talk to her. I'll tell'er you're really okay!"

He flew down the steps before she could give him a more formal message for Lee. But then, maybe his words were better than any she could come up with.

Knowing that sleep would be a while in coming, she grabbed her rifle and headed for her rock. It was hard to believe that Haven had almost been lost. It was hard to believe that Chris had just left. She really should hunt him down and kill him. Too bad she was a thief and not a gun for hire.

Without needing to think about it, she made her way to her favorite spot. She turned and faced home. From her perch, she could see the lights. She found Keith's apartment and smiled. At least two people in Haven were celebrating. She would have to check and see if Appleton had any reservations about letting Pete join security. Who could know? The kid might turn out to be interested in something totally different. At least here, he would have a chance to explore.

With a start, Alexia noticed a light near her bedroom window. It was only a pinprick really. If there had been fireflies in the area, she might have attributed it to them. "Now what?"

For a moment, she considered just sitting on her rock and watching. She simply didn't have the energy or inclination to deal with a thief. Besides, what in the world was left to steal? Could it be another of Keith's buddies?

Her next thought had her up and running. It might, if she was very lucky, be Lee.

Chapter 31

By the time Alexia reached the bottom of the mountain, ran to her house and through the gate, whatever had caused the light was gone. She was disappointed. Lee had probably knocked on the window and when Alexia hadn't answered, left.

Darn.

What were the chances of Lee trying again?

She let her rifle rest on the ground. Rats. Lee had broken through the security at Haven and shot a woman when necessary. The girl was intelligent and had potential.

Gasping in a few more breaths of much needed oxygen, Alexia went inside. Everything was just as she had left it. There were no notes waiting on her desk. Still...

He scared the hell out of her. As if her nerves hadn't been on edge for weeks, as if nothing at all untoward had happened, and as if he hadn't walked out on her, he strolled in from the kitchen, chewing on a carrot and waved. "Hey. Where you been?" He munched again and then added, "I knocked, and then tried the door codes. Noticed you didn't change them." He leered happily.

Alexia didn't have the strength left to lift her rifle and shoot him. She sat instead. "What are you doing here?"

Chris finally dropped his happy demeanor and looked a little guilty. He sat down across from her on the easy chair. "I couldn't do it."

"Couldn't do what?"

"Couldn't just walk away. I tried, but I couldn't do it. I didn't even know if you were okay." His green eyes held something of a plea in them.

Alexia fought the urge to stuff the remainder of the carrot up his nose. Words helped. "You mean you left before I even got out of your dad's office? No," she answered her own incensed question. "I checked on you so I know you saw me after that."

He snapped at her. "I don't mean that, dammit."

Alexia didn't feel like reading between the lines. She didn't want to guess what he was trying to say. Her own emotions were crazy enough.

She stared at him and wondered what in the world he was talking about.

He pulled his hair with both hands. "When I left, I told dad I'd be coming back. You know, from time to time. Keeping in better touch and all that." He waved his hands aimlessly. "But I didn't mean this soon."

"So? Why bother?"

"Because!" He realized he was standing and sat back down. "I don't know. You're the psychiatrist, you tell me."

Alexia crossed her arms. "No. If you want that kind of help, I suggest you look for a psychiatrist outside Haven. They're good at listening and helping you speculate yourself out of your problems."

"What if I need a real friend?"

She stared at him impatiently. "What are you asking for? You want me to sit here and wait for you while you go off and have your adventures? You want me to turn into your father?"

He tilted his head. The old smile came back for a moment. "Well, okay, that doesn't sound so bad. Except for the father part. I was hoping for something a little more intimate--"

She threw the couch pillow at him because it was the only object at hand. She would have preferred something a lot harder. It was apparent, from a medical point of view, that his head required some compacting. Maybe squishing his brains closer together would help some of the synapses connect.

"I supposed that is a no." His shoulders dropped, as did the grin. He turned serious again.

"Chris--"

"No wait," he held up a hand. "It's exactly what I expected. That's why I didn't stay before. I knew you would try and talk me into hanging around and playing the dutiful boyfriend."

Alexia was angry enough to stutter. "You...you...I never said that! Give me one good reason that I would waste my valuable time!" She stood and threw another pillow. He matched her motion, but didn't give her a chance to continue.

She had time for only a single squeak before he kissed her.

He pulled back almost immediately, but held her still with his eyes.

Of course, she should have continued to try and choke him or at least push him further away. She should sit him down and tell him all the reasons why she had not lain awake the last three nights thinking of him. She wasn't going to waste her time worrying about him while he ran off on his adventures. But inside, buried in a coffin that wasn't nailed tightly shut, she was glad to see him. The emotion raging through her pores was not just anger, it was an overwhelming need to answer the look in his eyes.

Chris let out the breath they had both been holding. "That's my reason," he finally said. He leaned in again, trapping her lips beneath his own. "I may be carefree, but this," he kissed her again, "this demands more than just a casual see you around."

Alexia pulled away. She tried to bring her analyzing skills to the fore. It was obvious she needed distance to examine the situation with less emotion. She sat slowly, controlling her movements precisely.

It didn't clear the fog that was threatening to feel a lot like happiness.

Chris helped clear her head with his next words. "Alexia, I love my work too much to give it up. But I have this feeling...I think I might love, like, well..." His brow furrowed with his effort to get the words out.

She stared up at him. "Love what?"

"You know."

"Nope." She put her hands around her knees and rocked back and forth and waited. No one had said that to her in a long time. But then, no one had said the other things Chris had said. Like the fact that she could trust him and tell him her secrets. And he had kept them.

He sat back down in the easy chair and fidgeted. "I'm not saying for sure. It's just that I might."

"Might," she repeated cautiously, tasting the hope that the single word created. Incredible how gullible the human mind allowed itself to be.

"Yes." He put his head in his hands as if he had announced a most terrible thing.

She dragged her doctor's face to the fore. "Well, speaking analytically, I might too." There. It was out. Then, her brow furrowed in concern. "It's going to be awfully hard to find out though if you're off in some other country hunting down the latest spy."

Chris lifted his head suddenly. "Really?"

"Of course really! How will we ever find out, if you're not here?"

"No, I mean, really the other."

"The other what?" Talking to Chris was like reading a comic strip that you had to keep rereading to get the joke.

With a good deal of male satisfaction he said, "That you really might care about me."

She glared at him. "But what's the point if you're not here?"

He gazed upwards for a long time, thinking. Finally he divined some wisdom from the ceiling. "Well, what if I based my operations from here? It certainly has the best security I've seen in a long time. And dad would be happy."

She studied him suspiciously. "And?"

He shrugged. "It might work."

"When would you be leaving?"

He got up and came around to kneel by her knees. "I don't know. I don't have another client yet. In fact, it would be good to lie low; pretend I'm staying here indefinitely." As he warmed to his subject, his eyes unfocused. He nodded suddenly as an idea took shape. "That's it! If everyone who knows my work is convinced that I'm staying here, when I do strike next, it will be as unexpected as when I started my career!" He rubbed his hands together. "I hadn't even thought of that benefit. My God, it's pure genius!"

She raised an eyebrow. "Be still my beating heart."

"Huh?" Sheepish, he remembered his original purpose. "Oh. Yeah. And we'll get a chance to...you know."

Alexia couldn't help it. She burst into giggles. "Chris, don't overdo the romance. You practically bring me to my knees." She rolled back on the couch before it came to that, but continued to laugh.

Chris stood up and fidgeted. "Well, it does happen to be a good idea."

"Fine. It's a good idea. But what will you do while you're lying low?"

He shrugged. "Darren's job needs filling. Dad has a few other things he wanted me to look into. That should leave plenty of time for us."

She stared back at him, the laughter gone. He met her gaze fully. He was serious. He was thinking of a way to stay around at least for a while. Of course, she needed time to analyze all the possibilities. Sort out how she really felt about him. She could take a few days and let him know later. Yes, that was the thing to do. Her training practically dictated such a safe way of thinking.

But then, there was Haven. It was a place to test theories, a place to follow instinct, a place to find something better than mere survival. A brilliant smile lit her features. She hadn't come to Haven for a cautious way of life. She had come here to grasp everything life had to offer. "I think that would be great."

Gleefully, she stood up on the couch and launched herself into his waiting arms.

The following is an excerpt from **Under Witch Moon,** an urban fantasy:

Under Witch Moon Summary

Adriel should have known that with a werewolf, it never stopped with just one body. She would have gone to the police after witnessing Dolores' death, but she wasn't certain the killer she saw was responsible for the other murders. Besides, the police didn't believe in werewolves, and they weren't going to believe she was a witch either so what could she tell them?

She kept her eyes and ears open while she tried to help her latest client escape the clutches of a voodoo witch, but things went from bad to worse when more bodies turned up. She was greatly relieved when she met White Feather, an undercover cop. Unfortunately, he wasn't convinced she was innocent of all wrong-doing.

It was going to take every spell she knew and a few she hadn't tried to solve the murders and stay alive.

Under Witch Moon

Chapter 1

Being a witch isn't easy. It's smelly, grueling work. I'm not talking about magic. Magic is a power that comes from natural forces. I'm talking about witchery, the chemical reactions for spells. Mind you, I dabble in magic; most witches do, but the bulk of my work involves a lot of formulas. It's a chore like any, much like caulking a house--messy, stinky and the results don't last forever.

Yes, spells wear out. They sometimes glue themselves to the wrong thing or dry too fast or don't dry at all. When I'm finished, I need a bath and in some cases, just as paint needs turpentine, I need special solutions to rid myself of the chemicals that have made themselves at home on my person.

At present, I was working on a spell for protection. It was an easy spell and thankfully cleaner than most. Salt, a purifier and element that worked well against rogue spirits, was the main ingredient. While it was wonderfully effective, it was unfortunately, quick to break down. The main job of a witch in this case was to make sure the salt didn't degrade too quickly. Rich patrons paid me to mix it in gold or silver.

I preferred silver myself. It provided additional protection against evil spirits, including vampires and shifters. Gold was better for other types of spells, plus it was coveted by all, which meant that patrons expected me to include a spell of illusion so that the protection object didn't get stolen--*but* those same clients wanted the object to be beautiful, so it was therefore coveted by anyone who happened to see it anyway.

Being a witch was indeed an onerous task. If people accepted us, they wanted the impossible. If they didn't, they wanted to burn us at the stake.

Never mind all that. The important thing when working with metals, as I was now, was to make certain of its purity. I didn't care if a customer told me he dug it out of a mountain with his bare hands under a full moon. Santa Fe, along with most of New Mexico, was chock full of old Aztec gold and silver, and let me tell you, those people could imbue nasty spirits like no other.

I had to burn my entire house to the ground once when working with contaminated gold. I still looked over my shoulder on moonless nights, because I wasn't certain I contained the evil spirit back in that lump of gold.

My new house had a special room made from concrete walls covered in adobe brick, covered in stucco. Mud had the wonderful ability to soak up any number of bad things. Stucco had only one important feature--chicken wire. When coated with the right ingredients, the wire provided a nearly complete mesh of protection against many a magical ill. I only wished I had been able to dip the mesh into silver such as I was using now, fresh from the U.S. minting office.

The mint did a great job of removing impurities, along with any bad spirits. Of course, in doing so they nearly removed silver's strong ties to mother earth. Part of my job was to make sure the silver linked again with the purity of earth. I melted it, salted it and strung it ever so carefully into magical fibers. The magic came from mother earth; it was part of the silver. And in truth, any witch worth her pay added a certain magic of her own, a heartbeat tied to mother earth, an aura if you will-- the magical quality of life.

The process of mixing, steaming, melting and salting took several days and exquisite timing. Moreover, when those things were done, I had to weave the silver thread into a careful pattern inside my chosen fabric. Given the trouble the woman was in, Dolores Garcia should have sprung for a fifty-strand liquid silver necklace instead. Such a necklace contained far more silver and wearing it would be an obvious message to a courting werewolf that she was not interested.

I finished my client's shirt on the night of a full moon, making sure the silver threads were placed correctly. As with any project, it felt good to finish, but I was tired. I planned to deliver the shirt the next day, but as I left my workroom, the phone rang.

"Adriel!" a voice sobbed my name and then choked to silence.

"Dolores?" I asked, although it could be no other.

"You must help me! Tonight. It's a full moon. It's…I can't control it, I saw him! I must have the shirt, finished or not, I can wait no longer!"

"Tonight?" Dismay colored my voice.

"It's a full moon! He's watching me, he's…" Her voice trembled with emotion.

"Oh for--"

"Please," she begged, naming a price that I could not afford to refuse.

"Fine." I sighed and then rolled my eyes as she dictated directions to a "safe" location. She insisted the exchange take place in the middle of the desert down in an arroyo so that we didn't stand out in the moonlight. In my mind, it would have been far less suspicious had she come over for a cup of coffee--or even met me at a donut shop.

Whatever. I had an image to uphold, and if the customer wanted me to traipse about the dusty desert after midnight, I just added it to the charge. If she didn't show up after keeping me up most of the night, I'd not only curse her, I'd sell the shirt to someone else, her silver or not.

I got traipsing. With the full moon, I managed to reach the location without too much trouble despite the fact that the spot Dolores had chosen was a mile from any paved road. To her credit, she was on time. From the looks of her though, I was a lot more agile in the dark.

She wasn't any older than me; somewhere in her twenties. She should have been able to easily avoid the prickly cactus, creosote and rocky terrain, but as she approached, she was limping rather noticeably.

She slid down into the arroyo and without ceremony, thrust out a tote bag weighted nicely with money. "Do you have it?" she whispered.

"You won't be able to wear this shirt every single day," I warned, prepared to sell her a kerchief as an additional security measure. "A werewolf is a dangerous--"

"Shhh," she shushed, despite the desert location.

"This shirt will be effective, but I would advise you to purchase some additional protection," I said, exchanging the plain wrapped package for the bag of money.

She grabbed the brown paper bundle from me and held it to her heaving chest like a long-lost teddy-bear. "At last!"

I frowned. I was accustomed to people being grateful, especially in the case of fending off evil, but her elation was almost giddy. "It will keep the werewolf away. Once you start wearing it, he will know that you know what he is. It will make it clear you are not interested."

She spun around in a circle, full Spanish skirts swirling around her legs. In addition to the dress, the idiot had actually worn sandals. Had she worn jeans and hiking boots like I had, maybe she wouldn't be limping.

"He will be mine now," she declared lustily. "I can date him without fear."

"What?" I forgot she wanted to keep our meeting a secret. "Are you crazy? He's an animal!"

"We're all animals! He just happens to be two animals, his were-person and his...person-person."

"That would be were-*wolf*," I emphasized. "Not were-person. The whole point is that he is an *animal* at times, with animal instincts and animal reactions."

She flicked long hair over her shoulder. It should have been as luminous black as mine from the usual mix of Spanish and Native American blood in the area, but she had bleached a gray streak across her forehead. Eagerly she gushed, "He's a person and very intelligent. I'm sure that I will be safe now."

"Nonsense." I shuddered at the thought of dealing with a werewolf in beast form.

She drew herself up tightly, thrusting out rather over-sized breasts. "Are you saying the protection I'm buying won't work?"

"Oh, the protection works. But you do realize that the werewolf will sense it, and it will automatically make you an enemy, especially to the wolf."

"He's human! He'll know that I need to be protected from the wolf. He'll be...attracted to the danger!"

"No. Animals are not attracted to danger. They run from it or they fight it."

She smacked away my hand as I reached for the goods. I had decided not to sell it to her.

"His human part will be wildly attracted to me!"

"Fool!" I declared. "His human part--"

She turned away in a swirl of skirts and ran.

Who in their right mind wore a skirt out in the desert? Some women had no sense.

Apparently I was one of them, but for different reasons. When Dolores had approached me about protection from a werewolf, I had hoped to keep her away from the animal, not bring her to it. While I worked on the spell, I kept my ear to the ground. Dolores had been keeping her distance from all men. Since I couldn't know who in her community was the actual werewolf, it only stood to reason that if she were interacting with none of them, she was indeed concerned for her safety.

"Drat your silly hide." I hurtled after her up the side of the arroyo.

Catching her should be easy. She gimped along, tripping in the dark. Her legs would be good and scratched and the skirt full of rips before she made it home.

I lunged at her, but missed. She was too stupid to stay where the path was clear. Worse, her limp made her run and weave like a drunk.

I dashed forward again, making a flying tackle at her legs. The skirt, with its billowing mass, misled me. I ended up on the ground with a large armful of material. "Stop, you fool! The werewolf is a dangerous animal!"

She yanked hard, showing desperation that should have been saved for the werewolf. "No!" The skirt was already half shredded from her run through the desert. It gave way with a low rumble of protest. "He'll be mine!"

I was left in the dirt holding a fistful of brightly colored material while she made it to her truck and peeled away into the darkness.

Thankfully, in my pocket was the kerchief I had also made her-- intending to tell her to wear it on her person at all times. The silver in the kerchief was from the same batch as the shirt. If I worked quickly, I could use the silver to make a witching fork, track the shirt, and steal it back. Maybe without the false sense of security, she'd give up her wildly stupid plans.

I sighed. It was obvious I could not enlighten her. Mind you, I had nothing against werewolves. I had no problem befriending their human side, but werewolves were werewolves. The animal instincts were there, and so was the animal power. While wolves have been known to fight on the side of humans, it was usually against a common enemy. They were still wild animals, with goals and instincts all their own.

I grumbled my way to my feet and pushed back the dark strands that had loosened from my ponytail. I had time. The moon would still be nearly full for the next couple of nights. No one would date a werewolf this close to a full moon. It would be even stupider than believing a mere shirt of silver and salt could save someone who jumped into the teeth of a wolf.

I took myself home to begin work on a witching fork. Since the silver was from the same batch as the shirt, my witching fork would act like a tuning fork. Only instead of music, the closer I got to the shirt, the better I would be able to hear the song of the mother lode.

My body demanded at least a few hours of sleep before concentrating on the difficult task of wrapping silver threads along a willow-branch fork. Every silver strand had to be exactly the same length and weight on each side of the fork. I didn't want false readings in the middle of the night while breaking into private property.

* * *

It took until dusk the next day before I was ready with Dolores' address in hand. A quick check with Lynx, my friend who lurked in the shadows of Santa Fe's streets, assured me that Dolores' parents were in town enjoying dinner. Lynx didn't come out of the shadows, but I could hear him chuckle. "I keep them busy for you," he whispered. "I pick up my pay tomorrow night."

"Make sure I have at least two extra hours," I whispered back into the darkness.

He didn't answer, but I knew he would be happy to make sure they were delayed while I visited the Garcia's hacienda on the outskirts of Santa Fe.

The trip, even after I stashed my dusty blue Civic on an unrelated side road and hiked up the short driveway to the house, took me under an hour.

The stucco estate was to my liking, mimicking the pueblos from the ancient past, with adobe walls forming a stepped design from the first to the second floor. The stepladder formation was a very good thing because the witching fork was pointing straight up.

I approached the walled-in garden with trepidation. At only five-five and maybe a half, I couldn't reach the top of the wall, not even on my tiptoes. I hated climbing. It was strenuous work, and I wasn't the most graceful of creatures. Thankfully I wasn't fat or the nearly six-foot barricade would have won.

The top was rounded, which kept me from piercing various body parts, but it was damned hard to balance on the thing once I straddled it. I wouldn't die if I fell, but as I shimmied toward the window ledge, I cursed the wall for not being high enough to allow me to easily reach the window.

I was sure of my destination. The fork was singing louder, a subtle vibration along my fingertips.

I clutched at the side of the house and groped upwards toward the open window. There wasn't going to be an easier entry. I put one foot in front of the other, took a deep breath and jumped.

Don't get me started about witches, broomsticks and being able to fly. I didn't know how to fly yet, and no witch in her right mind would use a broomstick these days. Why bother when there were more comfortable objects to levitate? If I ever learned to fly, I was going with a nice Arabian rug. Whoever spelled those magic carpets understood comfort.

I caught the sill with only one hand, flailing desperately. My next mistake was to try to climb with my hiking boots. Planting my feet on the wall pushed me away from the window. My hand scraped painfully across a metal rim before losing what skin was left to the stucco.

"Aeii!" I couldn't contain a stifled scream. My left foot landed on the wall, but the right kept sliding. A large chunk of adobe broke off under my boot and took me with it. One leg went left, the other right. I sat astride the wall like a drunk on a broomstick. One leg was painfully tangled in a rose bush.

"Why couldn't they have planted nice, safe, lilac bushes against the house?" Stifling a groan, I got up and used the side of the house to keep from falling again. If I kept sliding down and knocking chunks of the wall away, the Garcia's were going to end up with no wall. I would end up with no legs.

I jumped again, this time muttering the ingredients used in levitation spells. I didn't *have* any of the ingredients with me because the only one I was sure about was lodestone, but the list gave me confidence.

More stucco knocked free as I clutched the sill and dug my boots into the wall. The metal cut into my hands, but I kept climbing until I had a leg over.

It was then that I smelled him. Had he been in his human form, I might not have caught the strong scent, but wolves have a unique muskiness. A small light, maybe from a night light in the attached bathroom, gave off just enough of a glow to throw shadows.

"Aztec curses!" I swore in disbelief. "She wouldn't! The moon is practically full…"

One leg over the sill, I dared not move until I had my bearings. There was no sound of breathing other than my own, but if the man had turned werewolf, there had been an emergency or danger at the very least.

By the moonlight and the night light, I saw him. He was in the corner, half-changed to his coyote form. Most werewolves in the area were coyotes; at least the native ones. I hadn't known if I would be dealing with a local or not, but the color of his fur was definitely the dirty-blond of a coyote.

"It would be easier for you to escape as the wolf," I said softly, showing him that I was all about cooperation. I edged to one side of the window to give him plenty of room.

He let out a panting groan from the effort and pain of changing. His growl was a feral moan, but still a threat.

"You'll need to hurry," I advised. If I could talk him into leaving, I stood a better chance of coming out of the experience alive. His face was furry, but not much more than an overgrown, bushy beard. Ears were still poking through, but rapidly disappearing.

Because he was mostly human, I could see why the situation with Dolores had turned into such a problem. He was young. Very young. Eighteen if she was lucky. The barely grown man probably hadn't known how to deal with a flirtatious woman dabbling where she didn't belong. Perhaps he thought he could live in both worlds. Perhaps he was simply too young to understand she had been after him because he was a unique trophy prize.

"I would never have sold her the shirt had I realized she sought to control you with it. You have my apologies."

He was miserably human, shivering uncontrollably in the corner.

"You need to leave," I urged again. "Quickly." I moved away from the window without touching anything.

He bolted, buck naked, for freedom. I wasn't going to stop him. More stress might cause him to revert back to full wolf form, and that stupid I was not. Instead, I looked for the shirt.

It wasn't on Dolores, since she was completely naked. The problem with fabric protection was that it could be taken off and she had, after all, invited the werewolf into her bedroom. Had she somehow thought she could have sex with a werewolf partially clothed?

The scene in front of me was unpleasant, but for a panicked wolf, surprisingly lacking in blood. He had killed her, but crushed her throat rather than ripped it to shreds. There were more than a few deep scratches, as if the coyote had been trying to scramble away rather than do serious damage. From what was left of the shirt, it looked as though Dolores might have tried to wrap him in it.

The wolf had not been amused by the protection spell. I had seen at least two burns, one on his arm and another across his chest.

When it had finally rid itself of the touch of the garment, the coyote had soiled it with urine, destroying any of the spell that hadn't burned itself up when it came in contact with his skin. The silver that was left would have to be purified. Depending on the wolf's abilities…well, it was probably best buried.

I scanned the room one last time. There were two fancy shopping bags on a chair in front of the dressing table. The plastic one was the easy choice.

I held my nose as I bagged the shirt. I would have sighed, but didn't want to breathe deeply. Being a witch was a messy job. Being a witch wasn't easy. I had a bad feeling that retrieving the spelled shirt wasn't going to be enough to keep myself out of further trouble.

More Books by Maria E. Schneider

Most of my other works are cozy mysteries. Some contain magic, such as the anthologies: **Tracking Magic** (Max Killian Investigations) and **Sage** (Tales from a Magical Kingdom). The Sedona O'Hala series (**Executive Lunch, Executive Retention, Executive Sick Days**) is a series of contemporary cozy mysteries: Sedona must solve a few crimes while fighting her way up the corporate ladder--or dangling from a rung, whichever she's able to achieve on a given day. **Under Witch Moon** is a paranormal mystery.

To find out what I'm currently up to, visit me at: www.BearMountainBooks.com

www.ingramcontent.com/pod-product-compliance
Lightning Source LLC
Chambersburg PA
CBHW021033130626
46552CB00005B/1815